...y Slide

Lost Gay
Reference Guide to ...s
from the First Half
of the Twentieth Century

Pre-publication
REVIEWS,
COMMENTARIES,
EVALUATIONS . . .

"**A**nthony Slide has rescued some fascinating, frequently alarming, and occasionally absurd works of fiction from obscurity. Brave or timid, candid or hypocritical, they reflect the fears, inhibitions, and prejudices of the times, and with his comments on the writers and their critics, Slide sheds further light on growing up gay or homophobic in the first half of the twentieth century."

Gavin Lambert
Author, *Mainly About Lindsay Anderson, On Cukor,* and *Inside Daisy Clover*

"**L**ost Gay Novels fills a critical gap in the study of gay literature, reclaiming works written before the niche was named and `the gay consumer' became a publishing demographic. Here one will find many surprises, including expressions of a startling, pre-Stonewall gay sensibility. Anthony Slide has accomplished the herculean task of reading and analyzing hundreds of texts, rediscovering in the process the work of forgotten gay literary pioneers."

William J. Mann
Author, *Behind the Screen: How Gays and Lesbians Shaped Hollywood, 1910-1969*

Lost Gay Novels
*A Reference Guide to Fifty Works
from the First Half
of the Twentieth Century*

HARRINGTON PARK PRESS
Titles of Related Interest

Rough News—Daring Views: 1950s' Pioneer Gay Press Journalism by Jim Kepner

Before Stonewall: Activists for Gay and Lesbian Rights in Historical Context edited by Vern L. Bullough

A Sea of Stories: The Shaping Power of Narrative in Gay and Lesbian Cultures: A Festschrift for John P. DeCecco edited by Sonya L. Jones

Reclaiming the Sacred: The Bible in Gay and Lesbian Culture, Second Edition, edited by Raymond-Jean Frontain

Bisexual Characters in Film: From Anaïs to Zee by Wayne M. Bryant

Scandal: Infamous Gay Controversies of the Twentieth Century by Marc E. Vargo

Lytton Strachey and the Search for Modern Sexual Identity: The Last Eminent Victorian by Julie Anne Taddeo

The Empress Is a Man: Stories from the Life of José Sarria by Michael R. Gorman

From Drags to Riches: The Untold Story of Charles Pierce by John Wallraff

The Man Who Was a Woman and Other Queer Tales from Hindu Lore by Devdutt Pattanaik

Against My Better Judgment: An Intimate Memoir of an Eminent Gay Psychologist by Roger Brown

Rebel Yell: Stories by Contemporary Southern Gay Authors edited by Jay Quinn

Rebel Yell II: More Stories of Contemporary Southern Gay Men edited by Jay Quinn

Lost Gay Novels
A Reference Guide to Fifty Works from the First Half of the Twentieth Century

Anthony Slide

Harrington Park Press®
An Imprint of The Haworth Press, Inc.
New York • London • Oxford

Published by

Harrington Park Press®, an imprint of The Haworth Press, Inc., 10 Alice Street, Binghamton, NY 13904-1580.

Cover design by Jennifer M. Gaska.

Cover photograph: a scene from *The Strange One* (1957), based on Calder Willingham's *End As a Man*.

Library of Congress Cataloging-in-Publication Data

Slide, Anthony.
    Lost gay novels : a reference guide to fifty works of fiction from the first half of the twentieth century / Anthony Slide.
       p. cm.
    Includes bibliographical references (p.) and index.
    ISBN 1-56023-413-X (alk. paper) — ISBN 1-56023-414-8 (alk. paper)
    1. American fiction—20th century—History and criticism. 2. Homosexuality, Male, in literature—Bibliography. 3. English fiction—20th century—History and criticism. 4. American fiction—20th century—Bibliography. 5. English fiction—20th century—Bibliography. 6. Homosexuality and literature—Bibliography. 7. Gay men in literature—Bibliography. 8. Homosexuality, Male, in literature. 9. Homosexuality and literature. 10. Gay men in literature. I. Title.

PS374.H63 S65 2003
813'.52099206642—dc21

CONTENTS

ABOUT THE AUTHOR

Anthony Slide is the editor of the Scarecrow Press "Filmmakers" series and the author of more than sixty volumes on the history of popular entertainment, including *The Silent Feminists, The New Historical Dictionary of the American Film Industry, The Encyclopedia of Vaudeville, Early American Cinema, Great Pretenders: A History of Female and Male Impersonation in the Performing Arts, Silent Players,* and *Gay and Lesbian Characters and Themes in Mystery Novels.* In recognition of his work on the history of popular culture, Bowling Green University awarded Dr. Slide an honorary doctorate of letters in 1990.

Acknowledgments

My thanks first and foremost to the librarians in the Literature Department of the Los Angeles Central Library: Helene Mochedlover and her staff, Robert Anderson, Christine Bocek, Bill Jankos, and Bette McDonough. In an age of computers and digital technology, they remain the keepers of the book—and long may they endure. Gavin Lambert and William Mann provided helpful comments, and Raphael Kadushin at the University of Wisconsin Press offered initial support and encouragement. This book would not have been published without the efforts of Thomas L. Long, editor of *Harrington Gay Men's Fiction Quarterly*. I am grateful also for the help of Bolerium Books in San Francisco, Robert Gitt, Jane B. Smith, and André Soares; and, above all, I acknowledge a debt to Donald Webster Cory, whose pioneering text, *The Homosexual in America*, first made me aware of the substantial number of "lost" gay novels.

Introduction

Lost Gay Novels is a reference work for students and scholars in modern gay studies or queer theory, providing a unique record of fifty English-language popular novels from the first half of the twentieth century identified as containing gay characters, gay themes, or both. Each entry provides a detailed examination of the text of the novel, together with a sampling of contemporary reviews and pertinent historical information as to the author and the work.

The emphasis is on lost gay novels, by which I mean novels that are not generally known to modern audiences. The approach of the novelist toward homosexuality may not always be a positive one; in fact, it is almost always negative, but the works are important to an understanding of contemporary attitudes toward gay men and gay society. These novels, the majority of which qualify as second-rate literature, are fascinating examples of contemporary prejudices and both their authors' and society's inhibitions. They are worthy of study in relationship to the unapologetic gay fiction of high quality by such authors as Christopher Isherwood, William Burroughs, Dennis Cooper, Armistead Maupin, and John Rechy, published in the second half of the twentieth century.

The gay protagonists are generally young and stereotypical—drugs, alcohol, and drag play a major role in the lives of many of them—and ageism is prevalent in the thinking of many of the novelists. Homosexual men past the age of thirty are seldom seen in a positive light, although Willard Motley's *Knock on Any Door* and Rex Stout's *Forest Fire* discuss the love of an older man for a younger one. If nothing else, so many of the novels here—Myron Brinig's *This Man Is My Brother,* Richard Hull's *The Murder of My Aunt,* Blair Niles's *Strange Brother,* and others—illustrate the basic assumption that gay characters in literature must come to a tragic end. It is very much as if an early death is the only justification for the inclusion of a gay protagonist.

Death plays an important role in many of the titles. In both Isabel Bolton's *The Christmas Tree* and Ward Thomas's *Stranger in the Land* there is a neat twist, and it is the straight man who dies at the hands of the gay hero. In Charles Jackson's *The Fall of Valor,* the bisexual protagonist wishes he might have been killed. The central gay character in André Birabeau's *Revelation* is dead throughout the novel. Their gay protagonists might not die, but presumed gay (or at least bisexual) authors Stuart Engstrand and Harlan Cozad McIntosh, illustrating that life could indeed emulate art, chose suicide to end their own lives.

Some of these novels have been rediscovered in more recent years and reprinted; some remained in print for many years until supplanted by novels with more positive (and more explicit) gay texts, while others, rightly or wrongly, have simply been forgotten. Specifically not included here are the familiar gay novels of the period, such as Djuna Barnes's *Nightwood* (Harcourt, Brace, 1937), Truman Capote's *Other Voices, Other Rooms* (Random House, 1948), Carson McCullers's *Reflections in a Golden Eye* (Houghton Mifflin, 1941), and Gore Vidal's *The City and the Pillar* (E. P. Dutton, 1948). I have also chosen to ignore the many erotic novels of Frederic Prokosch, Carl Van Vechten's *The Blind Bow-Boy: A Cartoon for a Stained Glass Window* (Alfred A. Knopf, 1923), and Charles Brackett's *American Colony* (Horace Liveright, 1929). The last writer is worthy of additional study if for no other reason than as a gay man he posed as a straight (and married) Hollywood screenwriter and was a highly regarded president of the Academy of Motion Picture Arts and Sciences. Because it was published in Paris—by the Obelisk Press in 1933—and not in the United States, I have not included *The Young and Evil* by Charles Henri Ford and Parker Tyler.

This study is limited to novels from the twentieth century, in large part because they are more accessible to a modern readership. The gay novel can, of course, be traced back to the Greek and Roman Empires, and while the genre was relatively dormant in Western civilization for more than 1,000 years, it did reappear in Victorian England. Two prominent works from this later period are *The Sins of the City; or, The Recollections of a Mary-Ann* (1881), set in London's gay underworld, and *Teleny; or, The Reverse of the Medal* (1893), the story of a love affair between two young men, sometimes attributed to Oscar Wilde. The modern gay novel may be dated from E. M. Forster's

1914 writing of *Maurice,* but because it was not published until after the author's death, it does not belong here. As Roger Austen has noted, "The main reason for the dearth of explicitly gay novels in America from the nineteenth century up to 1920 is that sexual perversion was regarded as hardly a fit subject for fiction—or, for that matter, nonfiction."[1] He might have added that it remained a subject about which most Americans were happy to remain in ignorance.

Gay authors did not exactly flourish in Europe, but they must have been aware that, unlike their American counterparts, there was a strong possibility that they might able to find a sympathetic publisher. Robert Musil's *Young Torless,* Jean Cocteau's *Le Livre Blanc,* and Jean Genet's *Notre Dame des Fleurs* are examples of European gay novels from the period that would not find American publication. Scottish-German author John Henry Mackay published the explicit *Der Puppenjunge,* the story of a Berlin rent boy, in Germany in 1926, but it was not until 1985 that Hubert Kennedy translated it into English as *The Hustler* for distribution in the United States by Alyson Publications.

The majority of the authors represented here were probably not gay; those who were must, of necessity, remain closeted to the present, simply because it is impossible to identify them through the pseudonyms they chose to use or to determine their lifestyles through often limited contemporary reporting. Some, such as *The Night Air*'s author, Harrison Dowd, one assumes to have been gay; others, including *The Gallery*'s John Horne Burns and *The Fall of Valor*'s Charles Jackson were identified as bisexual late in life, and a handful, including *The Welcome*'s Hubert Creekmore and *The Invisible Glass*'s Loren Wahl, write so well of the gay experience that one hopes they might have been gay men and that in their private lives they achieved some measure of happiness.

In identifying the fifty gay novels under discussion, I have relied upon earlier published bibliographies, on a subject index compiled many years ago by unidentified librarians at the Los Angeles Public Library, and on my own good fortune in stumbling upon a few treasured volumes, such as Compton Mackenzie's *Vestal Fire.*

Often I have followed up on leads only to be disappointed by a singular lack of gay content in a novel that appears in most gay bibliographies. What, for example, is gay about Richard Pyke's *The Lives and Deaths of Roland Greer* (Albert and Charles Boni, 1929)? The title character is heterosexual and he has a love-hate relationship with his older brother—and that is all. If anything, Pyke is attracted to his brother's wife. Too much attention has obviously been paid by bibliographers to the novel's dust jacket and the publisher's claim that this is "the life of a spiritual hermaphrodite, where the masculine and feminine are fighting for control."

One must beware of dishonest claims by publishers. The dust jacket description of *Send Them Summer* by Hansford Martin (Harcourt, Brace, 1946) tells us that the principal character, "Banjo," is hated by the character "van Brunt" for "being normal." Yet "van Brunt," a fat, pasty-faced guy, is barely present, and is more despised by "Banjo" than the reverse.

Just as the motion picture has presented its share of "buddy" movies, such as *Wings* (1927), in which the love between two men is heterosexual, so has the publishing industry come up with its fair share of "buddy" novels. A fine example is John Kelly's *All Souls' Night* (Harcourt, Brace, 1947), in which two young men are in love with the same woman and also with each other. However, there is nothing overtly sexual in the men's relationship; they may share the same bed, but they keep their pajamas on and neither hug nor kiss.

Mainstream American publishers did not shy away from gay characters or themes, but the United States boasted no gay publishing house comparable to Britain's Fortune Press, which remained in existence from 1926 to 1970. The one U.S. publisher most associated with the gay genre from the 1930s through the 1950s is Greenberg, but the gay connection is unclear. The company was founded as Greenberg Publisher, Inc., in June 1924 by three brothers, David, Jacob, and James Greenberg. It published more than 1,000 titles, with the emphasis on nonfiction, and early made its reputation with the illustrated children's books of Tony Sarg. Among its most prominent writers were Max Eastman, Robert Graves, Betty Smith, and Deems Taylor, and among its best-sellers was *Freud: His Dreams and Sex Theories* (1949).

A gay editor must have been associated with the company, but his name is not recorded. One editor identified with some of the later gay works from Greenberg is Elliott W. McDowell (1903-1976), who came to the company in 1944 and became its editor in chief. The small amount of information accessible on his personal life gives no indication that McDowell was gay.

Ian Young notes that two lesbian novels by Anna Elizabet Weirauch were translated for Greenberg by Whittaker Chambers, who was a prominent figure in the Alger Hiss spy scandal, and who kept his homosexuality a secret.[2]

Also worthy of further study is New York publishing house William Godwin, Inc., founded in 1931. One of its leading writers was Gerald Foster, responsible for such suspiciously titled novels as *Lust* (1934), *Strange Marriage* (1934), and *No Women Wanted* (1936). The first, described by its publisher as "A book for harassed men and curious women," was reprinted by Balzac Press in 1949.

Just as so little is documented on the gay editors responsible for publication of America's first gay novels, so is there little available on the authors of many of those novels. They hid behind pseudonyms, with their real names unrecorded in the publishing records of the Library of Congress. Yet again, another aspect of gay society and gay culture remains firmly buried in the historical closet. Thanks in large part to prescient public librarians—many of whom were probably gay—the lost gay novels have survived (if seldom on the circulating shelves), but beyond what exists on the printed page must remain only supposition.

NOTES

1. Roger Austen, *Playing the Game: The Homosexual Novel in America*. Indianapolis: Bobbs-Merrill, 1977, p. 1.

2. Ian Young, "Some Notes on Gay Publishing," in *The Male Homosexual in Literature: A Bibliography*. Metuchen, NJ: Scarecrow Press, 1982, p. 291.

James Barr, *Quatrefoil*

Quatrefoil (Greenberg, 1950) is a novel that obviously meant much to the gay community when it was first published, but is, in hindsight, overwritten, overwrought, and peopled with characters that seldom break through the fictional veneer. The ending is weak and depressingly conventional for a work of gay fiction. *Quatrefoil* meets all the guidelines for popular romantic fiction of the day, with a gay couple substituting for the typical hero and heroine.

It is 1946, and Ensign Phillip Froelich is en route to Seattle, where he faces a court martial. He has disobeyed his captain's orders and, in order to get various jobs accomplished on board ship, he has fraternized with the men. Froelich comes from Oklahoma, but he is not a typical native of that state—his father is head of a bank and the family owns much of the town where he grew up. The twenty-three-year-old accepts a ride from Commander Tim Danelaw, a married man ten years his senior, who is able not only to get the charges against Froelich dropped but also to persuade the young man to cancel his wedding plans. It transpires that Danelaw's is a marriage of convenience, and in San Francisco, Danelaw lures Froelich into bed. The happiness that the two men share is brief, as they are discovered by a fellow officer.

Ultimately, after a trip by both to Oklahoma, a relationship develops and is sustained. Froelich keeps his belongings at the base, but spends his nights with Danelaw at his club in Seattle. "For the first time in his entire life, he [Froelich] felt individually free" (p. 353). The happiness of the pair is momentarily stifled when Froelich receives a visit from a sailor named Stuff Manus. At sea, the two men had become friendly, despite the difference in their ranks, and Stuff had, in a clumsy fashion, attempted to sexually assault the young officer. "He felt Stuff's firm mouth on his own, the man's tongue forcing itself into him," writes Barr (p. 72) in one of the few descriptions of physical sex in the novel. Renewing their acquaintance in Seattle, Manus again attempts to force himself on Froelich, but is again rejected. At one point, Danelaw contemplates what Froelich means in his life, commenting, "Had Phillip been of the other sex, his life would change little at this point. With its sanction, he would be tied to society a little more, but his vows would still be made." But, as with countless gay men before and since, "He was glad Phillip was what he was, for in loving him he withdrew farther from all men and saw them in greater perspective. Phillip was his last benevolent gesture, the crystallization of his nature" (p. 338).

Of course, in 1950, even in a novel authored by a gay man and aimed at a gay market gays could not find lasting happiness. Danelaw is killed in a plane crash. Froelich reads of the accident: "He had gambled with life for happiness, and miraculously enough he had won. But as he had put out his hand to receive his reward, it had vanished. Life and the game, both were a dream" (p. 372).

Froelich contemplates suicide, but perhaps because, again, this is 1950 and a gay-oriented novel, he stops, recalling the last words of Danelaw: "And now, my life is a part of ours, and your life is a part of mine. Never again shall we stand entirely alone" (p. 373). For Donald Webster Cory, writing in *The Homosexual in America,* "The note of hope on which this novel ends is perhaps its finest contribution to the literature on the subject."[1]

A subplot involves the Froelich family in Oklahoma, an overbearing and unsympathetic father, and the eventual discovery that the grandfather for whom Phillip Froelich is named was also homosexual. The family ponders whether Phillip has "inherited the taint?" (p. 323).

Neither Froelich nor Danelaw is a stereotypical gay man. As both have experienced sexual relationships with women, they might well be identified as bisexual. There is nothing feminine about either man, excepting that Danelaw is an amateur painter, and Froelich, "like most men of his class . . . considered art effeminate" (p. 122). When Froelich agrees to pose in the nude for Danelaw, the author is very much overreaching the bounds of possibility; a naval officer is very unlikely to agree to such a request by another, but it does provide an opportunity for an intimate description of Froelich:

> Tim watched the lithe, rippling muscles of the boy's splendid body. . . . He saw the white cups beneath the arms, the lean ribs,

> the ridiculously narrow waist and hips, the smooth, down-covered columns of the legs, the high white arches of the feet, and above everything else the graceful, straining, uplifted arms that framed a relaxed sensual face. (p. 165)

The description, with its lack of comment on either the buttocks or the sexual organs, is possibly a result of the mores of the times, but it might just as well be lifted directly from the pages of a modern Harlequin romance.

When they first meet, Danelaw asks Froelich if he has anything against Oscar Wilde. By discussing Wilde, Froelich realizes he has revealed much about himself, just as the supposedly idle comment demonstrates to a modern readership how two gay men might identify themselves upon a first encounter.

Quatrefoil was reprinted by Alyson Publications in 1982, with an introduction by Samuel M. Steward, who praised it as "a wonderful treatise on how to live happily in the closet in 1950." At this point, Alyson was unable to locate the author, but he resurfaced and wrote an epilogue for the 1991 reprint of *Quatrefoil*.

James Barr was revealed as the pseudonym of James Fugaté. He had apparently worked in the oil fields, and in 1951, he published (also through Greenberg) a collection of gay short stories appropriately titled *Derricks*. James Fugaté identified the central character, Phillip Froelich, as a fraternity brother, with whom he had had a brief and unhappy affair. Phillip and the author had both independently joined the Navy, where the latter frequently encountered the Timothy Danelaw "type"; "They were often brilliantly educated, frequently married, and usually completely bewildered at having found strong tendencies of homosexuality in their personalities."[2] The real Phillip was brutalized by his father, and committed suicide on his wedding day. When he was told by Fugaté that he was to be the central character in the novel, he asked only that he be made happy. In so doing, Fugaté escaped the stereotypical gay character of the period and the stereotypical gay ending that the real Phillip Froelich experienced.

NOTES

1. Donald Webster Cory, *The Homosexual in America*. New York: Greenberg, 1951, p. 297.

2. James Barr, *Quatrefoil*. Boston: Alyson Publications, 1991, unpaginated epilogue.

– 2 –

Larry Barretto, *The Great Light*

A gay man, Roswell Cleminshaw, dominates only one chapter of *The Great Light* (Farrar, Straus, 1947), but he is a pivotal figure in the life of the central character, Dirck Ericson. Just what the violent and confrontational scenes between the two actually constitute is somewhat difficult to understand or explain. Dirck is given to hallucinations, is seeking some kind of inner truth or beauty, and is never fully developed as a character. As critic "J. B." wrote in *The New York Times* (October 19, 1947), the author assures us that Dirck is "an extraordinary and sensitive person who is seeking for absolute beauty. Unfortunately, however, he succeeds in bringing Dirck to life primarily in those scenes where his conduct is anything but saintly."

Those far-from-saintly moments include not only the chapter with the gay man but also a deeply disturbing encounter that Dirck has in New York around midnight. Unable to sleep, he prowls the streets and meets a young man who asks him for a match. The guy may or may not be gay, but as he speaks,

> the words did not issue from that sweetly curving mouth. Instead it was the mouth of Roswell Cleminshaw whose sagging lips were trying to stiffen in an attempt at self-control, and it was Cleminshaw's effeminate face that was looking so intently at him. (p. 97)

"You God-damned fairy!" (p. 97) Dirck yells as he strikes and kills an innocent man. Dirck confesses this ugly truth to a friend, but there is no punishment for his crime, and neither the characters in the novel nor the author seem to care too much about the matter.

Dirck Ericson is a good-looking youth—a friend, admiring him in the showers, describes him as resembling "a Scandinavian God" (p. 22)—but he is abused by his father, reduced to poverty, and forced to work in a menial occupation. With friend Archer Paine (who later becomes a novelist), Dirck enlists as an ambulance corpsman at America's entry into World War I.

One of the men in his unit is Roswell Cleminshaw:

> Cleminshaw was not a man, he was an affront, and every member of the unit resented him. Somehow he seemed to reflect discredit on themselves even though he did his work a little better than well. He was a slim, pale boy with wavy blond hair, and a timid smile which faded soon after his arrival. His voice was soft, precise, unpleasantly artificial and complicated by a lisp which he could no more control than he could the involuntary gestures which he made with his hands. His shoulders were over-narrow for his frame and his hips were over-wide. In the shower the men stared at him with amusement and contempt. (p. 37)

It is Dirck, at the age of eighteen, who gives Cleminshaw the name of "Nelly," joking that if he met him on a dark night, "in the struggle my virtue might be impaired" (p. 38). However, it is Cleminshaw in action who proves his bravery, while Dirck, through no real fault of his own, appears to shun the fighting, preferring to go on K.P. and work in the kitchen. Still Cleminshaw is ridiculed by Dirck: "Well, Nelly . . . were you a brave girl at the front today?" (p. 44). When Cleminshaw accuses Dirck of cowardice, he is beaten up, but Cleminshaw has gained an inner strength: "You've beaten me up, but I've learned now there are other things worse than that" (p. 44). He has faced death, and he has a Croix de Guerre given him by a French colonel, who removed it from his own tunic, in recognition of his bravery. The hostility of the men in the corps is turned on Dirck, and the name Nelly is never again spoken.

"I truly believe that night was the turning-point in his [Dirck's] life" (p. 45), writes Archer Paine, but the turning point to what still remains obscure. Dirck wanders aimlessly through life, examining his emotional problems with psychiatrist Nevius Brooks. The latter discusses homosexuality with Dirck and his friends:

> I reviewed the history of homosexuality insofar as I know it, stressing the fact that it is believed all humans are born with a bisexual nature which sometimes becomes overbalanced, and is

even evidenced by physical characteristics of the opposite sex. . . . Speaking to Dirck, I said that this condition had been accepted in ancient Greece, and was even now more than tolerated in large sections of the modern world. (pp. 109-110)

One of Dirck's friends, banker Peter Fleming, who would rather die than take a blood transfusion from a "nigger," asserts that "all men like that should be shot" (p. 110). But tolerance grows in Dirck and he becomes obsessed with the mythical Greek character Andragathus, the presumed paramour of the poet Meleager. He has visions of Andragathus; in the features of the man he killed, Dirck more and more sees an archaic Greek lover.

When America enters World War II toward the close of the novel, Dirck addresses the troops, arguing against race prejudice and intolerance. The former he defines, but intolerance is left vague. Where there might have been gay propaganda, there is none. Again, neither Dirck nor the author appear fully able to establish a philosophy. The chapter dealing with Roswell Cleminshaw argues that gay baiting is wrong and that gays are as strong and courageous as any heterosexual soldier. There is a marvelous moment when the troops return to New York in 1918. Cleminshaw suggests doubtfully that he and Dirck might shake hands. The latter agrees, but notes that he will wear his glove. " 'Don't mention it,' Cleminshaw answered sensitively. 'I've kept mine on too' " (p. 84). Yet the story is not adequately developed from that point. Thanks to Cleminshaw, gays have gained in stature and respect, but what of Dirck? Is he a closet gay? He has married and separated in the course of the novel, but he has certainly not displayed any physical interest in any of his apparently attractive male associates.

Again, contemporary critics understood the problem with *The Great Light.* In the *New York Herald Tribune Weekly Book Review* (October 12, 1947), Rose Feld wrote that

Mr. Barretto has a philosophy, but it comes through somewhat vaguely. It is undefined, mainly because Dirck remains vague and unreal. He never reaches the stature of spiritual greatness indicated by his quest. Strangely enough, or perhaps because he is dealing with recognizable people, Mr. Barretto is highly successful with the secondary characters of the book, particularly with Archer Paine, the novelist, and Nevius Brooks, the psychiatrist.

The only positive identification of Dirck as gay comes with his death. World War II is over. Dirck is driving down a country road and tries to attract the attention of a nineteen-year-old youth in another car. Dirck believes the young man to be Andragathus and, perhaps in order to unite himself in eternity with the Greek lover, he crashes his car into a tree.

Archer Paine, who has earlier compared Dirck's nude body to that of a Scandinavian god, sees an affinity between Dirck and Andragathus, who was raised in a time of beauty. Was Dirck obsessed with Andragathus because he was pleading "for a group of men who . . . were either variants of their species or mentally ill?" (p. 279).

Who knows? Certainly not the reader, and perhaps not even the author, Larry Barretto (1890-1971), who was also a correspondent and critic, had been writing novels since 1925, and was not known to be gay.

Stuart Benton, *All Things Human*

On the surface, *All Things Human* (Sheridan House, 1949) is little more than an exploitation novel, the story of a man jailed for a murder he did not commit, a trashy melodrama with a substantial number of gritty prison scenes. What is surprising about *All Things Human* is the amount of homosexuality lurking within its pages. At first, the homosexual angle seems as exploitive as everything else about the plotline until, gradually, it engulfs the story, becoming a major theme.

The central character here is a millionaire banker in his early forties named Stuart Kent, who makes an enemy of a prominent political boss in the city of Midmetropolis (which sounds like something out of *Batman* but is presumably a pseudonym for Chicago). Kent has lost sexual interest in his wife and is finding his secretary more and more attractive. On a trip to New York he visits a medical friend, Dr. Brennan, in the hope of restoring his glandular balance and becoming more of a competent husband. While in the waiting room, Kent is amused by a pimply youth with a falsetto laugh, a mincing manner, who "would be more plausible in a frock than in trousers." "Presumably the mother hoped that Brennan's laboratory would supply the boy with hormones to strengthen the chain of masculine glands, hormones her own body had been unable to furnish when the embryo was in need of such nutrient" (p. 32). Thus the first reference to homosexuality—and a far from satisfactory one.

Despite, or perhaps because of, Dr. Brennan's "monkey gland" treatment, Kent visits his secretary's apartment and has sexual intercourse with her. The following morning he is arrested for her murder, which obviously took place after he left. Thanks to the city's political boss and a judge under his control, Kent is found guilty of the crime and sentenced to fifteen years in prison for second-degree murder. His wife leaves him, takes his money, and marries his defense attorney. Kent's daughter will have nothing more to do with him, and his sympathetic son is killed during World War II.

Much of the novel describes Kent's time in prison, beginning with his arrival, when he takes a shower and the other inmates find humor in comparing his genitals to those of a Negro sharing the facilities with him. It is generally assumed by the prison population that the younger man sharing Kent's cell is his "boy," but Kent avoids any homosexual contact. At the same time, he begins to display compassion for the gay activities around him. The sexual activity evokes no conscious personal reaction, and he claims his interest is purely scientific. Another prisoner warns him not to let the guards discover he has any sexual interest in another prisoner or he will be recorded as a "P" or a "D" (pervert or degenerate).

Kent enjoys the "graceful" nudity of the "colored boys" as they dash by in the hallway. He is attracted in the shower room to a young man, nicknamed Goldielocks, whose attributes are described in great detail: his lissome figure, blue eyes, long silken lashes, metallic hair like burnished gold, hairless chest. "The boy's legs were straight. Gracefully curved buttocks recalled Hadrian's Antinous. Muscles rippled under his skin without disturbing the perfect harmony of limbs tanned uniformly to a light, golden tint" (p. 112).

A strip search of the boy by a sadistic guard is equally detailed, as the youth opens his mouth, spreads his legs, bends over, and draws his cheeks while the onlookers snicker. "Goldielocks smilingly ignored the indelicate allusions and guffaws of the inmates. He found a recondite pleasure in his passive defiance and in the exposure of his anatomical charms" (p. 113).

Moved to the state prison where he is eventually allowed to work in the library, Kent meets a sailor arrested for vagrancy named Jack Reynolds. Half shy, half impudent, Reynolds reminds Kent of his murdered secretary and her "once adorable mouth" (p. 240). Kent becomes Reynolds' mentor, and begins to wonder whether he is in love with the young man. When Kent gives Reynolds a gift, the youth impulsively kisses him, a gesture that Kent finds innocent and spontaneous, "like a son's shy caress" (p. 244).

In the meantime, Kent's appeal against his conviction is upheld, the political boss has no further interest in keeping him in jail, and the banker is once again a free man. He is taken up by a rich, aging society woman named Ivy Randolph who installs Kent on her estate where both hetero- and homosexual activity abound. When Ivy asks that Kent choke her, as she believes he strangled his secretary, the banker rushes from the house in disgust.

He visits a Turkish bath, where an ex-convict gives him a massage and where Kent begins to yearn for prison life. He wonders about Jack, the "onlie begetter" of his affection. Kent, taking the name Jonathan Doe, is arrested for drunkenness and disorderly conduct and is reunited in prison with Jack.

The banker considers his intimacy with Jack, his "unsullied and genuine" affection. He reads Shakespeare's sonnets to the young man, pondering the "enigmatic youth" who lives eternally therein. Jack tells him that he does not miss women friends: "They're dirty. They smell. A man's body is clean, you can see all he's got. . . . After I've been with a girl . . . , I feel like kicking her out of bed. I get disgusted with her and myself" (pp. 316-317). When Jack is accused of rape, Kent decides to reveal his identity and arranges for an attorney to represent the young man.

Kent asks Jack why he is unwilling to defend himself against the charge, and the youth reveals his secret: Kent's secretary had been his girlfriend and, in a drunken stupor, he had killed her. Kent asks himself whether he should use Jack's confession to shame the city that convicted him, but while reason says yes, his heart says no.

Kent keeps quiet, but Jack is sentenced to the electric chair for the rape he did not commit. At the last minute, the real culprit is arrested and Jack is freed. Also, Kent reads an Associated Press story of a death in England, similar to that of his secretary, which explains that too ardent a caress can exert pressure on the nerve center and cause immediate death. Jack did not willfully kill the secretary!

After the two men leave prison, Jack disappears, and Kent, unable to locate him, moves to New York, recovers a portion of his wealth from his ex-wife, opens an office on Wall Street, and begins a relationship with a woman named Sylvia Sinclair. However, he still misses jail, which, of course, means that he misses Jack. Could it also be that Kent misses the all-male environment and the homosexuality of prison life? Dr. Brennan returns to the story, explaining, "Kent knows that man is basically bisexual, but refused to acknowledge the homo-erotic component in his own temperament" (p. 350).

After dinner with Brennan and Sylvia, Kent swallows a vial of morphine he has stolen from the doctor. While he waits to die, the night clerk rings up to his apartment that Mr. Kent has a visitor—Jack. The latter wants to apologize and to tell Kent that he now has a girlfriend. He still wants to be with Kent, to work for him, but Kent tells Jack that he is going away. In the meantime, Dr. Brennan discovers that the vial of morphine is gone and rushes to the apartment, where he meets Jack. Sylvia is called, and the three work to revive Kent. As Kent awakens, he hears Sylvia tell him, "Each of us loves you. . . . Our love calls you. Brennan and Jack . . . and I" (p. 383).

If nothing else, the author deserves praise for concocting such a preposterous story and for a sympathetic view of homosexuality—even if it does seem to thrive at its best only in a prison environment. He is clever in capturing the reader's compassion and support for the gay life. Stuart Kent's wife is quickly revealed as one of the villains of the piece. When the attorney suggests to her that Goldielocks is her husband's punk, she is quick to respond, "I had to tolerate his kept women. I will not support his kept boys. . . . I can forgive murder, but degeneracy—never" (p. 205). The speech speedily wins the reader's support for Goldielocks and his colleagues.

All Things Human is not well written, and the convoluted story line requires tolerance from the reader. Although, in all honesty, much of it is so outrageous that one cannot help but read on in awe at what the author will come up with next. Perhaps the worst moment in the book occurs when the author suddenly begins to quote an Associated Press news story, complete with footnote as to date. Is this an attempt to suggest that everything here could just as much be truth as fiction?

Stuart Benton was the pseudonym of George Sylvester Viereck (1884-1962), who published *All Things Human* through George Duckworth (1950) under his own name in the United Kingdom. Viereck's first novel, *My First 2,000 Years,* written in collaboration with Paul Eldridge, was published in 1933 and described as a "daring and fantastic set of historical variations on the eternal theme of man and human," a theme taken up again, but in a modern setting, in *All Things Human*. The publisher claimed that although the prison scenes in *All Things Human* were "not for the squeamish," they were "authenticated by the author's own experiences." Those "experiences" were the result of Viereck's pro-Nazi sympathies and his work as U.S. correspondent for a Nazi publication, for which he was jailed from 1942 to 1947. Presumably, he was somewhat notorious in the United States for being a Nazi and found it necessary to adopt the one-time pseudonym of Stuart Benton, whereas in the United Kingdom, Viereck's name remained relatively unsullied.

Born in Munich, Viereck came to the United States with his family in 1896, and, as in the later conflict, he supported Germany throughout World War I. Viereck's pro-Nazi stance led to an estrangement from both his wife and son, who, similar to his father, was a highly respected poet. Viereck was something of a scandalous poet whose verse dealt with sexual imagery. His poems often praised pansexualism or bisexualism, and there is every reason to believe that as his hero Stuart Kent may have been, Viereck was involved in bisexual affairs. When asked in regard to his poem "The Pilgrim" whether there was such a thing as perversion, he responded,

> Perversion is what the other fellow does and what we don't like in the technique of sexual acts. It is not important to anyone except himself and his partner or partners. The sole question is of the effect on the respective nervous and glandular system.

It is worth noting that this strange and unequivocal writer and propagandist (whose thinking on sexual matters seems far removed from Nazi doctrine) also edited an American edition of Oscar Wilde's *Panthea and Other Poems,* along with two volumes of verse by Lord Alfred Douglas. He is the subject of a little-read biography, *George Sylvester Viereck: German American Propagandist* by Neil M. Johnson (University of Illinois Press, 1972), and his papers (obviously worthy of further study) are housed in the University of Iowa Library.

– 4 –

Alvah Bessie, *Dwell in the Wilderness*

Dwell in the Wilderness (Covici-Friede, 1935) is one of those family sagas with which British and American literature is littered; it was described by Mary McCarthy in *The Nation* (September 4, 1935) as "a rambling family history, spirited but pointless," as, quite frankly, are most of the novels of this genre. The period covered is 1876 through 1925, and the family is that of Eben and Ameliah Morris of Michigan. What is pleasing about the narrative is that, as in any good modern family, one of the Morris children—the youngest, Dewey—is gay.

You sort of know Dewey is going to turn out gay fairly early in his life. As a small kid, he stops to watch a crowd of little girls at play. They grab hold of him, strip him of his trousers and underpants, and generally humiliate him. The reader knows what the future holds for this poor kid, even if he and his parents do not. Dewey is somewhat artistic and, as an adult, becomes involved in a small-time theatrical production. His sister, Martha, is an actress in the company, and she is attracted to a young man named Warren, who is also in the company and who shares Dewey's bed. When another young man, Sam Graham, joins the company and becomes Dewey's lover, Warren leaves and heads for New York with Martha.

The two take a hotel room, and the naive Martha believes that she has found a lover in Warren. Martha finds nothing odd in Warren's calling her brother Dew-Drop. On their first night together, they undress, stand naked holding each other—and Warren breaks down, sobbing that he is sorry he cannot continue. Later, he explains to her,

> There are many millions of men on this earth who are not men in the ordinary sense of the word, who are not women in that sense; the men cannot love women; the women cannot love men—they are lovers of their own sex. . . . I am such a person, . . . but I

thought there was enough in me of what the uninformed call "normal"; I thought because of my love for you that I could transcend the limitations of my kind—that I could make you happy. (p. 419)

Martha is remarkably understanding; Warren heads for Europe and leaves with her a copy of Edward Carpenter's *Love's Coming of Age*. Martha rents an apartment and is soon joined by Dewey and Sam. Dewey tells her,

There are all kinds. . . . Just the same as there are all kinds of men and women. You've seen a lot of them in the last week or so. Some of them are decent. . . . Some of them are bitches, just as some women are bitches and can never get enough of a man. (p. 447)

The three settle down together, working to create a new theatrical troupe.

It is all very civilized for its day, and free of any name-calling or gay stereotyping. The only complaint might be that the author deliberately avoids anything explicit in regard to the behavior of the three men—although Warren and Dewey do giggle a lot in bed as heard through the wall by Martha. The penultimate chapter in which everyone's homosexuality is revealed is delightfully titled, "What Would the Neighbors Say?"

Reviews were decidedly mixed. Louis Kronenberger in *The New York Times* (August 25, 1935) wrote that *Dwell in the Wilderness* "must be admired for the seriousness of purpose it so vividly communicates." Similarly, H. M. Jones in the *Saturday Review of Literature* (August 31, 1935) noted that "scene after scene is presented with loving fidelity and great vividness." But to the reviewer in the *Christian Science Monitor* (August 19, 1935), it was "a one-sided picture, and a continually unpleasant one. . . . He [Bessie] is too much like Coleridge's atheist, who closes his eyes and calls it night."

Dwell in the Wilderness was the first novel from Alvah Bessie (1904-1985), who is best known as one of the "Hollywood Ten" jailed for contempt of Congress after refusing to confirm or deny his membership in the Communist Party before the 1947 House Committee on Un-American Activities. The novel gives absolutely no hint that the author is a Communist who was to serve in the Abraham Lin-

coln Brigade during the Spanish Civil War. The blacklisting in Hollywood, which followed Bessie's imprisonment, formed the basis for
his 1965 autobiographical *Inquisition in Eden.* Among Bessie's films
(all Warner Bros.) are *Northern Pursuit* (1943), *Hotel Berlin* (1945),
and *Objective, Burma!* (1945). His 1967 novel, *The Symbol,* was
filmed in 1973 as *The Sex Symbol.*

André Birabeau, *Revelation*

The revelation of the title is that Dominique, the son of Madame Casseneuil, is gay. In her Paris apartment, the proud mother finds continued pleasure in looking at the photographs of her son, now living in Avignon; her marriage is not an unhappy one, but her husband, Jean, is a writer who spends most of his time abroad.

One of Madame Casseneuil's favorite photographs of Dominique shows him in his new car, and it is ironic that when the telegram arrives, reporting his death, it was in a motor accident. Madame Casseneuil visits Dominique's room in Avignon, holding and kissing a kimono that he had recently purchased, and discovers a cache of love letters. She is touched by the ardor of the letters, but puzzled by the use of the masculine gender until, suddenly, she realizes that they are from a man. "God! a man! . . . Dominique! Dominique! . . . The abomination of it! . . ." (p. 76).

Madame Casseneuil leaves Avignon to return to Paris, unable to reveal what she has discovered, even to her husband. He admits that he never really knew his son, and his wife desperately wishes to tell him that she also did not know Dominique. She longs to reveal to her husband, "You, a decent man, and I, a decent woman, we have only produced a perverted child. . . . The flesh of our flesh, the soul of our souls; the best of you and of me is nothing but a degenerate . . ." (p. 151). Madame Casseneuil cannot grieve as other mothers might grieve:

> She is completely void. Nothing in her heart either. A deathly chill, a chill like the chill of ether. . . . When she thinks of her son, it is not a weight of sorrow that rises to her lips but the irrepressible, sour foul regurgitation of utter disgust. (p. 92)

Not one happy memory remains for this mother; everything is soiled and tainted, every trust betrayed, the past ravaged, and not one pleasant thought left to her. As she thinks back on her son's childhood, Madame Casseneuil recalls that he was a weakling, unwilling to fight, that he would play with a little girl who would treat him as her slave, would strike him, pinching and scratching his arms. The more she broods, the more the mother sees her son as a victim; alone and weak, he had been easy prey for the other man, "That monster of depravity, that—beast! . . ." (p. 213).

That man is Gilbert Savinnes. "A beast may be slaughtered . . ." (p. 215), and Madame Casseneuil, armed with a newly purchased gun, seeks revenge. In Avignon, she discovers that Savinnes is a forage merchant, an ordinary, unromantic man who sells animal feed. He looks like any other male, not remarkably handsome. "Neither tall nor short, clean-shaven, about thirty years of age . . . he wears a very ordinary grey lounge suit. He does not even look wicked" (p. 229). As the two talk together, Savinnes reveals that he was devoted to Dominique, that Dominique used to sit where his mother is now sitting, that he has arranged for Dominique's grave. Suddenly, Madame Casseneuil is overcome with a new revelation—that here is someone who loved her son, who speaks lovingly of him, who makes her realize that a mother cannot despise her child and cannot leave off loving him. Here is the only one with whom she can speak of her sorrow, who can share her grief—she and Savinnes are the only ones who have loved Dominique—and Madame Casseneuil will return again to him. The mutual bond that existed (at least in the mother's mind) between Madame Casseneuil and her son is now transferred to Madame Casseneuil and her son's lover.

Revelation (The Viking Press, 1930) is unique for its time, and while the writing style is somewhat antiquated, it does manage to capture the grief, horror, and revulsion that a mother of the 1920s could well experience on discovering her son's homosexuality. Here, for the first time, is a novel that discusses homosexuality from the viewpoint of the mother. The final chapter in which Madame Casseneuil slowly shares her sorrow with her son's lover is not overwhelmingly moving. There is something wooden about Savinnes's response. He holds himself back while his lover's mother offers an outpouring of grief. In many ways, Savinnes is the more sensible of the two, taking care of the grave site, while Madame Casseneuil wanders around, lost in despair and revulsion.

In many respects, *Revelation* is a cold novel, for all the mother's emotional outbursts. Not once does the reader get an accurate description of the son. There are occasional glimpses—a reference to "beautiful long sweeping lashes" (p. 62)—but no reference to good looks or sensuality or any other attributes that might have made Dominique attractive to both women and men. In the presentation of the drama, André Birabeau is dispassionate, ultimately neither condemning nor praising Dominique's lifestyle.

The novel was first published in Paris, by Ernest Flammarion, in 1924 as *La Débauche*. Its author, André Birabeau (1890-1974), was a prominent French dramatist, responsible for some thirty popular comedies and farces, all far removed from the anguish and controversial subject matter of *Revelation*. A number of his works were produced on the New York stage: *Déjeuner de Soleil* (1925) became the musical *Lovely Lady* (1927), *Dame Nature* (1936) was produced under that title in 1938, and *Pamplemous* (1937) became *Little Dark Horse* (1941). Photographs of Birabeau show him as a slightly disheveled gentleman, with a thick black beard and piercing eyes.

Contemporary critical reaction to *Revelation* was positive. In a *New York Times* review (July 20, 1930), in which the son is described as homosexual, and with the correct usage of the word as an adjective and not a noun, Louis Kronenberger wrote,

> This novel, the work of a writer whose interest in an unusual human situation is equaled by his skill in dealing with it, differs from any previous treatment of sexual pathology in literature. . . . M. Birabeau's whole book is written with logic and detachment. However special its subject-matter, the author has made it a serious and dignified, if sometimes rather horrifying work.

In the *Saturday Review* (September 20, 1930), Osbert Burdett commented,

> It lives as a story, and it moves its readers because of the understanding and the imagination which have worked out every necessary detail of the picture and have omitted everything else. Being only the fulcrum, the son, except through his mother's eyes in his infancy and after his death, forms no part. That is

high praise for such a story as this. An erotic motive is not exploited, but used to show how average humanity behaves. These reactions are the marrow of the story, and the way in which they are woven into a living pattern is an object-lesson of narrative skill.

Kenneth White in *The New Republic* (August 13, 1930) opined,

Even a bad translation cannot conceal the excellence of Birabeau's study of a mother who discovers that her dead son has been loved by a man. The main excellence appears in the novel's complete escape from the circle of a scandalous social problem. . . . The faults of the novel lie entirely within the style. . . . What remains a sincere, good novel might, with a richer style, have been a profoundly moving one.

Despite no words apparently being absent, the translator or the novel's author is very fond of ellipses. There is hardly a sentence, once the mother discovers her son's true nature, that does not conclude with three or four periods. For dramatic effect, two chapters—18 and 25—consist of only one sentence. The first reveals the identity of the son's lover: "The name of the man is Gilbert Savinnes" (p. 179). The second alludes to the mother's response: "A beast may be slaughtered . . ." (p. 215).

The translator of *Revelation* is Una Vicenzo Troubridge (1887-1963), who promoted herself as Una, Lady Troubridge, despite not being born a lady and having no right to the title after she had separated from her husband. Una, Lady Troubridge, is, of course, the lover of *The Well of Loneliness* author, Radclyffe Hall, and her literary efforts include the biography *The Life and Death of Radclyffe Hall* (Hammond, Hammond, 1961).

– 6 –

Isabel Bolton, *The Christmas Tree*

It is Christmas 1945 and wealthy New Yorker Mrs. Hilly Danforth, recalls Christmases past, and determines that her grandson, Henry, shall have a Christmas tree. Henry lives with his grandmother because her son, Larry, and his wife, Anne, are divorced. As Anne explains it, "He was . . . the type she always fell for—the invert, the schizophrene, the artist. Men like that were never normal sexually" (p. 30).

Mrs. Danforth thinks back to the years that she and the youthful Larry spent in Paris. She remembers Larry's friend Pierre playing the "Moonlight Sonata," rising from the piano, and moving toward Larry, her "seeing them staring at each other; and divining instantly the truth about the boys' relationship" (p. 37). Now Larry is living in Washington, DC, with his friend, Gerald Styles. The problem for Mrs. Danforth is that Larry, Anne, and her new husband, Captain George Fletcher, all plan to visit her for Christmas.

The narrative voice switches from Mrs. Danforth to Larry in Washington, DC. He decides to ignore a telegram from his mother suggesting that it would be better if he not come. He has also decided to leave Gerald, whom he finds too possessive, and on whom he is taking out much of the animosity he feels toward his mother.

Larry leaves by train for New York, and Gerald follows him on the same train. While Larry takes time out to get drunk, Gerald goes directly to Mrs. Danforth's apartment, hoping to find his lover there. As Gerald tries to explain his presence, Anne, Captain Fletcher, and Larry arrive. Everyone, even Henry, is "in a queer way spelled and bound by him [Larry]" (p. 199). Henry goes out to the terrace. Larry, Ann, and Fletcher follow, and Larry tells Fletcher to leave. Larry pushes Fletcher off the terrace, sixteen flights to his death. Despite the insistence of both Anne and Gerald that it was an accident, Larry turns himself in to the police as a murderer. Mrs. Danforth, realizing she must stand in complete fidelity with her son, informs the police

25

they must abide by what Larry has told them. "His getting off to Sing Sing to pay the final penalty would be merely a part, an infinitesimal part of the monstrous, wholesale and unspeakable melodrama that was afflicting the world today" (p. 211).

The Christmas Tree (Charles Scribner's Sons, 1949) is a strange novel, its story presented in an extremely straightforward, matter-of-fact style with virtually no emotion from any of its protagonists. Only at its close do we have Mrs. Danforth presenting a somewhat muddled philosophy linking her son's killing of the captain to the latter's holding in his innocent, young, and heroic hands "satanic weapons," such as the atomic bomb. The mother feels pride at her son's confession, and the manner in which he has conducted himself with the police; his values and her values are one and the same. As the publisher notes, this is a strange and original book, in which a final tragedy is so exalted as to approximate a kind of joy.

At the novel's opening, Mrs. Danforth comments that the Christmas season "did queer things to you" (p. 3), and the number of times the author makes use of the word *queer* cannot be accidental. Larry Danforth is not once branded homosexual. The use of the term "invert" is very old-fashioned, but somehow appropriate here in that the Danforth family belong to another age.

A spinster who had the appearance of an old-fashioned schoolmarm, Isabel Bolton (1883-1975) was in her sixties when she wrote *The Christmas Tree;* she had already published five volumes of poetry and two earlier novels. As with *The Christmas Tree,* all of Bolton's books deal with the "leisure class," of which the author was very much a part. Isabel Bolton understood wealth and position, and had no problem developing the character of the mother in *The Christmas Tree.* However, she does not, perhaps, have sufficient grasp of the subject of homosexuality, despite living in Greenwich Village and, presumably, having some social intercourse with gays (although there is no evidence that she ever had a lesbian relationship). *Time* (March 28, 1949) complained that, "Whenever she tries to speak through a character who is not her own kind and her own sex, she loses her firm tone of voice."

There is some truth to that criticism and to the comment in *The New York Times* (March 19, 1949) that "Larry so often seems merely petulant and childish, and never quite important enough to justify all the emotion that is spent on him." At the same time, there is little that one can criticize about Larry or the author's presentation of him except his rather arbitrary dismissal of Gerald from his life. The latter act is one of pure selfishness that does not help win over many gay readers. Larry is a central gay character in a novel where homosexuality is almost an irrelevancy.

On the whole, reviews of *The Christmas Tree* were most positive. M. W. Stoer in the *Christian Science Monitor* (March 17, 1949) described the novel as "a morality play for moderns," adding, "In *The Christmas Tree,* the residue of thought or emotion, which remains, at the end, with the reader is liable to be simply one of pity. And pity is not enough." In *The Nation* (March 19, 1949), Diana Trilling wrote, "Dealing with that most hazardous of themes, the sources of homosexuality, it adds a whole new dimension of feeling to anything fiction has hitherto given us on the subject."

7

Vance Bourjaily, *The End of My Life*

Vance Bourjaily (born 1922) served as a volunteer ambulance corpsman in the Middle East and Italy from 1942 to 1944, and *The End of My Life* (Charles Scribner's Sons, 1947), the first of fourteen books, is obviously based on individuals whom he met during that period.

Thomas "Skinner" Galt is the principal character in the novel, a personable young man, an American civilian volunteer who drives an ambulance for the British. With him on a tour of duty in the Middle East are Robert "Freak" Lacey, Benjamin Berg, and Rod Manjac. Also in the corps is fifty-year-old Haldemeyer, described as "a queer" (p. 42), and an exceptionally effeminate boy named Billy, who "had a delicate, musical voice, with no trace of the simper and lisp which amateur and professional funny men insist is an attribute to all homosexuals" (p. 81).

Freak notes, "Gee, he's pretty. . . . I can see how, if you were off someplace, away from women, you might really go for him" (p. 82). Obviously there is to be a revelation here, but when it comes, it is a genuine surprise to the reader. One wonders about Skinner, whose reading matter consists of Christopher Isherwood's *Mr. Norris Changes Trains*. But no; Skinner learns that Rod plans to desert, disguising himself as an Arab and expecting to live as an Arab. "I'm in love," explains Rod. "A beautiful little someone right here. A little blonde someone . . . a lovely, blue-eyed creature, with crispy golden curls, and a nice little pink set of male genitals" (p. 198).

Rod had been having an affair with Billy. His interest in "punks" had developed when he lived and played piano in San Francisco. "Every now and then, maybe, you try spending an evening with a punk, just for the hell of it, but it's all right, because you're under control. You aren't doing it because you have to; you're doing it because you want to" (p. 199).

Without success, Skinner attempts to talk Rod out of leaving. "You know it doesn't make a damn to us," he claims, but, on reflection, admits, when Rod asks, "How would you like to have a nice fairy for a friend?," "I guess it does" (p. 202). Rod leaves, and Skinner remains silent as to the reason why.

The remainder of the novel follows Skinner from the Middle East to Italy, where he inadvertently lets an American nurse be killed by enemy fire. Skinner is court-martialed and sentenced to a year in jail. From there he ends an affair with his American girlfriend; "I'm becoming dead," he tells her (p. 276).

The End of My Life has a style evident of a debt to Ernest Hemingway. It captures the spirit of young men at war but, at the same time, there is very little war here. Only at the close does any fighting intrude on the story. It is the characters, their past and present lives, that are significant, together with the environment in which they find themselves. The reasons for their being there and what is taking place around them are relatively unimportant.

The homosexuality is dealt with in a frank and honest manner, with Skinner and his colleagues relatively tolerant for the times. The expressions "fag" and "fairy" are thrown around, but so, also, is "gay." Rod's acceptance of his homosexuality does not make particularly appealing reading:

> I could take a fag for an evening, or leave him alone. Or take a woman, and have just as good a time.... But more and more, the last couple of years, I've gotten so that women kind of revolt me. ... No girl ever affected me this way. (pp. 200-201)

Contemporary reviewers praised the novel, without emphasizing its gay element. In the *New York Herald Tribune Weekly Book Review* (August 24, 1947), Iris Barry, the founder of the film department at the Museum of Modern Art, described *The End of My Life* as "astonishingly civilized, earnest and illuminating." *The New Yorker* (August 30, 1947) commented, "Mr. Bourjaily is often startlingly perceptive, has a true sense of climax, and unquestionably knows how to write." A couple of decades later, Merle Miller was to "out" himself as gay. In the *Saturday Review of Literature* (August 30, 1947), he wrote,

I hope a lot of people will read *The End of My Life;* I'm sure almost everybody will enjoy it despite its faults, which are numerous and obvious, and I'm equally certain that Bourjaily is going to write other and better novels. He has done an almost first-rate job with this one.

8

Kay Boyle, *Gentlemen, I Address You Privately*

Kay Boyle (1902-1992) had been an avant-garde writer in Paris in the 1920s, and she based *Gentlemen, I Address You Privately* (Harrison Smith and Robert Haas, 1933) on individuals she and her first husband encountered in Le Havre and Harfleur in 1923 and 1924. Yet despite the apparent authenticity of the individuals that people the novel, one is hard-pressed to believe in either them or their situation.

The central character is named Munday, an Englishman who has been forced to leave the Church (presumably Catholic) because of some unexplained behavior. He is, apparently, a musician who has found insufficient romance in the Church and its music. Munday flees to the French coast and ekes out a living giving piano lessons. In the first chapter, a fellow Englishman with a cockney accent, named Ayton, whose sister is one of Munday's pupils, comes to his room. In true Gothic style, a storm is in full force outside. There are many clues to Ayton's character. His elegant hair is "curled tight as a woman's all over the crown" (p. 15). "His eyes fell shy as a girl's" (p. 17). "He sat shaking his wrists in the fire's light, stirring and preening like a vain woman with gems of value hanging on her" (pp. 132-133). Ayton is a sailor who has deserted his ship and is on the run:

> "It's queer, I don't doubt, to come to a stranger for help," he said, "but I couldn't turn to a woman. I know a few of them here, but it ruins a man to be with them. A man must stay to himself, away from them," he said, "if he wants to become anything at all." (p. 21)

By the close of Chapter 1, it is agreed that Ayton will stay the night—he sleeps on the bed, Munday on a mattress on the floor—and thus a relationship develops between the two men. It is gay, without the author's acknowledging the word "homosexuality," and without censure from any characters in the novel. The two men meet their neighbors: a squatter and his wife, and three lesbians. Nothing very much happens except that Munday hides Ayton from discovery by the police. He questions Ayton's morality. "What kind of life of abomination do you live! . . . What kind of evil are you trying to fasten on me?" (p. 103). It is not so much an attack on a fellow queer, but rather an inquiry as to Ayton's immorality and his obvious attachment to a life of petty crime. The concern here, as in many of Boyle's later novels, is with an individual's moral responsibility—and Boyle does not equate morality with sex. Ultimately, Ayton leaves with the lesbians, and Munday discovers that Ayton is the father of the squatter's child. For all his comparison to women, Ayton was also a man.

One is forced to agree with H. S. Canby in the *Saturday Review of Literature* (November 4, 1933), "This is no book to attract the sensualist or arouse the censor." It is all rather vague and romantically dated, although one might dispute Canby's comment that Ayton is nothing more than "a woman's conception of a fascinating man." Ayton's request to spend the night would not be rejected by any gay man.

Kay Boyle may be little more today than a footnote to twentieth-century American literature, but she was once fairly prominent in the field. She had been a prolific novelist, short-story writer, essayist, and poet, who lived in Europe until the outbreak of World War II, and returned to France in 1948 as *The New Yorker*'s European correspondent. Kay Boyle was fired in the 1950s because of her outspoken leftist views, and with her third husband, Joseph von Franckenstein, she was denounced and blacklisted by Senator Joseph McCarthy. Taking up residence in San Francisco, Boyle continued to write and turned to teaching. Her poems, published in 1955 as *Collected Poems of Kay Boyle* (Copper Canyon), are indicative of her continued support for gays and lesbians.

One noted critic, Katherine Anne Porter, wrote of Boyle's romantic style:

> Miss Boyle writes of love not as if it were a disease, or a menace . . . or the fruits of original sin, or as a bawdy pastime. She writes as one who believes in love so fresh and clear it comes to the reader almost as a rediscovery in literature.

How pleasant it would be to accept Porter's description of the gay romance in *Gentlemen, I Address You Privately,* but in reality there is little romantic description. The most detailed reads more like a Barbara Cartland romance, lacking in sexual detail or climax:

> After a little Munday knew that he would get up and follow Ayton up the spiral stairway. The door would close behind them and there they would stand, curiously altered, as if they had hung their own beings like cloaks without the door. The two strangers who had come there seeking a cigarette, or any other useless thing, would suddenly come face to face and sit down speechless, but crying out each other's names, upon the bed together. The tide would come, and the tide run out again for all they would know of its coming and going. But a clear strong sense, like a statue standing, would be hewed out of sleep. (pp. 134-135)

Louis Kronenberger, writing in *The New York Times* (November 12, 1933), was right in his assertion that "Because its theme never flowers, because its hero never breathes, this book for all its minor excellence fails to be important." However, Kronenberger and other contemporary reviewers found much to praise in Kay Boyle's prose style and her insights into the human character and the human failings. None of the reviewers made reference to a gag line spoken by Ayton, "There are fairies at the bottoms of our guardsmen" (p. 214), a parody of the title of the Beatrice Lillie song "There Are Fairies at the Bottom of My Garden," and which surely Kay Boyle must have heard at a gay gathering.

Gentlemen, I Address You Privately was Boyle's second novel, and also the one that held the most fascination for her. She returned to it at the end of her life and, in 1991, Capra Press in Santa Barbara published a completely rewritten version.

9

Myron Brinig,
This Man Is My Brother

In 1929, Myron Brinig published the highly regarded *Singermann,*
an autobiographical saga of a Jewish family in the United States,
based on his father's life. With *This Man Is My Brother* (Farrar &
Rinehart, 1932), Brinig returns to the Singermann family, the successful owners of what would now be considered a department store
in Silver Bow, Montana. The text concentrates on the Singermann
children and is told, in part, through the eyes of one of the sons, Michael, who drives from New York to Montana to visit with his family
and to gather material for his new novel.

It is Michael's brother, forty-four-year-old Harry, who has consoli-
dated four Singermann stores into one and built up a thriving business.
"His organizing genius drew all of the individualistic Singermanns into
one organization" (p. 27). It is Harry who is gay, identified here as an
"invert." The family, at least on the surface, is unaware of Harry's sexuality, but as Michael sits at dinner with his brother and the family, it is
more than obvious:

> Harry was interested in art and literature and was fond of travel.
> . . . Yet as Michael watched Harry, he was irked by a quick, em-
> barrassed discomfort. Harry was too flushed and effeminate.
> His long fingers were too solicitous of moods and objects both
> real and invisible. (p. 13)

Harry is particularly fond of his brother David's adopted Gentile
son, Richard. He goes swimming with the young man, keeps a photograph of him on his desk at work, and serves as his mentor, but is unable to express the true affection that he feels for him, in part because
Richard is his nephew: "True, he could not openly make known the

nature of his affection and was forced to bottle it up so that he suffered the tortures of the damned" (p. 180).

Richard goes east to attend college, and later journeys for a vacation in Florida, where Harry joins him. There is affection between the two, but Harry fails to realize that it is only the "love" of a nephew for his favorite uncle. On the last night of his visit, Harry is determined to restrain all the impulses that he feels, and says goodbye to his nephew with a farewell hand on his shoulder. But as he held Richard, "All he saw was the image of beauty before him, and he moved close to it and held it in his arms, close to his heart, and felt an answering beat" (p. 301). He looks into Richard's eyes—the happiness he feels at that moment is overwhelming—but the response from his nephew is only anger and disgust. The boy leaves.

The next morning Harry encounters Richard on the beach. The boy will not speak to him and swims away. Forsaken, Harry takes to the water; in his mind he wonders what is wrong at revealing one's love for a person of the same sex—where is the sin? He swims toward Richard, calling his name, desperate to speak with him. Two days later, Harry's body washes up on the shore and is identified by Richard, who cannot stop weeping.

The entire family gathers for Harry's funeral, with Richard overcome by grief and unable to utter a coherent word. Michael Singermann wonders if the future—in this world and in another—will solve Harry's "peculiar problems of conduct, of desire and anguish" (p. 309).

> They used to throw men like Harry into prison. We have made some headway in this regard. We are beginning to study the problems of men and women like Harry, and there is a certain tolerance manifested nowadays. It would be terrible to think that Harry went on living, suffering the selfsame torture he suffered on earth. (p. 309)

In amusing but at the same time incredibly moving language, Michael Singermann and the author consider Harry's arrival in heaven. Will he sidestep an interview with God in favor of the latest Rembrandt or El Greco exhibition? The weather there is the same as Los Angeles, "sunny and monotonous" (p. 313). Michael Singermann agrees that there is a hell, existing on earth and around us every day. He continues, "And I sometimes think that Heaven is also on earth, and that just before Harry died, he reached out for it and grasped it close to his expiring heart" (p. 313).

Harry's death is, arguably, formulaic and expected. At least it is not a gay suicide in the accepted literary style of the day. If the reader is irritated by Brinig's killing off of Harry, he or she is more than satisfied by the funeral and Michael Singermann's comments that follow. On the dust jacket of *This Man Is My Brother,* the publisher comments, "The book contains, among other things, as beautiful and delicate a handling of a homosexual tragedy as has yet appeared." Harry does not appear on every page of the book—there are many chapters from which he is absent—but he is the dominant figure in the novel. He holds the family together. He is the head of the Singermann empire and a benevolent figure both in the family and in the store.

Only once does Michael Singermann make a disparaging remark about his brother, when he thinks,

> Harry has all the aspects, the mannerisms of a "queer," yet he seems quite alive in his ideas, his brain is working all the time. . . . Again, Harry was in his forties, the time of life when inverts are supposed to go to pieces mentally, yet there seemed nothing cracked or illogical in his thinking. (p. 36)

Yes, there is some stereotyping here, but notice that "queer" appears in quotes. How many other writers from this period would so treat the pejorative term? In addition, Michael's respect for his brother grows as the story unfolds. By the day of his funeral, Harry has grown in stature and respect; unfortunately, it has taken Harry's death for Michael Singermann to put aside his prejudices.

Harry gives work in the store to an unemployed youth, Jim Shepherd, caught shoplifting. By chance, Harry comes upon the boy as the two walk to the store, and the youth proudly tells his co-workers what a fine man is Harry, how democratic, how decent and nice, willing to walk alongside and listen to a lowly employee. The other men laugh and whisper in his ear. "How different the world had become in just a few minutes," thinks Jim Shepherd. "I'm kind of glad I was never educated," he says (p. 81). It is the world around that seeks and finds fault in an act of friendship by a gay man. It is not Harry but the heterosexuals with their innuendoes who pervert the young man and destroy his innocence.

At night, Harry lies in bed, suffering, as the author points out, as many inverted types do. He worries that his "weakness" will be revealed and exposed. He recalls "certain adventures" in New York and London, and the potential for blackmail. He senses and rejects Michael's feeling of pity for him: "My life is often fascinating . . . beautiful . . . beyond your depth of understanding, clever as you are!" (p. 77).

This Man Is My Brother is, of course, about much more than Harry Singermann. Most family members receive equal time, and Brinig is highly amusing in his depiction of Harry's sister-in-law Daisy and her fixation with Hollywood. There is endless analysis, much of it thought provoking, on the attitude of Jews to Gentiles, and of Jews to Jews. Harry's other nephew, Ralph, points out that "A Jew without a problem is a sky without stars" (p. 218) and *This Man Is My Brother* offers an array of Jews with problems, all of whom are happily entertaining or moving.

Myron Brinig (1900-1991) has produced a novel that is compelling in its emotional strength. It is one of the few popular novels of its day that has stood the test of time, and one of the few family sagas of the past that is worthy of modern attention. Brinig demonstrates tremendous ability to stir one's emotions here, but in concentrating on the ultimate tragedy of Harry's life, one should not ignore the original humor with which the text is peppered.

Brinig was a prolific author; most of his work dealt with Jewish life in the United States, although he is responsible for a 1930 study of male narcissism, *Anthony in the Nude* (Farrar & Rinehart). *This Man Is My Brother* was compared somewhat unfavorably to the earlier *Singermann,* but contemporary critics did not slight the work. A reviewer in *The Nation* (May 4, 1932) described it as "A fine novel, quite out of the rut, profoundly moving if not completely satisfying." A reviewer in *The New York Times* (January 31, 1932) was equally fulsome in his praise of Myron Brinig, who "has abundant vitality and emotional power, combined with that invaluable knack of being always interesting."

10

Richard Brooks, *The Brick Foxhole*

According to the author's note, the brick foxhole is a barracks, in this particular context just outside of Washington, DC, within which are soldiers who, because of their special qualifications, will never be assigned to active duty in the war. "This is a novel about a handful of men who happen to be trapped in a brick foxhole" (p. vii). It might also be considered the story of the murder of a gay man and its aftermath.

The central character, Jeff Mitchell, is a former Walt Disney animator who is now assigned to draw maps for the military. Not only does he have an inferiority complex because he has not been allowed to fight and kill "Japs," but also he is obsessed with the notion that his wife back in Hollywood has had sex with another soldier in the barracks. Mitchell's best friend, Pete Keeley, is disturbed at Mitchell's emotional state and so telephones his wife, asking that she come immediately to Washington, DC.

As he waits for a bus to take him into the city, Jeff is accosted by two of his fellow soldiers, Monty Crawford and Floyd Bowers. They have been picked up by a Mr. Edwards, "a simply wonderful interior decorator" (p. 86), who invites them back to his home for a drink. The men accept, knowing fully that Mr. Edwards is gay. Jeff goes along despite being concerned with what he knows "about the pastime of some soldiers. Their treatment of sexual perverts" (p. 88). A sickness arises in Jeff as Floyd whispers to him, "I ain't beaten up a queer in I don't know how long" (p. 89).

As the soldiers get drunk, the situation deteriorates. Monty asks Mr. Edwards to dance with him. Floyd takes off his trousers. Mr. Edwards sits down on the floor and cries, "I have such a bitchy life. . . . I don't think anybody in the world loves me" (p. 93). Jeff leaves, visits a bar and then a brothel, where he has sex with a good-hearted prostitute named Ginny, who gives him the keys to her apartment. Jeff heads there, lets himself in, and meets Ginny's husband, who has problems of his own, being one of her ex-clients.

In the meantime, Pete Keeley's poker game at the Stewart Hotel is interrupted by the police, who inform Keeley that Mr. Edwards has been murdered and that Jeff's furlough bag has been discovered at the Edwards' residence. The police and the press are more than interested in the case when it is discovered that Edwards is the son of a New York millionaire.

Unaware that he is wanted for murder, Jeff wanders into a hamburger joint. There he meets Max Brock, a Jewish soldier with whom he is friendly, and is shown the newspaper headline, "Prominent Decorator Found Murdered in Sordid Sex Orgy" (p. 176). Max helps Jeff hide out in a movie theatre and seeks out Keeley, who has gone to meet Jeff's wife. The police have already located Mary Mitchell, but a deal is worked out whereby she can talk with her husband before he is arrested.

Jeff is forced to tell his wife that he has an alibi in the prostitute Ginny, with whom he was having sex at the time of the murder. Mary Mitchell visits Ginny and persuades her to testify on Jeff's behalf. Keeley tracks down Monty, whom he realizes to be the murderer, and who has since murdered Floyd, the only witness to the crime. The racist Monty calls Keeley an "Irish sonofabitch . . . [a] Jew-lover . . . a Papist bastid" (p. 224), just before he is killed by Keeley. With the evidence of Ginny and her husband, Jeff is released by the police, and is accepted by Mary, who now has a new understanding of soldiers such as her husband and Keeley.

The Brick Foxhole (Harper & Brothers, 1945) is an intense novel, but not quite as hard-hitting as its author intended it to be. As Walter Bernstein wrote in *The New Republic* (July 23, 1945), "This is a pretentious book, tough on the outside and soft on the inside." The author is angry with a racist society that condones anti-Semitism, racism, and even homophobia, but the arguments put forward against these conditions by the two decent characters in the book (along with Max Brock), Jeff Mitchell and Peter Keeley, are weak and inconclusive. At times, it seems the police here are more tolerant that the men of the U.S. armed forces.

It is a gay man and his murder that serve as catalysts for the healing process between Jeff Mitchell and his wife and, to a lesser and rather uninteresting extent, Pete Keeley and his wife. Yet the gay man receives little sympathy from the author or from any of his characters. Edwards is a stereotypical gay man, who plays the complete score from *Oklahoma!* and insists his guests listen to his favorite recordings by Hildegarde. Police Captain Finlay looks at Edwards's friend, Palmer, who has discovered the body: "Finlay has marked him as a sexual pervert immediately upon seeing him. Now he was wondering why a man became one of 'those.' Was it environment or heredity?" (p. 155). Jeff describes Edwards to Max Brock as "Hell of a sweet guy. Kind of queer" (p. 176). That is about the best that gay men received from *The Brick Foxhole*.

Of course, when all is said and done, straight men fare little better. A more unpleasant bunch of soldiery it would be hard to imagine than these inhabitants of this specific brick foxhole. As Hubert Kupferberg wrote in the *New York Herald Tribune Weekly Book Review* (May 27, 1945),

> This is a somewhat unusual thesis and Sergeant Brooks could have made it stronger by peopling his brick foxhole with a less discreditable array of characters. The soldiers in *The Brick Foxhole* have already so far deteriorated that when the reader meets them it's hard to feel sympathy for them.

The proximity to the South results in the most offensive of language directed toward African Americans, who virtually do not exist in *The Brick Foxhole*. They come out late at night when all the white soldiers have returned to barracks. Anti-Semitism is rampant, particularly among the crowd of soldiers early in the novel, watching a boxing match wherein Max Brock is one of the losing contenders. At one point, it is noted that Monty is strongly American: "Frenchmen were frogs; Negroes, niggers; Poles, Polacks; Italians, wops; Chinese, Chinks; Jews, Christ-killers" (p. 30). Prejudice abounds here, and an argument might be made that there is no reason why gays should not suffer as much as Jews or Negroes. It has validity, except that no Jews or Negroes are actually murdered within the pages of *The Brick Foxhole*.

The Brick Foxhole is not a great novel of World War II. Lurking behind the façade of toughness is a mundane story line involving a man wrongly accused of a crime, a staple of popular fiction. Contemporary reviewers were very mixed in their reactions. In *The New York Times* (June 3, 1945), D. S. Simon wrote,

Mr. Brooks is an angry man and he seems to have spent great energy in his writing; his prose jerks across the page like a horse being whipped. His subject matter is highly interesting and he writes out of a first-hand experience. Yet the effect that he achieves is dim, cheap and second-hand.

Hamilton Basso in *The New Yorker* (June 2, 1945) commented,

This is a good theme for a novel, and, since it must have occurred to any number of writers in the armed forces, a good novel may someday be written about it. The field is still wide open. Mr. Brooks, having come upon the theme, does little more than kick it around.

On the positive side, screenwriter Niven Busch in the *Saturday Review of Literature* (June 2, 1945) described the novel as "angry, rapid, stream-lined, and beautifully written; it is tough without self-consciousness and bitter without irritability and it has a mood in it which looks like the mood of the best of the new stuff coming out of this war."

The Brick Foxhole was Richard Brooks's first novel, followed by two others, *Boiling Point* (1948) and *The Producer* (1951). A former reporter and radio writer, Brooks served as a sergeant with the Marine Corps and, although he denied that the novel was autobiographical, it is obvious that the character of Pete Keeley is based on him. Richard Brooks (1912-1992) went on to become a major Hollywood screenwriter and director, responsible for such classic motion pictures as *The Blackboard Jungle* (1955), *Cat on a Hot Tin Roof* (1958), *Elmer Gantry* (1960), *Lord Jim* (1965), and *In Cold Blood* (1967).

Of the filming of *The Brick Foxhole* as *Crossfire*, Alvah Bessie wrote in his autobiography, *Inquisition in Eden*, "This was probably the first Hollywood film ever to make an outright attack on anti-Semitism, an interesting thing in itself, considering the fact that the novel dealt not with anti-Semitism but with homosexuality."[1] Well, yes and no. The novel does deal primarily with homosexuality, but there is also much commentary on anti-Semitism in *The Brick Foxhole*. It is, of course, not surprising that Hollywood (in the form of producer RKO) would shy away from the homosexual murder, and it is creditable that a group of filmmakers—producer Dore Schary, screenwriter John Paxton, and director Edward Dmytryk—should have sufficient courage to tackle the subject of anti-Semitism at a time when Hollywood's Jewish moguls feared antagonizing American moviegoers with any film that might show up their religious background.

The murder victim in *Crossfire*, released in 1947, is Joseph Samuels, a draft-dodging "Jewboy." The Production Code Administration, whose staff read *The Brick Foxhole* and initially found it unacceptable for adaptation to the screen, required that there should be "no suggestion of a 'pansy' characterization about Samuels or his relationship with the soldiers." Perhaps because of the date of the film's production, the leading characters are now former members of the military, and for inexplicable reasons Jeff Mitchell becomes Arthur Mitchell, a relatively minor character; Pete Keeley becomes Felix Keeley, played by Robert Mitchum; and Monty Crawford becomes Sergeant Montgomery, played by Robert Ryan. The central character here is the police captain, played by Robert Young, who dominates the film.

NOTE

1. Alvah Bessie, *Inquisition in Eden*. New York: Macmillan, 1965, p. 129.

11

John Buchan, *Greenmantle*

John Buchan (1875-1940) has been the subject of many biographical and critical studies. A major figure in the British establishment, a director of intelligence at the Ministry of Information during World War I, Buchan was named Baron Tweedsmuir in 1935, and that same year appointed governor-general of Canada. A surprising number of his books have been reprinted, and there is even a *John Buchan Journal,* but if he is remembered at all by the average reader it is because of the 1935 film *The 39 Steps.* The production is supposedly based on the first of four adventure-thrillers featuring Richard Hannay published in 1915 as *The Thirty-Nine Steps,* but the plotline has virtually no similarity to that of the novel and is the work of screenwriter Charles Bennett. It is ironic that Buchan's best-known story line is the creative work of another writer.

Richard Hannay, who is regarded as the prototypical John Buchan hero, appears in four novels, published between 1915 and 1924, in all of which he is a gentleman spy working in the best interests of Britain and the Empire.

In the second book, *Greenmantle* (George H. Doran, 1916), Hannay is now a major in the British Army and is investigating German attempts to incite a jihad or holy war. Throughout, it is apparent that Muslims rate even lower than Germans in Buchan's estimation. Hannay's work takes him to Germany and through the Balkans to Constantinople.

Greenmantle is surprising in that Hannay's nemesis, Colonel Stumm, is quite obviously gay. After being captured, Hannay is taken by the German to his room. Hannay writes,

> At first sight you would have said it was a woman's drawing-room. But it wasn't. I soon saw the difference. There had never been a woman's hand in that place. It was the room of a man

who had a passion for frippery, who had a perverted taste for soft delicate things. . . . I began to see the queer other side to my host, that evil side which gossip had spoken of as not unknown in the German army. (p. 101)

"Perverted." "Queer." Buchan leaves little doubt as to Stumm's character. He even manages to get in a dig at the Germans, then Britain's enemy, suggesting that a fair number of them have similar tastes to Stumm, thus placing gays on the same level as Germans, Muslims, and other enemies of the Empire. Unfortunately, Hannay escapes prior to experiencing what is obviously to be some very kinky torture that Stumm has planned. At the novel's climax, the two meet up again, and at Stumm's death, Hannay delivers what may be considered a somewhat sympathetic tribute, "He was a brute and a bully, but, by God! he was a man" (p. 342).

Despite the pejoratives in the text, Buchan does deserve some credit for his depiction of Colonel Stumm. This is no stereotypical queer. He is gay, but he is not feminine or mannered in any way. Rather, Stumm is ugly, strong, violent, a brave and courageous fighter, and, ultimately, a worthy opponent to the handsome young Englishman.

Colonel Stumm was basically ignored by contemporary critics reviewing the novel, all of whom echoed the praise of *The New York Times* (March 4, 1917) that *Greenmantle* was "a story full of spirit and swing and high heroism." Contemporary critics saw the thrillers of John Buchan as dramas for schoolboys and others with adventuresome spirits. Few noted the remarkable lack of women in the stories. There are virtually none in *The Thirty-Nine Steps*—the Madeleine Carroll character in the film was created by Charles Bennett—and in *Greenmantle,* there is really only one, the dominating, Teutonic, and stereotypical Hilda Von Einem.

"Women had never come much my way, and I know as much of their ways as I know about the Chinese language," (p. 167) whines Richard Hannay, as he falls under the spell of Von Einem. She is as commanding as any of the men in Hannay's acquintance, and thus she replaces the male colleagues in his affection. If anyone is a stereotypical latent homosexual, it is Richard Hannay.

In recent years, commentators have been quick to point out the singular lack of women in all of Buchan's novels. "Buchan's is a man's world and that fact is merely underscored by supplying a restricted number of restrictedly drawn women with pivotal plot roles (this is especially true if the plots themselves become subject to accusations of thinness)," writes one modern critic.[1] The author quite obviously has a problem with female characters. His is a male world, one in which he feels comfortable, and although one can hardly label John Buchan as a latent homosexual, one must wonder at his unease with the feminine sex and his love of handsome, young, male heroes, be it Richard Hannay and his colleagues Peter Pienaar and Sandy Arbuthnot, or the central characters in other series, Dickson McCunn and Sir Edward Leithen. Indeed, Sandy Arbuthnot's love of Arab attire has one pondering if there might be a similarity between him and Lawrence of Arabia, a later hero with more than a passing knowledge of gay sex.

NOTE

1. Clive Bloom, *Spy Thrillers: From Buchan to Le Carré*. New York: St. Martin's Press, 1990, p. 69.

12

John Horne Burns, *The Gallery*

Based on the one and a half years that John Horne Burns (1916-1953) spent with the military in Italy, *The Gallery* (Harper & Brothers, 1947) was named "Best War Book of the Year" by the *Saturday Review of Literature*. It is more a series of short stories than a novel in the established sense, providing portraits of various Americans and Italians who come together in the summer of 1944 in a Naples arcade called the Galleria Umberto Primo.

Time (June 9, 1947) described as "first-rate" the sections dealing with a venereal disease hospital and a homosexual hangout, praising the best writing in the book as "descriptive reporting." The chapter titled "Queen Penicillin" is certainly the most disturbing, as it follows a young American sergeant whose blood tests positive for venereal disease and who is subjected to all manner of humiliating medical procedures. Heterosexual sex in war-torn Italy can have very unpleasant aftereffects. The most entertaining and, arguably, the most highly descriptive chapter is titled "Momma." Twenty-eight pages long, it describes Momma's bar, a hangout for gay soldiers and civilians in Naples.

Unlike other areas of military occupation, there is no discrimination at Momma's. Italian men fraternize openly with American, British, Australian, and South African soldiers. There is even a Negro second lieutenant present: "He seemed to have the idea he was stepping onto some lighted stage. He moved his hips ever so slightly and carried his pink-insided hand tightly against his thighs" (p. 134). He admires Momma's hats, asking if they are the work of Britain's Queen Mary.

The soldiers appraise each other openly, but few, if any, lasting relationships are formed. Momma's is a place for gossip and relaxation: "At Momma's most of her customers talked like literature salesmen who cunningly invited you out to dinner—all the time you knew that they were selling something, but their propaganda was sparkling and insidious" (p. 134).

Two English soldiers have the mannerisms and talk of old women, primping themselves in front of a mirror, referring to each other as Esther and Magda. There is one lesbian, Rhoda, a WAC with a page-boy bob. Looking at her, Momma wonders if, with women such as this, romantic love is on the wane in the United States, while the soldiers pointedly ignore her presence. The Italians behave like a bevy of Milan shop girls at the end of a busy day. A plump grenadier guardsman introduces his wife, a South African lance corporal, to Momma.

An American major and second lieutenant arrive at the bar late in the evening, wearing identical gold wedding bands on their fingers; "They came in a little flushed, as though they'd been surprised in a closet" (p. 146). There is some talk of morality and the law as it relates to the homosexual male. A British soldier ponders how one can speak of sin in regard to homosexuality "when thousands are cremated in German furnaces, when it isn't wrong to make a million pounds, but a crime to steal a loaf of bread" (p. 150).

His friend points out, "in relation to the world of 1944, this is just a bunch of gay people letting down their back hair" (p. 150). This is the second use of "gay" in the modern sense to be found in the chapter. Earlier, the author describes the crowd in the bar as "cajoling and tender and satiric and gay." It is unusual to find the adjective so used at this time and is arguably revealing to the reader of the author's true sexual identity. Equally unusual is the author's spelling of "queen" in reference to some, but not all, habitués of the bar. They are "queans," an archaic term for wenches or sluts.

The author of *The Gallery* displays an obvious sympathy for the regulars at Momma's bar, just as his compassion is more with the Neapolitans than with the occupying American soldiers. John Horne Burns captures the brutality, the crudity, and vulgarity of the military, and is very comfortable with it, but at the same time he never loses his understanding of higher human qualities. As Richard Sullivan in *The New York Times* (June 8, 1947) noted, "There is a fervent sensitivity, a passionate sympathy in the writing of these intimate studies." In the *New York Herald Tribune Weekly Book Review* (June 8, 1947), J. D. Ross described *The Gallery* as, "A novel of extraordinary skill and power . . . Mr. Burns writes unevenly, perhaps deliberately so, sometimes using the shock technique of photographic realism, sometimes employing a kind of stylized symbology." Edmund Wilson in *The New Yorker* (August 9, 1947) described it as "a remarkable book."

The gay military at war and at ease with itself is well documented in *The Gallery,* but that is not surprising in that it is the work of a gay novelist, obviously familiar with the scene. Burns revealed his homosexuality to Gore Vidal and Christopher Isherwood in 1947. The latter described Burns as drunk, hostile and tiresome, but he did admire *The Gallery.*[1] Burns decided to "come out of the cloister," as he described it, with his second novel, *Lucifer with a Book* (1949).

The hero here is Guy Hudson, a World War II veteran, the left side of whose mouth is scarred as a result of a mortar attack, and who becomes a history teacher at an eccentric American private school, The Academy. The male faculty are described as both "virile and swishy" (p. 39), and among the latter group are Dr. Sour, the head of the department of modern languages, who offers private tuition to some of the boys at nude parties in his quarters and who tries to pick up two sailors in Washington, DC, "who were not so compliant as his boys at The Academy" (p. 279), and a closeted old queen, Philbrick Grimes, who is the school's second in command.

There are quite a few gay youths among the students, notably "The Abbot" and "The Abbess" who host a salon, attended by "The Body," who edits the school newspaper; a muscular Alabaman named Mung; and "The Bishop," who wears a cope of gaudy cloth and gives lollipops and smacks on the rear end to younger boys who embrace his religion. The habitués of "The Abbey" dance to the music of Ravel and enjoy mutual masturbation. A muscular eighteen-year-old student, in need of higher grades, appears in Guy Hudson's room wearing tight silk pajamas and attempts to seduce the teacher: "You are different from most of the fairies they've got on this faculty. . . . I thought maybe you and me could be friends . . . real friends . . ." (p. 104). Hudson is more attracted to Brown's roommate, the sensitive, violin-playing Ralph Du Bouchet:

> He caught himself teaching only for the response of Ralph. The boy lay open to him like a maiden. He had the reflexes of a lover in bed. . . . The arrowlike beauty of Ralph brought Guy Hudson back to those slim boys of Normandy who in 1944 had mascoted themselves to the American Army for food and secu-

rity. And he himself had had a young friend, Marcel Bonné, to whom even now he sent CARE packages. (p. 84)

The boy, in turn, has a crush on Hudson. In the showers, he watches as the teacher dreamily soaps his genitals, impressed by Hudson's red hair and extremely hairy body. However, when Ralph returns to school in the spring, Hudson notes a change in the boy, and a curious conversation takes place:

> Ralph: "You know, it was sort of wonderful, those days when you and I were friends. . . ."
> Guy: "Can't we continue to be?"
> Ralph: "Not the way we used to be. . . . How silly I was about you! I guess I had what my mother would call a crush. But you were silly about me too. . . ."
> Ralph gives Guy a sidelong glance, and the teacher understands, "O, I see. You've finally discovered girls? . . . Good. That's the way it should be." (p. 287)

Guy Hudson has also discovered a girl, Betty Blanchard, and the two are to marry. That's the way it should be in mainstream novels of the 1940s. Yet throughout, the author has offered lingering doubts as to Hudson's sexuality—and he has spent too much time with Hudson and the boys in the showers to leave doubt as to the author's own interests.

Lucifer with a Book is the story of a heterosexual relationship but, as Maxwell Geismar comments in the *Saturday Review of Literature* (April 2, 1949),

> The central love affair of the novel, through which Guy Hudson finally realizes the difference between sex and love, is not altogether convincing. What is apparent, however, is the dominant sexuality of the novel, and a sexuality that finds expression in harsh and even violent terms.

The reviewer in *Catholic World* (June 1949) was even more outspoken and considerably more outraged: "the book is filled with cynical obscenities; and Krafft-Ebing, who is named only once, seems to have inspired the author frequently."

Many gay critics have claimed that Guy Hudson is a gay character whose sexuality is "modified" to suit the readership of the period. As presented by John Horne Burns, he is certainly a most ambiguous individual. On vacation from The Academy, he spends every night in New York in bed with a different sex partner (gender unspecified), and then returns for three months of celibacy, surrounded by eighteen-year-old males who are more than eager to offer the teacher sexual relief.

According to Gore Vidal, Burns himself found some sexual relief in the 1950s, living with an Italian veterinarian in Florence. "They had a rather stormy relationship, but nothing sinister about it," Vidal told *Fag Rag* (Winter-Spring 1974). "One day he was drunk at a bar, wandered out in the hot midday sun and had a stroke. Cerebral hemorrhage. . . . I think he wanted to die." Burns is the subject of an obscure tribute volume, *John Horne Burns: An Appreciative Biography* by John Mitzel (Dorchester: Manifest Destiny Books, 1974). *The Gallery* was reprinted in 1950 as a Bantam paperback, containing some revisions and expansion by the author.

The Gallery is not the only novel concerned with the liberation of Italy. *All Thy Conquests* by Alfred Hayes (Howell, Soskin, 1946) is set in Rome, but is very similar to *The Gallery* with its individual chapters devoted to specific characters. One such character is the Marchese Aldo Alzani, a blond, indolent, thirty-three-year-old gay aristocrat, who has spent the war in exile in Switzerland. He returns to Rome and generally makes himself obnoxious, attracted to pretty boys rather than the pretty young sisters they are trying to "sell." Alzani is not a major figure in the novel, and he is a far from entertaining one. Similar to John Horne Burns, Alfred Hayes (1911-1985) served with the U.S. military in Italy, and as in *The Gallery, All Thy Conquests* is a first novel. Both books were praised, but it was Hayes, the straight guy, who went on to enjoy a successful career as a writer, journeying to Hollywood and working on scripts for *Clash by Night* (1952), *Island in the Sun* (1957), and other well-known titles.

NOTE

1. Katherine Bucknell (Ed.), *Christopher Isherwood: Lost Years, a Memoir, 1945-1951*. New York: HarperCollins, 2000, pp. 137, 140.

– 13 –

James M. Cain, *Serenade*

Homosexual males first made an appearance in American mystery fiction in Dashiell Hammett's *The Maltese Falcon* (Alfred A. Knopf, 1930), in which the characters of Joel Cairo, Casper Gutman, and his gangster sidekick Wilmer are all presumed to be gay. The sexuality of the characters is somewhat muted in that Knopf editor Harry Block asked Hammett to delete the "to-bed and homosexual parts." Hammett complied to a certain extent, but did leave in a number of clues for more perceptive readers, the most famous of which is Sam Spade's reference to Wilmer as a "gunsel" (the slang term for catamite).

Raymond Chandler, who may well have been a latent homosexual, provides readers with suggestive gay characterizations in *The Big Sleep* (Alfred A. Knopf, 1939) and *Farewell, My Lovely* (Alfred A. Knopf, 1940), and it has been suggested that his detective hero Philip Marlowe might well be gay. Cornell Woolrich, who was a self-loathing homosexual male, includes gay characters in a number of his short stories, and features a gay actor who gets himself beaten up in *Manhattan Love Song* (William Godwin, 1930). Both Chandler and Woolrich had strong masochistic streaks in their nature, taking enjoyment from writing scenes in which their male protagonists receive beatings.

The best known mystery novel with a primary gay character from the first half of the twentieth century is Patricia Highsmith's *Strangers on a Train* (Harper and Brothers, 1949), which is too well known for inclusion here. Although the 1951 screen adaptation is vague, the novel is explicit in its identification of Charles Anthony Bruno as gay. Highsmith's characterization of Bruno and the subject of his misguided affection, Guy Haines, is relatively free of homophobia. The same cannot be said of the other gay characterizations in American mystery novels, and most certainly not of the leading gay character in James M. Cain's *Serenade* (Alfred A. Knopf, 1937).

Narrated in the first person, *Serenade* opens with opera singer John Howard Sharp, whose voice has failed, living in poverty in Tupinamba, Mexico. He teams up with a young prostitute, Juana Montes, and, with her, he returns to the United States. The pair moves to Hollywood, where Sharp finds work as a singer on radio and then, in a highly unlikely circumstance, takes over the lead in a production of *Carmen* at the Hollywood Bowl. He stars in a feature film, but rejects Hollywood for New York, where he goes to resume his operatic career in the company of Juana Montes.

Just as his success seems assured, Sharp receives a letter from the producer of the Hollywood film, reminding him that he is still under contract. At the same time, conductor Winston Hawes comes back in Sharp's life. Hawes had been fixated with Sharp; he had earlier promoted the singer, but at the same time, as Sharp puts it, "What I meant to him and what he means to me were two different things" (p. 206). As a result of Hawes's attention, Sharp's voice had cracked up.

In New York, Hawes has with him the same mob with which he surrounded himself in Paris:

> gray-haired women with straight haircuts and men's dinner jackets, young girls looking each other straight in the eye and not caring what you thought, boys following men around, loud, feverish talk out in the foyer, everybody coming out in the open with something they wouldn't dare show anywhere else. (p. 209)

Sharp is determined to resist the advances of Hawes, but discovers that his is the financing behind the Hollywood producer, and only by agreeing once more to become Hawes' protégé can Sharp get out of his film contract and sing in opera. At a party hosted by Hawes, emigration officers, alerted by him, arrive to arrest Juana Montes. She kills Hawes and escapes to Mexico with the help of the ship's captain who had earlier brought her and Sharp to the United States.

Eventually, Sharp joins his lover in Mexico, but she is killed by a corrupt official whom she had earlier antagonized. The novel ends with Sharp at the funeral of Juana Montes, receiving a blessing from the priest: "I knew, then, I had made a confession, and received an absolution, and some kind of gray peace came over me" (p. 314).

Serenade is not a typical mystery novel. There are far too many convenient plot contrivances; sea captains who appear at just the right moment and singers who suddenly are incapable of performing. The only mystery is how James M. Cain could get away with his offensive treatment of homosexual men. But then perhaps the gay community does not fare too badly in *Serenade* compared to the manner in which Mexico and its citizens are treated, with virtually all of the latter presented in the most derogatory of terms. Mexico is insulted throughout half of the novel, and gay men should be happy that they receive relatively few pages of condemnation. The gay theme is crucial to the plotline, but dwelt on only briefly.

This is a drama of the fight between homosexuality and heterosexuality, of the trauma that a gay relationship can cause—in this case the loss of a great singing voice—and how only the love of a woman, no matter how impure the woman may be, can restore a man's artistic abilities. It seems irrelevant to Cain that the first sexual encounter between Sharp and Juana Montes can be considered nothing less than technical rape. The novel is, of course, based on the preposterous theory that an individual's sexual persuasion can directly affect artistic capacity. James M. Cain was adamant that the theory had been proven correct, insisting that he had correspondence with doctors confirming such a claim, and boasted that *Serenade* served as a textbook on homosexuality in medical schools. He expanded on the theory in a letter to literary critic H. L. Mencken:

> The lamentable sounds that issue from a homo's throat when he sings are a matter of personal observation. . . . But the theme demanded the next step, the unwarranted corollary that heavy workouts with a woman would bring out the stud horse high notes.

Cain used Juana Montes to present his theory when she tells Sharp, "Hoaney, these man who love man, they can do much, very clever. But no can sing. Have no *toro* in high voice, no *grrr* that frighten little *muchacha,* make heart beat fast. Sound like old woman, like cow, like priest" (p. 227). In one paragraph, offensive of itself in the presentation of a comment by a Mexican, Cain manages to insult gays, the aged, the clergy, and even cattle.

As one might expect, Cain cannot resist stereotyping gay men, who are described here either as "fags" or "pixies." Sharp attends one of Hawes's parties:

> the worst drag was going on you ever saw in your life. A whole mob of them was in there, girls in men's evening clothes tailored for them, with shingle haircuts and blue make-up in their eyes, dancing with other girls dressed the same way, young guys with lipstick on, and mascara eyelashes, dancing with each other too, and at least three girls in full evening dress, that you had to look at twice to make sure they weren't girls at all. (p. 242)

What seems to insult Sharp most at the party is that the pianist is playing not Brahms but jazz. "The whole thing made me sick to my stomach as I looked at it" (p. 242).

The critics loved *Serenade.* "If you read for excitement *Serenade* is built to order," wrote J. D. Adams in *The New York Times* (December 5, 1937). "I defy you to lay it down," exclaimed W. R. Benét in the *Saturday Review of Literature.* In *The New Republic* (December 8, 1937), Dawn Powell commented,

> Mr. Cain's secret lies not so much in what he tells or in his prose as in a brilliant manipulation of story and a dexterous staggering of terror effects—from rape and murder to the frou-frou of pixie petticoats. His words are simple but inflate with horror, the story grows in memory; its minor implications will roam through your dreams for days to come. There is nightmare material here for a whole winter.

Despite the hard-boiled quality of the narration, there is an operatic sense to the story line. Some might argue that *Serenade* is melodrama, but, in reality, it is opera—much along the lines of *Carmen.* There is even a bullfighter—Mexican—in the first chapter. *Serenade* is the most important of Cain's novels with operatic themes, but opera is also featured in the magazine serial, "Career in C Major" (1938), *Mildred Pierce* (1941), and *The Moth* (1948).

James M. Cain (1892-1977) may be a great novelist and occasional screenwriter, but he was also a homophobe. As modern critic Paul Skenazy observes, of all Cain's novels *Serenade* is "the most difficult for a contemporary audience to accept . . . based on what today is recognized as an entirely false premise."[1]

Serenade was included, along with *The Postman Always Rings Twice* and *Mildred Pierce* in *Cain Omnibus* (The Sun Dial Press, 1943), and was reprinted by Vintage Books in 1978. It was filmed in 1956 as a vehicle for Mario Lanza, but with the gay angle removed and the story now involving a singer torn between two women.

NOTE

1. Paul Skenazy, *James M. Cain*. New York: Continuum, 1989, p. 54.

14

Clarkson Crane, *The Western Shore*

There is a pervasive quality of homosexuality in *The Western Shore* (Harcourt, 1925). It seems always just under the surface, begging the reader for recognition, and occasionally breaking through. There is only one obvious gay character here, but there are two or three others who might well be labeled as such—if not at this point in their lives then at least a little later. A San Francisco setting, a fraternity initiation, fun and games among male students around an outdoor swimming pool, young men sleeping three to a room, a young male college professor who finds a bed in his home for a younger male student—these are just a few of the areas touched upon by *The Western Shore*. Noted University of California scholar and administrator Lawrence Clark Powell wrote that *The Western Shore* "was one of the first and remains the best novels about university life in Berkeley." He might also have added that it is proof that Berkeley was as lively in the 1920s as it was in the 1960s, and that modern readers might well ask what type of activity was nurtured at Berkeley all those years ago.

The Western Shore provides character studies of a group of individuals, the majority of which are students at Berkeley. (The published title does not make much sense and, apparently, the author intended the novel to be called *Scenes of Student Life*.) Introductory chapters deal with each major character and, indicative of the novel's lack of any real plot construction, the chapters are identified as "episodes."

Milton Granger is a shy youth from a wealthy Santa Barbara family who spends a little too much time glancing at other young men. He meets Tom Gresham, a twenty-three-year-old ex-student who has seen service in World War I, and who introduces Granger to Alpha Chi Delta. Granger is invited to join the fraternity and, as part of his initiation ceremony, he is ordered to strip naked along with a group of other captivating nude freshmen, and is forced to take a cold-water bath, held under by members of the fraternity.

Tom Gresham is unhappy with life as a businessman and decides to return to Berkeley to study law. One of the attractions of campus life is the fraternity house, to which he returns. A young English instructor at Berkeley is Phil Burton, who was with Gresham in the same army unit. Burton is obviously gay—"it was rumored that he had made advances to a freshman whom he had invited to his rooms" (p. 103)—but pretends to others, and perhaps even to himself, that he is shortly to be married. He is never quite able openly to express his feelings to those students to whom he is attracted, due in large part, obviously, to the fear of rejection and the subsequent consequences of his exposure as gay.

Burton invites George Towne, a poker-playing, lazy, and unmotivated student, but also blond, well-built, and good-looking, to share his house. Towne is presently sharing a room with two other students—they in the bed and he on the couch—and so decides to take up Burton on his offer. He is a little concerned about the gossip he hears and the looks that he receives from Burton, but is reassured by the talk of Burton's impending marriage. Towne recalls a Sunday School teacher with a squeaky voice and plucked eyebrows who had approached him in his hometown of Lander, Wyoming, a man who "always had his left palm against his hip. . . . Burton was not effeminate. 'He's not that way,' George thought, standing on his threshold. . . . 'Naw,' George thought, 'he's not queer. All that stuff's bunk'" (p. 106).

When Towne does move in with Burton, nothing does happen between the two men, and the reader can only assume that Burton has better taste than to become involved with someone as uncultured and boorish as Towne. Or, as Burton explains, "The country is full of men like him. False beginnings. A momentary flicker. Nothing more" (p. 300).

Milton Granger is out walking in the mountains one day when he meets an older man who strikes up a conversation with him. The man admires Granger's tan and "drew his hand several times up and down his arm, fondled his wrist" (p. 226). Granger does not respond, and the man, feigning indifference, watches him depart. Later, at the Berkeley swimming pool, in the company of Gresham, Granger is reintroduced to the man, who is revealed as Phil Burton.

Gresham tells Granger that Burton would like to know him better, but ultimately Granger decides to spend the summer with his aunt. "You're a nice boy. I'm awfully glad I met you," says Burton (p. 281). Granger appears somewhat hurt to learn that Burton plans to spend a two-week walking trip with another student, a friend of Granger's, Aaron Berg, and yet Granger seems to be denying Burton and a potential relationship:

> It was almost a relief to be alone again and not have Burton around: there was something so patiently attentive about him; sometimes Milton felt that Burton agreed too easily with what he had said, or approved too warmly of verse he had written. And that caressing habit of his became a bore. (p. 285)

What is one to make of all this? Here, we have George Towne on the threshold, but the threshold of what? There is a momentary flicker there that intrigues Burton, but is it an intellectual or a homosexual flicker? Does Burton decide to take Aaron Berg on a walking trip to spite Granger, who would rather spend time with his aunt? Earlier, Berg had been presented as an outsider—a Jew—who despises the notion of fraternity houses, to which he cannot belong, but a student with whom Granger has instant rapport, and one who demonstrates an astute understanding of everything on campus. Is there more to the relationship? Is Berg an outsider not only because he is a Jew but also because he is gay?

Gay sex is in no way present and, curiously, none of the heterosexual male students initiate sexual encounters. Sex is represented in *The Western Shore* by Mabel Richards, a student taking creative writing, and who moves along from one sexual encounter to the next. It is she, and none of the males, who is there at the novel's conclusion, sizing up a new potential sexual partner.

Contemporary reviewers did not think too highly of the novel. *The New York Times* (May 10, 1925) described it as "realistic, brilliant and sound, without being great or important in any respect." The critic for the *Saturday Review of Literature* (May 2, 1925) commented,

> One does not expect to see life steadily and whole through a first novel. One does, however, expect to find revealed a fresh and vivid personality, that of the author. In this, Mr. Crane dis-

appoints us. He fails to realize the tragedy or the pathos of the lives he depicts. It is permissible that Mr. Crane should acquiesce to such lives. He is under no moral obligation to protest. As an artist, however, he is under obligation to give line to his chaos, no matter how dull and meaningless that chaos may be. That obligation Mr. Crane has not fulfilled.

On the whole, reviewers ignored the homosexual aspects of the novel. In *The New Republic* (May 20, 1925), Paul Rosenfeld wrote only of "childish fantasy" and "a tragedy of youth." In the *New York Herald Tribune* (March 29, 1925), poet and dramatist Stephen Vincent Benét was of the opinion that *The Western Shore* would secure Clarkson Crane "a distinctive place in American letters," but did go on to warn that the novel contained passages that "might well prove distasteful."

When *The Western Shore* was reprinted by Salt Lake City-based publisher Peregrine Smith Books in 1985, it contained a lengthy introductory essay by Oscar Lewis, which makes no reference to the novel's gay content. Lewis refers to "good-humored realism" and suggests that the individuals here are "the stock characters that have long been the mainstays of college fiction" (albeit presented in nonconventional style).

In reality, there are no college dramas of the 1920s or earlier with gay professors or potentially gay students. The humorous realism is, presumably, a reference, in part, to the fraternity initiation, which illustrates the need of college boys to see their colleagues in the nude and in humiliating situations, and, if nothing else, shows that the infamous fraternity paddle was not in use at Berkeley at this time.

Apparently, the great aunt, F. B., to whom the book is dedicated in thanks for a monthly stipend of fifty dollars she provided to support the author during the creative process, denounced the novel for ridiculing fraternity and college life. Clarkson Crane (1894-1971) came from a wealthy Chicago family, enrolled at Berkeley in 1916, and may well be the basis for the character Milton Granger. He wrote *The Western Shore* while living in Paris in the winter of 1923-1924. The novel was not a commercial success, and Crane did not publish a second novel, *Mother and Son,* also set in Berkeley, until 1946. It and third novel *Naomi Martin* (1947) failed to find an audience, and Crane decided not to pursue publication of any of his other writings.

Clarkson Crane did not marry—similar to Granger and Burton, he enjoyed walks in the country—and one has every reason to suspect that he was gay. His closest friend was historian and critic Van Wyck Brooks, eight years his senior, to whom *Mother and Son* is dedicated. Clarkson Crane was very much a loner, an outsider, and he remains as such in the literary world today. He is well deserving of resurrection as a lost gay author.

15

Hubert Creekmore, *The Welcome*

It is summer in Ashton, Mississippi. James "Jim" Furlow, a young lawyer, is not particularly happy in his marriage to Doris, a selfish wife who agrees to have his child only if he will buy her a new car. A more happily married couple is ex-college football player Gus "Tray" Traywick and his wife Bea. Into this stifling Southern atmosphere, with its racist attitude toward the Negro members of the community, its small-town bigotry, and its stultifying lack of cultural amenities— only the local movie house offers any escape from Ashton—comes Don Mason, who had been a school and college friend of the two men, but had left Ashton in favor of life and employment in New York.

It is obvious that Jim resents Don's return, and only slowly does it become apparent that the reason is because of his love for the other man. Tray does not understand Jim's distancing himself from Don until, in a drunken stupor, Don asks, "do you want me to tell you everything?" "I guess you don't have to now, Don," replies Tray softly (p. 199).

The relationship between Jim and Don was far from physical. After leaving a dance together, they would sit quietly in the moonlight. When the two went to the lake with their "girls," it was no different. They would horse around together in the water "until they gradually came to feel, self-consciously, that they had ignored their dates." In a canoe, with the girls in front and Jim and Don paddling at the stern, "they shared the same secret pleasure—Don more than either of them must have felt it—of their physical closeness; shoulders, thighs, arms brushing together as they pushed through the water" (p. 247).

Don has broken free of Jim, but the latter still believes that Don belongs to him: "Jim couldn't understand to what compulsion he had yielded that made him forsake the so close to perfection of those days for marriage with Doris" (p. 247). In despair and drunk, Jim confronts Don, asking that the two go off together. Don refuses, in part because he has decided to marry Isabel Lang, a woman who lives a semi-Bohemian life (or what passes for Bohemian in the South), and with whom Jim was once in love. Don explains that it is too late for him and Jim:

> No one in the world has ever meant more to me than you did, Jim—and still do. Maybe no one ever will. During all those years behind us, I loved you. But you always threw it away, because you could always be sure it was there. (p. 256)

Don accuses Jim of cowardice. When he was young, it was an act of cowardice to marry. Now that his marriage has failed, he has returned to Don in the hope that his friend will rescue him.

At the wedding, Jim refuses to see Don off on his honeymoon, refuses to wish him and the bride good luck. Tray tries to reason with Jim, but the only response is an angry accusation, the cry of a frustrated queen, that Don is a "damned little fairy" (p. 306). Jim sobs in the arms of an embarrassed Tray, who laments, "If only people could forgive each other for loving" (p. 307). As Tray speaks the words, he wonders what he really means. It is his very "straightness" that helps Tray stand as a pillar of strength to which both Jim and Don turn. In a way, it is his very awkwardness, perhaps his lack of total understanding at what he is learning, that prevents Tray from being judgmental.

The novel is very much about cowardice. Jim is a coward, unable to articulate his love for Don when his friend first leaves town. Later, when he, Tray, and Don are on a hunting trip, Jim considers ending his life. He is too much of coward himself to commit the act, and Don is not capable of shooting him.

Here is a love that dare not speak its name. There is no reference anywhere to homosexuality. The author does not even find the need to use "queer" as an adjective. Tray accepts that there is something special between Jim and Don, and has no problem with it. With the exception of Isabel, and she is after all something of a free spirit, none of the women can understand what is going on between the two men. *The Welcome* (Appleton-Century-Crofts, 1948) is a gay novel that makes no effort to announce what it is all about. Yet in many respects, as a study of gay love in the South, it is far more revealing and far more impressive than, say, Thomas Hal Phillips's *The Bitterweed Path,* published the following year. One can understand why *The*

Bitterweed Path should have been reprinted and acknowledged in the 1990s as a gay novel, just as one comprehends why *The Welcome* will never be reprinted and never receive recognition for what it is. Here there are no men in bed, with or without physical contact. Words do not need to be spoken. Descriptions are more than adequate, and what the author describes is never explicit. Not once, for example, do we really know what Jim and Don look like. Yes, we know Jim is handsome, and we assume Don is also, but what of their physical size, their height, their weight, their hair coloring, their eyes? We don't know them and, finally, we don't really care that much about them because they are not gay as we in the twenty-first century perceive "gayness." At the novel's close, they are both married—in some respects both alone—and they will remain closeted, happily or unhappily married, for the remainder of their days.

    The Welcome was Creekmore's second novel. In 1946, he published *Fingers of Night,* also set in Mississippi. The trade publication *Kirkus* (October 1948) described *The Welcome* as "A precise handling—neither clinical nor sensational—of a marital as well as a psychological theme, this offers a well integrated novel of characters as well as emotion." There is no documentation on Hubert Creekmore. Neither is there any record of Ted Rearick, the man to whom he dedicates *The Welcome.*

16

George Davis, *The Opening of a Door*

The Opening of a Door (Harper & Brothers, 1931) provides character sketches on the members of the MacDougall family who have
moved to the United States from Canada. The principal young personality in the novel is Edward Turbyfill, who has gone to live with
his aunts in Chicago following the death of his grandfather.

> Edward was known in the family as a hard boy to make out.
> Subdued, almost languid, he showed—though rarely at least to
> them—flashes of deeper nature, incandescent, exciting, and not
> really likable, so they felt. There was something too . . . well,
> "introspective" was the word they hit upon to describe what they
> meant. (p. 44)

Edward works as a clerk in an iron foundry, but dreams of becoming a novelist. He tells the plotline of his novel, *The Travelers,* to his
Uncle Daniel. It is the story of a band of young men who distinguish
themselves from others by the red bands they wear. They are asked by
their elders to give up their distinctive red bands and the books they
carry, but the young men refuse to compromise. They are killed. Uncle Daniel sponsors Edward's education at Ohio State University.

The gay characters in *The Opening of a Door* are shadowy figures
indeed. Neither Edward nor Uncle Daniel is identified as such. Only
drunken Uncle Lincoln seems able to understand what they are:

> Mother, mother . . . that boy in there, do you know what he is?
> He isn't fit, he's a monster . . . do you hear me, mother? He
> should be thrown from the house, driven into the streets,
> scourged with whips! Along with that other dirty one in San
> Francisco . . . they aren't fit to live among decent men and
> women! (p. 135)

How Uncle Lincoln can so identify the pair is hard to comprehend in that the reader is provided with inadequate evidence. Edward neither looks at nor expresses any interest in another male. There is certainly no suggestion of a budding relationship between Edward and Uncle Daniel. The latter confesses to Edward that he is unhappy with his life and urges Edward, just like the band of young men in his novel, not to compromise. He asks Edward where he wears his red band, where does Daniel? The boy flushes, but claims not to know. Daniel tells Edward that if he chooses to write to him from college, he will be very happy. He asks that Edward understand, but Edward—similar to the reader—does not.

If *The Opening of a Door* is in any way autobiographical, it is obvious that George Davis (born 1906) is Edward. In hindsight, this first novel is not a great work of fiction, but on its initial publication, it evoked strong praise. In *The Nation* (October 14, 1931), Clifton Fadiman wrote,

> The most important fact about this first novel is that it was written by a young man of twenty-four. The smoothness of the prose, the unity of the tone, the author's calm refusal to pose any difficulties of whose solution he is not wholly confident: these are all the marks of a practiced craftsman. *The Opening of a Door* is one of the most unfirstish first novels I have read. It is difficult to believe it is the work of one so young. . . . An injection of vigor and warmth would have lifted *The Opening of a Door* out of a class of the merely admirable into that of the really moving. Perhaps in his next book, Mr. Davis will not be so fearful of letting go.

17

Michael de forrest, *The Gay Year*

The "gay year" chronicled here is that of Joe Harris, a twenty-three-year-old living in a small New York apartment, who has his first sexual encounter of any kind with Roger Stuart, a narcissistic young man living with gay actor Teddy Watson. Prior to his night with Roger, Joe was adamant that he was not gay, and he still denies he is even after a series of sexual encounters with Roger. Among Joe's acquaintances are painter Lou Franklin, who marries African-American Nella Webb and has a child by her. Living in the apartment immediately above Lou Franklin are Wally Steinman, Charles Evans, and Harold Price. Wally and Charles are very gay, and Harold is—well, confused.

Joe is infatuated with Roger, but the latter goes off to Hollywood with Teddy and, as a result, Joe decides to continue his gay education. He is picked up by Donald K. Jeffries, a divorced male with two children, who later kills himself by jumping into the East River. Joe becomes the kept boy of theatrical entrepreneur Reginald F. Hartley, a far from arduous position which allows him time for other gay encounters.

When Hartley fails to give him the promised lead in a summer stock production of *Night Must Fall,* Joe attempts suicide at Malument on the Eastern seashore. He is rescued by Katherine, a young woman with a daughter whose husband is dead. Katherine tries to "straighten out" Joe, and appears to be succeeding until Roger Stuart reappears on the scene.

It is back to New York for Joe, who is again deserted by Roger, but finds new faith in himself singing in a recently opened gay nightspot, where his former neighbor Wally is the pianist. Thanks to his success there, Joe auditions for a musical. The novel closes with Joe's gay year ending, Katherine planning to come to town for his opening, and our hero considering the possibility of "a girl I'll love who'll love me" (p. 267).

Many novels from the first half of the twentieth century have negative gay connotations, but *The Gay Year* (The Woodford Press, 1949) must be the only book aimed at a gay audience while being so offensively filled with such a large array of gay stereotypes. Roger is described as helping to develop Joe's awareness of his inversion. He is setting Joe out on the "dark road" that gays must travel. It is a road Joe will conquer: "He paves his lane with satin, silk, lovers, perfumes, clothes, antiques, jewelry" (p. 57)—everything that a stereotypical gay man might enjoy.

In addition, the stereotypical gay men here are all effeminate. Wally and Charles address each other as "girl." To them, Joe is "Josephine." Charles is a chorus boy, who boasts of sleeping his way into the chorus line and is now sleeping his way through it. He keeps a gauzy white tutu, ballet slippers, and two dreamy ostrich feathers in his closet, and restores his spirit by dancing in them in the privacy of his bedroom. Wally and Charles know nothing of love; for them, there is only sex.

Young gay men set fashion trends. One year it is loafers and the next eyeglasses. Joe and company are youth oriented. Elderly gays are unattractive and distasteful. Reginald Hartley is described as "unhandsome" (p. 83), in his early forties, a cockatoo face with round, beady, black eyes and a curvaceous nose, and thus expected to pay dearly for Joe's affection. Joe watches a hustler in Times Square pick up "a fat old man" (p. 259), and his "stomach contracted with the thought of the frail boy sleeping with that lardy creature" (p. 260).

Suicide is never far away here. Joe attempts it in a somewhat half-hearted fashion. It is most tragic in regard to Donald K. Jeffries, who had taken Joe in after finding the kid half drunk in the street. He provided warmth and love for Joe, but Joe did not even bother to provide him with his name or address. Jeffries feels he has failed as a husband and failed as a father, and, with Joe, "He has even failed as a homosexual" (p. 53).

As to the most distasteful scene in the entire novel, it is surely when Roger picks up Kenneth, a fifteen-year-old mentally retarded boy. "Just relax and enjoy life" (p. 186), Roger tells him as he proceeds to deflower the boy. The most offensive aspect of all in *The Gay Year* is the concept that homosexuality is something that can be picked up and discarded at will. As Katherine explains to Joe,

> Well, some people, who discover themselves to be what are commonly called "inverts" are merely following a natural or conditional bent. It is the only valid way of life for them. While it presents certain problems, I imagine, still, anything else would amount to actual inversion for them, while others, who are not really like that, who try to adjust to such a life find it no life at all. (p. 173)

Confused? Well Joe and Harold certainly are. Poor Harold gets beaten up by "queer bashers" despite his doubts as to whether he is really gay. After all, as he explains to Joe, he has slept with a woman who found him cute, he hates Wally who is "swishy" and a "goddamed fairy" (and should have been beaten up in his stead), and all he is really seeking is love. "Lie to me and kiss me and tell me you love me!" he demands of Joe (p. 202). It's the mental institution for Harold—self-admitted, of course.

As for Joe,

> He remembered Roger saying that every time God created a homosexual he laughed. . . . Who created homosexuals? Maybe parents who failed to understand their sensitive sons, maybe the boys created themselves, maybe too stringent taboos on natural instincts—whatever it was, Joe concluded, it wasn't God. (p. 212)

Readers may take some comfort in the happiness that Lou Franklin and his African-American lover find; they are, of course, straight but at the same time, in their interracial relationship, they are unconventional and antiestablishment. Of interest also are Lois and Hi Sweeney— she a former dancer and he a crewman in a Chicago theater— who decide to open a gay bar, the Club des Arts—and make a success of it. Those seeking titillation in *The Gay Year* will find none. No sexual encounter is described in any detail; there are no references to sexual organs. Hair is ruffled, knees are patted, and Teddy does have a one-night stand with a soldier whose muscles are well defined. Most of the attributes of the young men remain hidden. About all we learn of any of them is that Harold has no hair on his chest.

Teddy is an actor, and the author devotes some space to Hollywood, including the need for leading men to hide their homosexuality. *The Gay Year* must have found some market within the film community. It was advertised in *The Hollywood Reporter* (July 22, 1949) as "A novel about the men who travel a strange side-road of human behavior," a phrase that might just as well be applied to all those who labor in the studios of Hollywood.

The Gay Year was the latest in a very short line of novels intended primarily for a gay audience. Robert Scully's *A Scarlet Pansy* (Faro, 1933) is supposedly an amusing account of the outrageous life and career of one Fay Etrange; to gay readers, if not others (and there probably were not others), it is obvious that Fay is no lady, but a gay man. There was less doubt as to the sexual identity of the leading character in Kennilworth Bruce's *Goldie* (William Godwin, 1933), with the dust jacket advising the reader that "Not since *The Well of Loneliness* has the delicate theme of sexual inversion been handled so artistically." Handsome and athletic Paul Kameron becomes "Goldie" after dying his hair, embarking on a part-time career as a New York hustler, and working in a gay Greenwich Village restaurant (where he organizes a gay liberation club).

18

Harrison Dowd, *The Night Air*

"Add another—and an excellent—volume to the lengthening shelf of novels about the homosexual in our society," wrote E. J. Fitzgerald in the *Saturday Review of Literature* (September 16, 1950). *The Night Air* (The Dial Press, 1950) is certainly one of the better gay novels of the late 1940s and early 1950s, lacking in sensationalism and homosexual stereotyping. The hero's despair is one with which many gay men can empathize, as he constantly searches for a happiness that appears beyond his grasp either in the big city or the countryside of his roots. The word *homosexual* does not appear in the novel, and *queer* is used only once or twice. There is much here that a gay reader in 1950 could enjoy, and little to which a gay reader a half-century later can take offense.

Andrew "Andy" Moore is a forty-three-year-old New York actor, who had brief success in 1940 as a composer of a song cycle, the lyrics of which were written by his wife, Kathrine "Kit" Slade. Kit, who is uncritically devoted to Andy, comes from a prominent Maryland family and it is her money that pays the rent while Andy searches for acting jobs. All too often, he is rejected as too old or not sexy enough for a part.

When he does obtain a role, it is a small but "flashy" one, in which his accomplishment as a pianist is used to advantage. On tour prior to a Broadway opening, Andy shares a hotel room with twenty-one-year-old Quentin Burke, who plays the role of a bus driver in the play. Between the two, a friendship develops that grows into love. Quentin, whom Andy refers to as the "boy," is admiring of the older man and asks that he sleep with him when disturbed by a nightmare. The first (and perhaps only) sexual encounter between the two takes place when both are drunk. However, Andy's growing love for Quentin forces him to reassess him marriage and to break up with Kit. When the play reaches New York, he and Burke decide to share a one-bed-room apartment.

It is obvious that Andy is homosexual, but Quentin is not, and the young man begins an affair with the play's leading lady. The discov-ery of that affair and Andy's increasing dependence on alcohol leads the two to split up and Andy to be fired from the production. The past with Kit is obviously dead, and Andy discovers that even the apart-ment building where the two lived has been demolished. In despera-tion, he returns to the now-deserted family farm in Vermont, seeking if not a new life at least a new beginning.

Andy Moore cannot be described as a latent homosexual. Early in the novel, he encounters an aging lesbian painter, Beryl, and through her the reader learns of Andy's gay past in Europe. There, he met Kit, whose flat chest and masculine looks had inadvertently led Beryl to believe she might be a lesbian. It is an angry and sick Beryl who dis-misses Andy's heterosexuality: "You can't make up your mind which sex you belong to" (p. 240).

Kit is aware of Andy's past; she meets his ex-lover, Sam North, who refers to her husband as "the toast of Vienna, the pet of the Prater. Handy-Andy, the boy who obliges." The drunken North re-calls Andy's love for a "big" sailor and points out that, as has Kit, he also had kept Andy some twenty years ago.

At first, it seems that Andy is attracted to Quentin because he is re-minded of Kit, but later he is able to accept his love of the boy as that of a man for another man. His love needs no justification or excuse. Andy's fixation with Quentin can be linked to his first love, a trol-leyman in Hollywood (where Andy had been a child actor) named Harold. Harold was a man, but Quentin is a baby: "I didn't want a man; this time I said I wanted to be the man. Husband, if you like. I was tired of being a wife, Kit's wife" (p. 273).

The uniform, the public transport driver motif, runs throughout the novel. Andy's first love in Hollywood is a trolley driver. Quentin plays a bus driver in uniform. In New York, Andy eyes with apprecia-tion the muscular shoulders and uniform of a bus driver, "the large ex-pert hands lying relaxed and possessive on the wheel. It was a plea-sure he found he could at last accept without furtiveness or apology" (p. 203). Later, a blond and good-looking bus driver does not escape Andy's attention as he travels across snow-covered New York State.

There is equal pleasure for the reader in discovering a middle-aged gay man who is not dismissed, as in so many novels of this period, as old and unwanted, but actually gets to bed a guy who is young enough to be his son. Not once does the author make an issue of the age difference. Neither man is presented as effeminate. When they decide to share accommodation, an elderly character actress comments, "If you both weren't such masculine types I'd be worried" (p. 139).

It is Quentin who makes the first move. He is grateful for Andy's help with his performance. He squeezes Andy's arm, telling him, "From now on I'm your boy" (p. 157). Andy's response is one of initial anger as he pulls his arm away. Later, he gives Quentin a birthday present of an antique cigarette case, thus formalizing the relationship. Andy recalls for Quentin the two gay men that they had passed on Boston Common,

> Unless you're one of those who haven't anything to lose, there's always fear. So you pretend, and if you're like me hate yourself for pretending. Finally, because hatred is somehow easier to put up with than fear, you come to value it. (p. 170)

Burke's response is simple and naive: "Don't talk like that; you're a man, not a creep. You talk like a man, look like one, walk like one. You haven't got anything to be afraid of" (pp. 170-171).

Quentin's response to Andy's homosexual overtures may in part be linked to his having a twin brother, Dan, who was gay and who committed suicide. Both were the subjects of sexual advances from an older man with an interest in bondage and discipline. It is obvious that Burke is a bit of a cock-teaser, leaving the bathroom naked, standing in the doorway in front of Andy as he pats himself with cologne. When the two first meet, he tells Andy of his need for female companionship, and also tells Andy that he likes him and asks why they should not make a foursome.

"Everybody's queer. Except thee and me," says a drunken Andy to Burke (p. 149). As far as their relationship goes, there is some truth to that comment. It is a remarkable coupling that is neither based on homosexuality nor male bonding. It will go nowhere and, ultimately, end in hurt and hatred.

After Burke has ended the relationship, Andy rapidly descends into alcoholism. His openness about his homosexuality leads him more and more to reveal his feminine side. He sings, in French, the once-popular Fannie Brice number, "My Man," and even appears at a gay gathering in semidrag. He has a brief, drunken affair with a guy named Mike, and meets up again with Sam North, who calls him "a no-good faggot" (p. 300).

When Andy returns to Vermont, it is with the memory of the happiest years of his life, of his grandmother's kitchen, and of his cousin, Harold, who "taught him other things, as frightening as they were pleasant, sinful too in a way" (p. 145). He recalls that in his youth he traveled from Vermont to Hollywood, where his parents were living. He was accompanied by a friend of his mother, Mr. Nickle, who did "something" to him that made him throw up. Mr. Nickle represents the change from the happiness of Andy's childhood with Harold to the confused sexuality of his adult life.

Back in Vermont, Andy is able to reject his alcoholism. He does not, however, reject his homosexuality. He is driven to the family farm by a young boy, Harold's son, and as Andy looks at him, he thinks of himself now as the Harold of his childhood. Andy has come home but, ultimately, Vermont is not his home. It offers no real answers to his future life, which can only be back in New York.

The Night Air was generally well received by contemporary critics. The reviewer in the *New York Herald Tribune Book Review* (September 24, 1950) wrote

> Harrison Dowd is a forceful writer, and there is tolerance as well as truth in this study of defeat and moral bankruptcy. The minor figures—producers, agents, floozies, failures—are drawn to the life, and the tensions of theatrical rehearsals and opening nights are conveyed with skill. *The Night Air* is a novel about tramps as Broadway understands the word, and the tramps are of both sexes.

The critic for *The New Yorker* (September 9, 1950) was not quite as positive, noting, "Mr. Dowd's writing is less than distinguished, and his characterizations for the most part are thin, but in the case of the actor he has succeeded in giving a heartbreaking picture of a human being in need." The distinguished theater arts librarian from the New York Public Library, George Freedley, reviewed *The Night Air* in *Library Journal* (November 15, 1950) and recommended it for librarians, a surprising acclamation for a gay novel of 1950.

The Night Air is the only novel by Harrison Dowd (1897-1964), a character actor who was active on the Broadway stage from 1929 through 1960. Dowd had neither the time nor the inclination to work in films or television, but he does have some impressive New York theater credits, including *Kiss Me, Kate* (1956), *The Visit* (1958), and major revivals of *Morning's at Seven* (1955) and *Our Town* (1959).

19

George Eekhoud, *A Strange Love:*
A Novel of Abnormal Passion

Georges Eekhoud (1854-1927) was a prominent Belgian novelist, short-story writer, and critic, active from 1877 until his death. He was an iconoclast whose works generally espoused the pariahs and criminals of society. The characters in his novels are generally in revolt against bourgeois uniformity and are frequently evocative of the author's ideology. According to the 1947 edition of the *Columbia Dictionary of Modern European Literature* (one of the most recent reference sources in which Eekhoud appears), he was "the fanative lover of independence and of 'irregulars.'"

Eekhoud was virtually unknown in the United States until 1917, when Duffield published his novel *La Nouvelle Carthage* as *The New Carthage,* and Americanized his name from Georges to George. Set in Antwerp where Eekhoud was born, the novel deplores the modernization of the city and presents a hero who objects to a social reformer's notion to save what can be saved of the population and to ignore "the hopelessly depraved."

The New Carthage might well have been the only one of Eekhoud's works to be translated into English had not the Panurge Press discovered his 1899 novel, *Escal-Vigor,* and published it in 1930 as *A Strange Love: A Novel of Abnormal Passion* (The Panurge Press). The uncredited translation is unspeakably bad, replete with antiquated phrases and slang, and it is difficult to know to what extent criticism of the novel should be directed at Eekhoud or at his translator—perhaps both are at fault.

Told in the most heavy-handed of fashions, *A Strange Love* is a fairy tale (no pun intended) set in an unidentified time period, in which footnotes explain untranslatable Belgian terms or identify Flemish artists. The central character is Henry de Kehlmark, the young Count of the Dike and the lord of the castle Escal Vigor, which is presumably located somewhere in the region of Belgium or the Netherlands.

The Count is attracted to a farming youth named Guidon Govaertz:

> He had rounded hips, an amber-like complexion, eyes of velvet under long black lashes, red fleshy lips, nostrils dilated as by some mysterious sensual olfactiveness and thick black hair. . . . The sculptural contour of this young rustic, who united the muscular relief of his compeers to a certain correctness of outline, recalled exactly to Kehlmark the Pipe Player of Frans Hals. . . . His heart tightened, he held his breath, a prey to overpowering emotion. (p. 51)

Fending off the ministrations of two women, Guidon's sister Claudie and the servantlike Blandine with whom he has a season of carnal love, the Count is eventually able to get together with Guidon. "Their eyes met and seemed to put to one another a poignant and subtle question" (p. 128). Guidon visits the castle daily and the Count shuts himself up with him for long hours in his studio, supposedly teaching the young man the finer points of art and literature. Blandine refuses to believe the obvious, that the Count "is fonder of the brother's breeches than the petticoats of the sister" (p. 155).

Seated one evening, holding hands, the Count tells Guidon the story of young Stephen and young Gerard, who are enveloped by heaven's fire after Gerard, unable to restrain his love for Stephen, burns Stephen's betrothed to death. The Count tells the story of Gerard's love:

> When they bathed in the Démar, Gerard admired this youthful frame, so slender and graceful, and knew no pleasure comparable to that of embracing the boy's warm and supple body, carrying him in his arms a long time and very far, deep into the midst of the woods, where they would finally roll about amongst the ferns and mosses. Gerard would tickle Stephen by passing his lips over his rosy skin. And the child would laugh, would attempt to escape, kicking out with his tiny feet, or else would bestow hearty slaps on the robust hinderparts of the big boy, who took these blows as caresses. (p. 160)

The Count reveals that he loves Guidon as much as Gerard loved Stephen. Nestled, shivering against the Count's breast, Guidon announces, "Thou are my master and my love. Do you with me whatsoe'er thou wilt. . . . Thy lips . . ." (p. 167).

Claudie and her lover Landrillon plan revenge on the Count and Guidon. At the annual fair held on St. Olfgar's Day, the young women of the community are given the opportunity to declare themselves to any youths they might encounter as potential husbands. Guidon is confronted by a group of women and asked to make his choice. He is attacked by the mob, bound hand and foot, and stripped. When the Count tries to rescue the boy, he is also attacked. As the couple die, the Count turns to Guidon: "Then, his lips joining again the lips of the boy, which were eagerly presented to him, Guidon and Henry mingled their breath in a supreme kiss" (p. 252).

That is about it for the gay sex in *A Strange Love*—nothing more than one supreme kiss. There is far more sensuality in the scenes where Guidon is attacked by the women. "The erotic clowning," as it is described (p. 245), has a naked-and-bound Guidon the subject of what can only be described as male rape. The women rub their buttocks against him, thrust their breasts in his face, and then, "the claws of these harpies violated in turns the unhappy youth's unwilling and horror-stricken flesh" (p. 244).

The violence and excess of his characterization, for which George Eekhoud was noted, are present in *A Strange Love,* but missing is much of that strange love. It is positively pure and innocent in comparison to the heterosexual abandonment of the women at the fair. It is hard to believe that the novel could have created the slightest controversy upon its initial French-language publication, but according to an introduction to the American edition, signed by one "Gauntlet," the book was seized from a store in Bruges and the author brought to trial:

> The case of *A Strange Love* was fought to a finish. After hearing all the witnesses, listening to expert medical evidence of the subject of abnormality, and the impassioned orations, for and against, the Jury came unanimously to their decision. George Eekhoud was acquitted! . . . *A Strange Love* was exculpated from the accusation of intentional pornography and its gifted author came little short of apotheosis on the spot. Thus it ever is and must be![1]

At this point, "Gauntlet" gets completely carried away with himself, ranting and raving in positively biblical fashion against the heathen. Equally remarkable is that *A Strange Love* should have been resurrected for republication in 1965 by the Washington, DC-based Guild Press. The original Panurge Press edition was limited to 1,000 copies. As was the better known Falstaff Press, Panurge was a mail-order publisher, specializing in sexology and anthropology. It was closed down as a result of a U.S. postal service investigation, finding Panurge guilty of "pandering," a charge perhaps more appropriately directed not at *A Strange Love* but at the press's best-known publication, *The Satyricon*.

NOTE

1. 1965 Guild Press Edition, pp. 10, 13.

20

Stuart Engstrand,
The Sling and the Arrow

The Sling and the Arrow (Creative Age Press, 1947) is a drama of latent homosexuality, and the chilling (not to say murderous) effect it can have on a marriage. The novel explains to the uninitiated how one may determine if a partner is potentially gay, although all the signs of such a condition are here guaranteed to insult and offend any gay male. So blatant is the sexual stereotyping of the latent homosexual that a reader with no immediate knowledge as to the book's subject matter would be hard pressed not to identify its principal character, Herbert Dawes, as gay.

Herbert Dawes designs women's clothes and is very successful at it. He is married to the lovely Lonna, who has narrow hips, minimal breasts, and is dressed by her husband in attire that makes her look like a boy. The stylish blouses she wears hide her femininity. When Herbert has an argument with the next-door neighbor, a bullying milkman, the poor guy is revealed as such a coward that he runs and hides to avoid a beating. Lonna is desperate to have a child, but Herbert is positively offended by the suggestion, in large part because it will force him to admit that she is indeed a woman; the child will destroy the illusion of his wife's maleness. Herbert is very happy at playing house, particularly if he is allowed to keep it clean and spend many thrilling hours in the kitchen. As a boy, Herbert prayed to Jesus to take away his penis and give him breasts, and when he was twelve, his father caught him and a neighbor boy playing man and wife. He will never forget his father's comment, "I would rather see you dead than see you a lover of men" (p. 349). Herbert is obsessed with his mother, a domineering woman who still tries to organize his life.

Herbert and Lonna live in an unidentified, affluent beach community, which must be somewhere between Los Angeles and San Diego. Herbert is fighting his unacknowledged homosexuality in highly melodramatic style. With his wife, he goes into the ocean to spear fish, and attempts to spear her. Looking at himself nude in the mirror, he admires his good looks, ignoring the slight double chin and the equally slight paunch that his wife notices, but is repulsed by the dark hair covering his chest. "It was shockingly out of place. Why did a man have to have a mat of hair there?" (p. 151). Herbert takes a razor and shaves himself.

As the novel progresses, Herbert sees himself more and more as a female character:

> He gave out a cry of sheer delight as he stared at his chest. To him, it was no longer flat, there was no stubble of hair. The nipples were not small and meaningless. Instead, he saw that he had breasts, white, sweet, round breasts. . . . He pinched at the nipples, and sensations of delicious pain shot to the juncture of his thighs. (p. 191)

Just as quickly, the euphoria fades away. His chest is flat, his nipples flat, and "the loathsome cylinder of his masculinity could not be blinded out" (p. 191).

Herbert becomes obsessed with Mike, the Coast Guard brother of the milkman, and spies on him and his girlfriend, Pauline. He makes drawings of the two nude, and as his fixation builds, he has sex with Pauline, asking her about Mike, and spying on the two. When Pauline, in all innocence, remarks, "You're sort of queer, aren't you?" Herbert misunderstands, his anger building (p. 126).

Herbert is shocked to discover that Lonna also knows Mike—she is having an affair with him and considering a divorce. He acquiesces to the relationship but, ultimately, the only course open to him is to kill Lonna, particularly after he has invited Mike to stay for dinner with the words, "We women would like a guest" (p. 244). The Freudian slip creates great amusement.

Through the family doctor, Lonna is introduced to a psychoanalyst, Dr. Kahn, who explains to her: "Your husband, Mrs. Dawes, is suffering from a sexual aberration. . . . He is, I believe, a latent homosexual. Suppressed. And up to now, unconscious. But I am afraid that it is breaking into his conscious" (p. 94).

The family doctor demurs, suggesting that it is Herbert's artistic business that has given rise to such a suggestion: "Art or no art, homosexuality is something I can't stomach, much less condone. . . . There isn't a perverted atom in him" (p. 95). But the good Dr. Kahn continues, pointing out—in italics—that Herbert is filled with an intense hate of his mother, that she has taken away his masculinity. Lonna's response is one of disbelief: "Herbert . . . a fairy?" (p. 96).

By the novel's close, Herbert has gone completely over the top. He fires the maid and takes on all the household duties, delighting in scrubbing the floors. Lonna reveals she is pregnant with Mike's baby; Herbert envisions her bulging breasts suckling a child, and breaks her neck. He had designed an ill-suited dress for a new client. He now realizes he had made it for himself. He adds lipstick, powder, rouge, a sweater, and stockings to the ensemble, and heads out on the road, only to be stopped by the police, who lock up all fairies. In jail, accused not only of being a fairy but also his wife's killer, Herbert descends deeper into femininity. He imagines Lonna in the prison cell with him, her hair as short as a boy's, her chest flat, and "the vigor of her manhood" visible through the tight-fitting trousers (p. 354).

A subplot, heavy with pseudopsychosexual undertones, involves Herbert's keeping a rattlesnake as a pet. He likes to watch it and listen to its rattle. When his mother comes to stay, she drowns it. All the viciousness and hatred that Herbert felt had been transferred to the snake, but now it was part of his psyche again.

The Sling and the Arrow is quite outrageous and, as might be expected, created a firestorm of criticism on publication. The trade journal *Kirkus* (April 30, 1947) noted that earlier novels had been concerned with physical love and "the preoccupation maturates here in a full blown novel of sexual perversion, and doesn't miss a chance to fictionalize—feverishly—psychosexual performance. . . . A sensational exploitation of scientific case history material, this is unnecessary." *Library Journal* (April 15, 1947) advised its readers, "We have here a book that does not belong in public libraries. . . . No library can stock this until it has been read word by word."

The nontrade critics compared *The Sling and the Arrow* to Charles Jackson's *The Fall of Valor*, and were not generally impressed. In the *New York Herald Tribune Weekly Book Review* (May 4, 1947), Hiram Hadyn wrote,

> Mr. Engstrand forgets that he is telling us a story about people. We follow Herbert Dawes down his dark road of violence, fear and compulsive hatred. But always we are uncomfortably aware of the clinical text beside Mr. Engstrand's and our elbow. . . .

The result is, of course, that we are never moved with pity and terror.

In *The New York Times* (May 11, 1947), Helen Eustis commented that, "If Mr. Jackson's novel is on the one hand more tightly composed and graceful, on the other hand we must give Mr. Engstrand the credit that is due his book for being more extensive and more courageous."

Thanks to the cautionary reviews, *The Sling and the Arrow* became an instant best-seller, going through some five printings. Curiously, its biggest market constituted women readers, some of whom, presumably, had doubts about their husbands. The publisher, Creative Age Press, was founded and owned by Jean Lyttle, who earlier had authored another novel, *Sheila Lacey,* with a major gay character.[1]

Stuart Engstrand (1904-1955) is a writer worthy of additional study. His early life was spent hiking around the United States, working on a freighter bound for China, as a truck driver, and climaxed by three years of semi-isolation, living in a self-built shack in the Wisconsin woods. His first novel, *The Invaders,* was published in 1937, two years after his marriage. His last novel, *More Deaths than One,* was published in 1955, simultaneous with his suicide. Engstrand walked into the MacArthur Park Lake in Los Angeles and drowned himself—an action that might well be interpreted as one of anguish over a failed marriage and latent homosexuality.

NOTE

1. *The Sling and the Arrow* and *Sheila Lacey* are not the only novels from Creative Age Press to contain gay characters. In 1946, the company published *Temptation* by John Pen (the pseudonym of John Szekely), translated from the Hungarian by Ralph Manheim and Barbara Tolnai, a sweeping and passionate novel dealing with the life of a young Hungarian male from 1919 to 1929, told against a background of poverty and politics. The narrator-hero works as a bellboy in a Budapest hotel, and one of the other bellboys, a "girlish-faced" boy named Ferenc, earns extra money by servicing wealthy male guests. As Ferenc explains it, "Some are born that way, and some only do it. I only do it. . . . You know, that's not so bad either. And why shouldn't I do it if I get something out of it?" (pp. 320-321). The hero has no problem with Ferenc's attitude.

21

John Evans, *Shadows Flying*

Jacob is in love with David Runyon, and that love is, in some strange way, returned. When Runyon moves into the house that Jacob has inherited from his uncle, he asks a question that is also a statement, "You love me, don't you, Jacob?" When Jacob makes an enthusiastic response, with tears in his eyes, Runyon says,

> Well, come now, that's fine, and I'm glad of it. But let there be an end to this misery I see in you. Love is no unhappy thing, and, besides, I can't bear the smell of unhappiness. I am glad you love me, and I hope you will keep on. In my fashion, I suppose I love you. . . . But I must tell you now, I will not be possessed. Love me all you want, but don't ask me to give what I do not give without the asking. (p. 19)

When Runyon suggests that Jacob accompany him on a visit to his mother and sister, Jacob is thrilled, for his meeting with Runyon's family will surely make the union complete. The two men set off to hike the 100 miles down the California coastal range to Runyon's family home, which is isolated and curiously built in the style of a Southern mansion.

From the start, it is obvious that Runyon and his sister, Fern, are very close, but that Runyon despises his mother, who is emotionally starved and desperate for some affection from her son. Runyon and his sister take Jacob to a bowl-shaped depression at the top of a hill, their favorite place when they were kids which they nicknamed the Teacup. Despite the idyllic surroundings, Jacob is very much aware of a tension within the family. Runyon asks if Fern may be allowed to come and stay with them for a while, because he is desperate to get his sister away from his mother, and Jacob is happy to agree.

On the day that the three are to leave, Jacob arises early and decides to walk up to the Teacup. When he reaches the top of the hill, he looks down and sees Runyon and Fern making love. "Alas, poor Jacob! Here lies your hope and your salvation! Here lies Runyon! And here, as well, lies Fern . . ." (p. 262).

Jacob leaves the two and begins the slow walk back to reality, seeing only emptiness ahead. "Paradise was not for him" (p. 262).

There is no great shock ending here, for the relationship between brother and sister is pretty much signposted by the author. The explosive ending is, therefore, somewhat softened, and as the reviewer in *The New Republic* (July 1, 1936) commented, "It seems curious that an author who accepts inversion calmly should become morally outraged at incest."

Most surprising is the frankness with which the author discusses the relationship between Jacob and Runyon. It is in the open from the first chapter—never hidden from view and constantly in the thoughts of the innocent Jacob, if not the more sophisticated Runyon. At the same time, it is a curious relationship. At no point do the two men share a room, let alone a bed; if there is any sexual contact, it is skillfully hidden by the author. Jacob and Runyon are a modern equivalent of David and Jonathan. The relationship is pure and even wholesome until the arrival of a woman—in the form of Fern—who welcomes Runyon back to his past life as her lover. If Jacob is a substitute for Fern, he is perhaps a poor one in that he offers Runyon no sexual release. In the manner in which he clings to Runyon, he is in many ways closer to Runyon's despised mother than to Fern.

When he discovered his love for Runyon, Jacob also accepted that "he belonged in a certain physiological group" and that now he might surrender to his impulse to love without shame (p. 213). From that moment on, he thanked God for giving him Runyon, the only one of God's creatures capable of filling his heart and soul with love.

To Runyon, Jacob is a "poor little man . . . half a burden, half a joy" (p. 41), whose thin, sensitive face reminds him of one of the pharaohs. Jacob is noble and sensitive, but he might as well have been dead for 5,000 years. Jacob's feelings toward Runyon are less esoteric and far more physical:

> That was it—the love beyond analysis, the intangible, satisfying essence of love, distilled, not from the heart, not from the head, but straight from the life-center, the tremulous, exquisitely sen-

sitive solar plexus. . . . He looked down at Runyon almost beneath him, fascinated as ever by the corporal appeal of the other's long body . . . the wide, flat shoulders, the narrow flat hips—Runyon's beautiful body. . . . Even when he is not near, I can produce his image at will, and feel my vitals quicken! . . . How perfect it would be . . . if I could own him! (p. 67)

Jacob is a sad case, searching for love and trying to erase the memory of an unhappy childhood—when he was branded a sissy and when his football hero of a father gave him a doll as a birthday present, deliberately provoking laughter from the little girls present. From that point onward, Jacob came to loathe women and at the same time wish that he was not so terribly like them in many ways (pp. 96-97). Had Jacob discovered Runyon making love to a local youth rather than his sister, might Jacob's response have been less hysterical? His hatred of women was a fair one—too bad he did not include Fern in their number.

Contemporary reviewers were not overenthusiastic, and took to far more moralizing than can be found in *Shadows Flying* (Alfred A. Knopf, 1936). In *The New York Times* (April 6, 1936), Harold Strauss wrote,

> Mr. Evans dwells by preference in the twilight world of tortured and over-refined sensibilities, analyzing subtle human emotions in a style that is as meticulous as it is musical. . . . It is painful to see a writer of Mr. Evans's accomplishments impelled toward sensationalism. Maturity and the fullness of living itself should do much to help him find more wholesome fictional material.

Fanny Butcher in the *Chicago Tribune* (April 11, 1936) was of the opinion that

> John Evans . . . is not supremely gifted, either as a psychologist or as a writer, and his novel has exactly the reality of its title. His characters are shadows, not real people, and his style is a cloudlike shadow of good writing.

Only Mary Ross in the *New York Herald Tribune Weekly Review of Books* (April 5, 1936) was sympathetic:

Mr. Evans tells the story with discrimination and restraint, unleashing his rage only at the smug and deadly mother whose emotional starvation is responsible for the corruption of Runyon and his sister, Fern. Like most of the other recent novels dealing with sexual abnormalities, the story is anything but lascivious. ... As the story takes form one feels more and more clearly the beat of disaster, like a tom-tom, sounding doom for three gifted, sensitive and intelligent young people not only in terms of the world's disapprobation (which they had accepted long since) but in terms of themselves. Theirs is an isolation, a death-in-life, beyond that of even the most painful humdrum lives about them.

John Evans (born 1902) wrote only two novels, *Andrew's Harvest* (1933) and *Shadows Flying*. The latter shows the influence of his friend, the commercially successful poet Robinson Jeffers who, as did Evans, lived in Carmel, California. Evans was the son of Mabel Dodge Luhan and her first husband, Carl Evans, and it is highly possible that he must have met many prominent literary figures, including D. H. Lawrence, as well as a number of gay men, at Luhan's home in Taos, New Mexico.

22

Waldo Frank, *The Dark Mother*

The Dark Mother (Boni & Liveright, 1920) is an early example—perhaps the definitive one—of a novel in which two men are in love, but in which the homosexual nature of the relationship is never revealed. In *The New Republic* (December 29, 1929), Stark Young wrote one of the few complimentary reviews of the novel, remarking,

> One thing Mr. Frank does do: he brings home to us anew in this book the very valuable reminder that there are vast areas of life that our literature has not yet known how to include. In that sense this novel in places may be called a creditable experiment in material.

The two men in question here are nineteen-year-old David Markand and the somewhat older Thomas Rennard, who meet in a small town. Rennard is a visiting lawyer from New York, and Markand, following the death of his mother, is about to leave for New York to work for his uncle.

An intimate relationship develops between the two, and it is nurtured in New York when both men decide to share an apartment. Both have close female friends, and both lead semiseparate lives, coming together at night but sleeping in separate bedrooms. Rennard is very much obsessed with Markand who, in turn, does not understand the feelings that the other man has for him and gives an impression of naiveté.

When he first returns to the city, Rennard tells his artist sister Cornelia that he met somebody interesting on his vacation. When she asks was it the girl at last, he responds, "No—not the girl" (p. 50). Rennard attempts to explain his feelings to Markand by telling him the story of a man who loves his friend:

The man loved his friend and a woman came into his life whom he also loved. He asked for her in marriage, and she gave her promise. So he went to his friend and told him. And the friend cried, "Do not wed her. Remain with me!" And the man said, "I love this woman but you are my friend. I remain with you." He dismissed the woman whom he loved. . . .

One night as the man slept an angel came to him. The angel said: "Thou who art so loyal to thy friend, name a wish and it is granted." The man, half-unknown to himself, cried out: "Make a miracle! Make one my friend and my lover. Then I may be loyal and yet be happy." The angel smiled. "So it is already." The angel disappeared. . . .

. . . He ran to the sleeping chamber of his friend, expecting to behold a miracle. It was his friend, his unchanged friend who slept there. The man cursed and smote his breast. Then a great light came to him. He understood. (pp. 88-89)

Markand sits there and listens in silence, perhaps unwilling or unable to comprehend what his friend is telling him, but Cornelia understands. She accuses her brother of corrupting Markand, to which Rennard responds, "I may be queer. . . . I guess I am a man of action" (p. 154). Later, he admits to Cornelia that there is something perverse within him.

When Markand wishes to enlist to fight in the Spanish-American War, Rennard argues against it, aware that his behavior is womanish. A three-page letter that Markand writes while on a business trip to Chicago is nothing more than a love letter.

As for Markand, he is warm and alive with Rennard. After an argument, Rennard tells Markand that he is "my better self, my decent self" (p. 211), and Markand takes Rennard's hands in his, his eyes full of tears, and forgives him. Earlier, Rennard had taken Markand's hands, looking almost fiercely into his eyes, until uneasiness forces Markand to draw back. These are the most emotional moments between the two in *The Dark Mother,* a reminder that those readers expecting any remote suggestion of sexual activity between the two men will be sorely disappointed. The two spend their evenings sitting together, smoking their pipes, and viewing each other in a far from detached manner. Markand lies on his back on the floor, and Rennard contemplates placing his foot on the younger man's stomach: "David lay prone and altogether passive: he was a little like a flame that had been extinguished" (p. 179).

Even as Markand prepares to leave Rennard, he sits across the room and looks at him: "And it was sure in David that if ever he had loved, this was the loved one. There had been women whom he had embraced, close of kin who had housed him. This was a mere comrade, a mere fellow-man: his handclasp was the strongest of all" (p. 363).

Ultimately, it is Cornelia who urges Rennard to let Markand go. When her brother insists he is slowly bringing Markand up, Cornelia asks, "Bringing him up to what?" (p. 323). She sets up Markand with a female friend, setting in motion a final act that finds Markand leaving Rennard to take up single residence elsewhere. Rennard warns him not to marry a good and beautiful woman because he will be unable to break away (when he discovers the truth about himself?), but the novel closes with Markand embracing such a woman and looking forward to getting to know her family.

The Dark Mother is a long, heavily descriptive novel, with much informative material on New York, its businessmen, and its politics at the turn of the twentieth century. Much content is related to the parents of both men, in particular their mothers. To Markand, the world is the Dark Mother of the title.

Most critical response to the novel was negative, with reviewers complaining of the writing style—short sentences—and the scenes of sexuality between David Markand and various women. "Of all kinds of sophistry the most insidious is that coming from an eloquent writer who is the unconscious victim of unsound thinking," wrote *The New York Times* (November 21, 1920):

> Mr. Frank is perhaps unduly preoccupied with the world and the flesh, but it would take a psycho-analyst to gauge his intention in dwelling upon them. To give the author his due, it must be said that he impresses the reader rather as a man groping for ethical convictions. Mr. Frank's powers of characterization deserve high praise.

The Nation (October 27, 1920) complained:

> He has chosen a highly impressionistic method of conveying his perceptions and observations. There are few or no connectives.

Sentences and paragraphs stand alone and unfriended. Individually they are pitched in an extremely high key. The result is both nerve-racking and, in the end, without true effectiveness.

The Dark Mirror is the second novel of Waldo Frank (1889-1967), described by one critic as " 'a man of letters' in the old sense of that phrase," who is largely forgotten today.[1] Frank, who was twice married, had two children, and is highly unlikely to have been gay, published *The Dark Mother* in 1920, a year in which he claimed to have had mystical experiences and in which he converted to Judaism. Frank described *The Dark Mother* as an experiment that did not succeed as a novel,[2] but he resurrected its principal character, David Markand, in *The Death and Birth of David Markand: An American Story* (1934). The latter is a complex book, dealing with such social issues as the International Workers of the World (IWW), striking coal miners in Kentucky, and the treatment of African Americans. Thomas Rennard also reappears in the novel, after a twelve-year break from David Markand—he is hired to take care of the latter's investments.

NOTES

1. Paul J. Carter, *Waldo Frank.* New York: Twayne, 1967, Preface. See also Gorham Munson, *Waldo Frank: A Study.* New York: Boni & Liveright, 1923; and William Bittner, *The Novels of Waldo Frank.* Philadelphia: University of Pennsylvania Press, 1955.
2. Alan Trachtenberg (Ed.), *Memoirs of Waldo Frank.* Boston: University of Massachusetts Press, 1973.

23

Ernest Frost, *The Dark Peninsula*

Ernest Frost (born 1918) was an English novelist and poet. The setting of his first novel, *The Dark Peninsula* (John Lehmann, 1949), is southern Italy toward the close of World War II. A group of British soldiers are occupying the region, and the first two to be introduced are Lieutenant "Mully" Mulholland and Private Arnold Thompson, who enjoy an uneasy friendship. Something is obviously strange here, when the latter looks at Mulholland and wants "to run his fingers over the jaw, to feel that light stubble of beard which glinted in the daylight" (p. 12). The reality is that Mulholland does not care for Thompson, grows genuinely to dislike him, and that both men are heterosexual. The gay member of the group is their commanding officer, Colonel Judd. A publisher before the war, he had been in love with a young poet, identified only as "A," whom Mulholland also knew and admired. Thompson makes no secret of his hatred for Judd, who has fallen in love with the young private and who secretly rescues him from drowning:

> A bobbing head I swam to, and it was he whom I love. How can you, you say, a man of my age love the least of these? But I'll tell you for why. . . . He couldn't recognize me. Not him. He thought I was someone else, someone kind and nice. He doesn't like me, but he never thinks I see in him the real need to continue. (p. 112)

The affection is not returned by Thompson, who sees in Judd only "a rotten predatory spoiler of young men" (p. 194). It is Thompson's rejection that leads Judd to force himself on another private, little more than a boy, named Kent. "There was something very lithe about his movements, something that made Judd continue to stare at him closely. The face came out of nostalgia. It surely had an element of

A's profile" (p. 169). A hopelessly lost and despairing Colonel Judd, who hates the war and the situation in which it has placed him, sexually assaults Kent, although the circumstances of the attack are not revealed. Judd is reassigned, and Thompson, without the unknown protection of the colonel, is sent to the front line.

The poetry that is inside each of them has ultimately destroyed them. For as A had told Mulholland, the poet "is the outlaw, the terrible leper in a London square, the misfit, the beggar in Battersea Park" (p. 224). The analogy between the poet as outcast and the gay man as outcast is very obvious; it is there without being written on the page. Each man kills the thing he loves. Judd, by allowing his physical desire briefly to overwhelm him, by losing his position of power, by no longer being the protector of Thompson, has sent the young man to his certain death. Thompson uses the colonel, accepting an offer to be his personal secretary with the promise of a visit to Rome. He still despises Judd not because he understands the colonel's inner feelings, but because he believes the officer is in love with a Danish woman whom Thompson regards, prematurely and incorrectly, as his mistress.

Thompson tries to explain his confused feelings to a young Italian doctor's wife:

> Our lives are dark peninsulas. . . . They run into the sea of experience we try to relate, but fail. War occupies part of this peninsula, but it is the war of our desire, our petty power, our dislike for the stranger. We prey on each other, for the enemies are around us, working with us. But if we looked into our mirror perhaps our true enemy would be there. We'd like to make a truce with him, eh! But we can't. (p. 192)

The Dark Peninsula is a novel in which homosexuality is not once mentioned by name, but one in which it is all-pervasive, both dangerous and desirous. In a unique sense here, it holds the power of life and death. The love of Judd for Thompson is a beautiful thing. When the colonel briefly takes Thompson's hand, "The body, supple and necessary, lay on his longing like a rose" (p. 130). As he walks with the unknowing Thompson, Judd recalls A's coming to his cottage in the Cotswolds to read his elegies. "And now, magically perpetuated, the past and present interwove the voices, the poems, the excitement"

(p. 130). It is powerful narrative, intense poetry, a drama between the two that transcends the mere physical.

Despite going through at least two printings, *The Dark Peninsula* appears to have made little impact on the gay community in the United States. It was little reviewed here, and the author remains unknown to an international readership.

24

Henry Blake Fuller,
Bertram Cope's Year

As the title suggests, the novel documents a year in the life of Bertram Cope, a twenty-eight-year-old English literature instructor at a Midwestern university, Churchton (presumed to be modeled after the University of Illinois at Urbana-Champaign). He becomes friendly with the literate and aging Basil Randolph and becomes a protégé of middle-aged widow Medora Phillips, who hosts salons to which local and visiting representatives of art and literature are invited.

Bertram Cope becomes engaged to and then disengaged from a young lady of Mrs. Phillips's selection and invites a young friend, Arthur Lemoyne, to join him at Churchton, and to enroll as a student of psychology. Within the year Lemoyne leaves the university in disgrace, Cope goes off to his parents' home, and the members of Churchton society await with interest Cope's return for the next school year.

The story, consisting of a series of incidents, basically one per chapter, is told in an ironic, comic style, somewhat similar in cynical approach to that adopted later by E. F. Benson. Reading *Bertram Cope's Year* (Ralph Fletcher Seymour, 1919) is rather like reading a play by Oscar Wilde that is devoid of any quotable witticisms.

What is most remarkable about *Bertram Cope's Year* is that the novel can be read on two levels. To the average heterosexual, it is a minor, vaguely amusing story of small-town university life. To a gay reader in 1919, its depiction of gay life in the same environment must have been quite exciting. To a gay reader in early twenty-first century, *Bertram Cope's Year* is possibly a bit of a bore—easy to read but not really worth the effort. The gay angle is not always blatant, and there is a danger that an overenthusiastic gay man might find more here than the author originally intended. The reader should take warning from critic Edmund Wilson that "though it involves homosexual situations, it is not really a book about homosexuality. It has a kind of philosophic theme."

The author provides what might be clues for the homosexual reader in his narrative, but are they genuine? Why does he make reference to an entertainment with the very obviously nongay ladies at Mrs. Phillips's home as being "an afternoon in Lesbos" (p. 23)? When he writes of Mrs. Phillips's entertaining the "Eminent and the Queer" (p. 13), in what capacity does he use the latter word? The term "gay" in reference to a homosexual man was, supposedly, not introduced until the 1920s, and yet the author has Bertram Cope commenting, "Well, I could be pretty gay too with a lot of money behind me; and I think that, for another year or so, I can contrive to be gay without it" (p. 49). When Lemoyne is cast in a female theatrical role, he exalts, "This is a gay life! . . . Just the life I have come down here to lead" (pp. 208-209). The number of times that "gay" is used in the text seems overabundant and in no way accidental.

Is Bertram Cope gay? Yes, but very much at ease with himself and in feminine company (even if members of the company are determined to snare him into marriage). That he can allow himself to become engaged suggests even that Cope lacks any sexual identity. Is Basil Randolph gay? Perhaps. Certainly, he enjoys the company of Bertram Cope and other young students, but he is very much one of nature's bachelors in need of no obvious sexual relief from either gender. He is happy to be an exalted observer at Mrs. Phillips's soirées and equally happy in the enjoyment of his collection of "curios." Much has been made of Randolph and Cope swimming nude in the lake, but such an occurrence would not be unusual at that time. Randolph does pick up a handful of sand and apply it to Cope's bare shoulder, but this is hardly an act of homosexual love or obsession, and the author singularly ignores the opportunity to dwell narratively on the naked bodies of either man.

Is Bertram Cope's friend, Arthur Lemoyne, gay? Definitely! Both Lemoyne and Cope are obviously sharing a bed at the latter's apartment and also one night at Mrs. Phillips's home. After an evening stroll together, Lemoyne puts his arm around Cope's shoulder "and Urania, through the whole width of her starry firmament, looked down kindly upon a happier household" (p. 211). The relationship between the two is well recorded by the author:

If Cope settled down in a large chair, Lemoyne would drape himself over the arm of it; and his hand would fall, as like as not, on the back of the chair, or even on Cope's shoulder. And when he came to occupy the piano stool, Cope standing alongside, would lay a hand on his. (p. 192)

When Lemoyne despairs of life in Churchton, Cope puts his arm around his shoulder, and Lemoyne presses his hand on Cope's (p. 227).

Lemoyne is somewhat effeminate—his "slightly affected movements" indicate possession of the "artistic temperament" (p. 183)—and quite happy to offend any member of small-town university society. Neither the author nor Basil Randolph seems to like Lemoyne, quite obviously because of his effeminacy. Lemoyne quickly becomes engrossed in playing a feminine role in the student production of *The Antics of Arabella*. Bertram Cope explains to Mrs. Phillips and her social secretary, Carolyn, who has become infatuated with him, that the play has absorbed Arthur completely.

> "Men in girls's parts are so amusing," said Carolyn. . . . "And when they speak up in those big deep bass and baritone voices. . . . !"
> "Arthur will speak in a light tenor."
> "Will his walk by heavy and clumsy?" asked Mrs. Phillips.
> "He is an artist," replied Cope. (p. 257)

Lemoyne becomes a little too obsessed with the feminine part, acting the role both on and offstage, and "in his general state of ebulliency he endeavored to bestow a measure of upwelling femininity upon another performer who was in the dress of his own sex" (p. 270). The young gentleman and the college authorities are outraged, and the hapless Lemoyne is told to return to his hometown of Winnebago, Wisconsin.

As a gay couple, Cope and Lemoyne are curiously uninteresting. The reader never really gets to know them. One has no sense of their physical appearance. We know almost nothing of Cope's build, height, or looks. We know Lemoyne is inclined to "flutter," that he has dark, limpid eyes and dark wavy hair, while Cope appears to often to be auditioning for a role in a second-rate touring production of *The Importance of Being Earnest*.

Mrs. Phillips and Randolph are obviously suspicious of the Cope-Lemoyne relationship, but it is Mrs. Phillips's wheelchair-bound half brother, Frank, who identifies Lemoyne as gay: "always hanging over the other man's chair; always finding a reason to put his hand on his shoulder . . . they brought the manners of the bedroom into the drawing-room" (p. 200).

Henry Blake Fuller (1857-1929) was a major American writer, relatively forgotten today, who was also a gay man. In a photograph from later years, he appears to be a very Edwardian and a forlorn-looking, heavily bearded gentleman. Rather like E. M. Forster, Fuller did not acknowledge in print any interest in homosexuality while a young writer although at least unlike the English novelist of *Maurice,* Fuller did have the courage to publish *Bertram Cope's Year* while still alive. Fuller was sixty-two when the novel appeared. No New York publisher had expressed any interest in the book, and eventually it was brought out in Chicago by Ralph Fletcher Seymour, with whom Fuller was friendly. *Bertram Cope's Year* received scant critical attention. With some truth, *The Bookman* (February 1924) commented that the novel "though filled with dynamite scrupulously packed, fell harmless as a dud." The lack of interest, either commercial or critical, hurt Fuller—he purchased and destroyed all unsold, unbound copies of the novel—and he was to publish only two more books.

Henry Blake Fuller, while certainly not faced with any financial problems in his life, was not a happy individual. He was an American who craved the European lifestyle. The happiest time of his life was spent at the Allison Classical Academy of Oconomowoc between 1873 and 1874. There he shared a room, and perhaps more, with five other boys, one of whom, Frank L. Donaldson, is in all probability the basis for Arthur Lemoyne.

The author is the subject of two very unsatisfactory critical studies, neither of which makes reference to his homosexuality and the earliest of which finds nothing gay in *Bertram Cope's Year*—*Henry Blake Fuller: A Critical Biography* by Constance M. Griffin (University of Pennsylvania Press, 1939) and *Henry Blake Fuller* by John Pilkington Jr. (Twayne, 1970).

– 25 –

Richard Hull,
The Murder of My Aunt

The first gay characters to be found in the mystery genre of the twentieth century appear in Arthur Conan Doyle's short story, "The Man with the Watches," first published in *The Strand* magazine, and reprinted in *Round the Fire Stories* (Doubleday, 1909). They are a young American named Edward, who has taken to dressing in female attire and is referred to as a "Mary Jane," and his "mentor," the criminal Sparrow McCoy. The first gay character in a mystery novel can be found in John Buchan's *Greenmantle* and the first lesbian featured in a mystery novel is "Everard Mountjoy" in Gladys Mitchell's *Speedy Death* (Victor Gollancz, 1929). "Everard Mountjoy" is revealed as a woman when she is murdered by her fiancée, Eleanor Bing. Bing, in turn, is killed by the novel's heroine, Mrs. Bradley, who comes up with the ultimate solution to "sexual perversion," and is acquitted at a trial in which her defense is handled by her son. *Speedy Death* is the first of sixty-five novels to feature Mrs. (later Dame) Beatrice Adela Lestrange Bradley, a nasty, homophobic creature who bears no resemblance to the character played by Diana Rigg in the popular BBC series *The Mrs. Bradley Mysteries*.

The best, and by far the most entertaining, of the early English mystery novels with a gay angle is Richard Hull's *The Murder of My Aunt* (A Minton Balch Book/G. P. Putnam's Sons, 1936), first published in the United Kingdom by Faber and Faber in 1934. This is certainly the first novel of any genre to feature a gay narrator, in the fat and greasy shape of Edward, whose one desire is to murder his Aunt Mildred. Edward (no last name supplied by the author) is quite nasty, something of a buffoon, and also quite witty, rather in the style of Oscar Wilde. Of Wales, where his aunt lives, Edward writes, "Miles and miles of hills and woods, all looking exactly the same. No man has ever taken this meaningless jumble created by nature and made everything of it. It needs forming" (p. 4).

Because his aunt is rich, because he is forced to rely on her support, living with her in her Welsh cottage—and because she calls him "a namby-pamby little pansy boy" (p. 193), Edward determines to murder her. The first time, when he tampers with the brakes of her car, he is almost successful. It transpires that Aunt Mildred has figured out what Edward is up to, thanks to some friendly advice from a Dr. Spencer. (The last chapter, a postscript, is written by her after she has disposed of Edward by tampering with the brakes of *his* car.)

One might argue that Edward, as he is presented or rather as he presents himself, is a very obnoxious homosexual male, but there is something rather likeable about him, pimples, extra pounds, long hair, puffy face, and all. Aunt Mildred deserves to die; she is too perfect.

Contemporary critics on both sides of the Atlantic Ocean praised *The Murder of My Aunt* for its originality and the unique manner in which it presented its story. The reviewer in *The Times Literary Supplement* (October 4, 1934) wrote, "Mr. Richard Hull's novel will delight and amuse all nephews and aunts, and all other relations to the tenth remove and beyond. A brilliant piece of serious fooling." In *The New York Times* (January 20, 1935), Isaac Anderson commented, "The author is to be congratulated upon having produced a completely merciless and, at the same time, amusing portrait of a perfectly worthless human being."

Richard Hull (1896-1973) was the pseudonym of Richard Henry Sampson, the author of fifteen mystery novels, published between 1934 and 1953. One of the most highly praised of these books is *My Own Murderer* (1940), in which the decidedly unpleasant narrator is named Richard Henry Sampson. Sampson was a confirmed bachelor (as certain gentlemen were once characterized) who described himself in 1950 in the third person to critic Howard Haycroft:

> In fiction, he specialized in unpleasant characters because he says there is more to say about them and that he finds them more amusing. In life, he pleads a kind heart as a set-off for an occasional flash of temper and an endless flow of conversation. For many years he has lived almost entirely in a London club, qualifying, as he says, as the club bore. He is convinced that his photograph would be detrimental to his sales.

Edward in *The Murder of My Aunt* is also a member of a London club, and there is obviously more than a fleeting similarity between Edward and his creator. The life in a London club, devoid of women and any sexual activity or comment, must have been most appealing to Sampson. Almost all of Richard Hull's later mystery *Keep It Quiet* (A Minton Balch Book/G.P. Putnam's Sons, 1936), is set within the confines of London's Whitehall Club. The villain of the piece, Dr. Anstruther, is exposed by the club's secretary, Ford, described by the former as "a sniveling old woman . . . whose black silk petticoats one can hear rustling as you walk" (p. 223).

The Murder of My Aunt has twice been reprinted. In 1968, it was reissued in hardcover as an entry in the Seagull Library of Mystery and Suspense, published by W. W. Norton, with a lightweight introduction by James Nelson. In 1979, it appeared as a paperback from International Polygonics, Ltd., with a better introduction from a writer/editor with the curious (and unlikely) name of Burke N. Hare.

The book is not the only English mystery novel of the 1930s to feature a major gay character. In 1937, Doubleday Doran published *A Bullet in the Ballet* by Caryl Brahms and S. J. Simon, the first of a series of novels to feature the Stroganoff Ballet Company. Not surprisingly, in view of the ballet background, there are two principal gay characters here, both of whom end up murder victims. The attitude of their fellow dancers toward the men's death is not particularly sympathetic. The prima ballerina is angry that the first victim continued to like men after she had taken the trouble to seduce him. Of the second victim, an older male dancer comments that his liking of men was a misfortune, but his claim that he could dance *Le Train Bleu* better than Anton Dolin was intolerable.

As with *The Murder of My Aunt,* there is much humor in *A Bullet in the Ballet*, but it is often strained and dated, with the authors addressing the reader directly. On the plus side, the novel does boast a very friendly attitude toward gay men, except for one passing reference to a "homosexual" and one to a "pervert." As with *The Murder of My Aunt, A Bullet in the Ballet* was also reprinted by International Polygonics, Ltd., in 1984.

26

Charles Jackson, *The Fall of Valor*

Charles Jackson (1903-1968) is best known as the author of *The Lost Weekend* (1945), his first novel, which was filmed by director Billy Wilder in 1945 with Ray Milland as the central character, Don Birnam. The novel, which is too well known to belong here, documents the five-day binge of an alcoholic, and is obviously semi-autobiographical. What is missing from the screen version is the strong implication that Don Birnam is a latent homosexual, whose alcoholism directly relates to his inability to accept his sexual identity. This is emphasized in *The Lost Weekend* when, at one point, a gay orderly in the alcoholic ward, Bim, whispers that he "knows" Don.

The Fall of Valor (Rinehart, 1946), Jackson's second novel, takes its title from Herman Melville's *Moby Dick*. Its pivotal character, John Grandin, is a "valor-ruined man," who, similar to Don Birnam, is presumably a semiautobiographical figure. (As is Charles Jackson, Birnam is an academic and a writer with two children—Jackson had two girls; Birnam has two boys.)

It is June 1943—for Americans, the second summer of World War II. John Grandin is in New York, his wife Ethel is in Boston, visiting her parents, and the two plan to meet at Woods Hole and take the boat for a vacation on Nantucket Island. As the trains carry the Grandins to their first meeting after a few weeks of separation, the sexual tension slowly and quietly mounts. The somewhat shy Ethel is surrounded by servicemen and cannot help but notice the sailor opposite, "the fly-less front of his dark pants . . . stretched tight across his abdomen and groin" (p. 36). John Grandin is also surrounded by servicemen, although in a more congenial situation—unlike his wife, he is traveling in a Pullman car. There is the paratrooper, "handsome in a lean-faced way" (p. 30), the photograph in his copy of *Life* showing four dead marines, "the pants and shirts tight with the already swelling bodies" (p. 27), and above all the athletic, blond, and blue-eyed Captain Cliff

Hauman. Grandin looks with an outwardly vague but highly descriptive eye at all around him. It is not coincidental that the forty-four-year-old Grandin has taken only one book with him, *The Collected Poems of A. E. Houseman,* the verses of an older academic fixated with a youthful, unconsummated love for a fellow undergraduate.

Just as the apparently unimportant sequences on board the two trains hint at a sexual climax, so does the boat trip to Nantucket suggest the emotional detachment of John and Ethel Grandin. They become acquainted with Hauman and his new bride, Billie, who was one of Grandin's students, and also meet another middle-aged couple, Bill and Sadie Howard. Only in the presence of the others do the Grandins seem able to conduct a civilized conversation. When the Grandins arrive at their hotel, Ethel points out the sterility of their marriage, that John has failed to show any physical interest in her for some considerable time, and that their relationship is basically a loveless one.

At the insistence of the Haumans, the two couples spend more and more time together. John Grandin is slowly becoming fixated with Cliff Hauman, misreading his behavior. The two men change into swimming attire together and Hauman carelessly walks naked around the room (although Jackson refrains from any description of the marine's naked body). Hauman showers and towels himself off in front of the older man. Grandin misunderstands when Hauman gives him his pale khaki marine cap as a "souvenir":

> John Grandin felt sick at heart. He wanted to say—he felt it impossible to keep from saying, Cliff, I'm very fond of you. The words stuck in his throat, he would never be able to get them out, never in a thousand years; and he was glad that this was so. (p. 186)

To John Grandin, Cliff Hauman is noble, considerate, and eloquent. He hears no coarse words from the mouth of the marine. Yet he is shocked when Hauman jokes about a young interior designer, Arne Eklund, who is also staying at the hotel with his mother. Hauman's wife has already identified the man: "Blindfolded you could tell he's 4-F—and why" (p. 162). Gleefully, Hauman yells at Bill Howard, "I want you to lay off that pretty boy over there, the fag. You can't have him—he's mine!" (p. 202).

When Ethel Grandin discovers Hauman's cap in her husband's luggage, she comprehends the reason behind his lack of physical contact. She understands now why, hidden in his study, he had kept a photograph, clipped from a newspaper, of a young marine, "a very rugged, masculine, and mature-looking young man" (p. 55). "It's a perversion," she cries out (p. 255), but Grandin tries to explain:

> Perhaps it's been due to happen for a long time, I honestly don't know; and it took Cliff to bring it out. Maybe it's a definite part of me, part of my nature. But till now, my love for you has kept it in the background where it belongs. Our love can do it again. (p. 255)

Ethel leaves him; Sadie Howard believes it is because of Mrs. Hauman until she sees the two men together. "All along I thought it was Billie. But it's Cliff, my god. . . . The poor guy" (pp. 273-274).

As Grandin prepares to depart Nantucket, he has a desultory conversation with Cliff, who tells him of an English professor named Scotty that he had in college.

> One night when we were sitting at the desk in his apartment, just he and I—I'd gone over to his place so he could help me study— do you know what he did? Scotty put his hand on my knee, his whole hand, and left it there for a second. Can you beat that, Johnnie? . . . Gee, it was too bad, because he was really a wonderful guy. (pp. 267-268)

John Grandin is not so much disillusioned as confused by Cliff Hauman's conversation and behavior. Ultimately, he misreads the situation. Hauman visits him in New York, and his first request is that he may have a shower. Here, as it has appeared so many times throughout the novel, the reader is forced to conjecture that Hauman is nothing more than "a cock teaser." For Grandin, this is so obvious, "such a cheap invitation to sexuality" (p. 303). But as with so many of Hauman's actions, it is nothing of the sort. Grandin is in love and past caring. He places his hands on Hauman's solid but slender waist, declaring, "Cliff, I've grown very fond of you, I can't help it . . ." (p. 307).

Cliff's body freezes, his blue eyes blaze with anger, and he seizes the brass-handled tongs in the fireplace—the tongs that Charles Jackson had introduced to the reader, as if foreshadowing their significance in the first chapter, when they fall down as Grandin prepares to leave the apartment. This time they fall on Grandin. Drenched in his own blood, Grandin crawls to the door, where lies a letter from Ethel, a letter reassuring him of their love, telling him that Cliff was nothing more than an episode in their past. As he reads the letter, John Grandin's "sole emotion was a passionate regret that Cliff had not finished the job" (p. 310).

Charles Jackson displayed considerable courage in writing a novel such as *The Fall of Valor.* As one critic pointed out, the theme was so sensational that the author was foregoing such lucrative subsidiary earnings as radio, films, book clubs, and serialization. (Library sales were in doubt when the leading publication for professional libraries, *Library Journal,* in its issue of September 15, 1946, warned, "Subject, and especially bluntness of presentation, limit library use. Read before purchase.") The author was also putting his innermost thoughts, his yearnings, his emotional soul on paper. Here, for really the first time, we have a major American writer opening discussing homosexuality—not just between two well-suited men, but the love of an older man for one almost half his age—with little self-censorship. Only Arne Eklund is presented as a gay stereotype, and it might well be argued that he is here to signify that such types do exist, but that there are others, such as John Grandin, who carry none of the baggage, the mannerisms, and the behavior generally identified by the contemporary reader with a homosexual man.

Contemporary critics were positive in their response to *The Fall of Valor,* but not necessarily in their interpretation of homosexuality. To all, it is nothing more than a disease, and one that needs to be controlled rather like smallpox or malaria. In *The Nation* (October 19, 1946), Diana Trilling wrote,

> In writing a story of this kind Mr. Jackson has set himself a task which is extremely difficult on two scores. He has the initial problem of making the evolution of Grandin's homosexuality, and Ethel Grandin's reaction to it, psychologically convincing. Then he has the problem of making his study something more meaningful than a case history. For, after all, scientific literature is full of psychologically sound records of the homosexual neurosis, and if we are to read Mr. Jackson's novel rather than a textbook, it must be because its study of disease will tell us

about more than disease, enlarging beyond the usual limits of a case history our understanding of the world in which illness exists. *The Fall of Valor*, however, seems to me to miss fire on both these counts.

In the *New York Herald Tribune Weekly Book Review* (October 6, 1946), Clifton Fadiman offers his theory on homosexuality:

> Mr. Jackson tells his story swiftly, cleanly, humanely, without a word of psychoanalytic jargon, making no explanations that are not implicit in the action. The speculative reader, however, may draw from the tale two conclusions that the author himself does not draw. The first is that the homosexual component overdeveloped in John Grandin partly because his marriage was a bore and a failure—rather than the other way round. . . . The second feeling some readers are likely to have is that John Grandin's disease is not a hateful aberration (as our Victorian grandfathers—and contemporaries—would have it) but is rather somehow connected with a larger and more pervasive disease or our time, a universal failure of nerve.

In *The New Yorker* (October 5, 1946), Edmund Wilson commented,

> What has been done here by Mr. Jackson is . . . so far as I know, something which has not been done before and something which perhaps needed doing. He has made homosexuality middle-class and thereby removed it from the privileged level on which Gide and Proust had set it. *The Fall of Valor* thus suffers from a handicap that *The Lost Weekend* did not have. But it does, like its predecessor, create apprehension and suspense. One used to feel about the characters of Hemingway that their nerves were just about to give way, that they were hanging on the edge of a precipice. The characters in Charles Jackson's novels are already falling over the precipice.

John Grandin is, of course, middle class because Charles Jackson was middle class. He inhabits an environment with which Charles Jackson was very familiar. What the critics failed to realize was that Jackson had more than a slight affinity with his central character. No one was more wrong than R. G. Davis, when he wrote in *The New York Times* (October 6, 1946),

> Charles Jackson, for his second novel, has hit upon a subject that has been treated by experts. Such an expert, in the precise sense of the word, Mr. Jackson quite obviously is not happily for himself, and unhappily for *The Fall of Valor.*

Very unhappily for himself, Charles Jackson was a little too much of an expert on the subject of closet homosexuality. In appearance, he was very much the dapper college professor, with suit and bow tie, the sort of individual who might have been portrayed on screen by the waspish and gay Clifton Webb. Only in old age did Charles Jackson try to come to terms with his sexuality. Again an alcoholic, he became estranged from his wife and children. In 1965, he rented a New York apartment with his male lover. He died three years later from an overdose of sleeping pills, having published only two further novels, *The Outer Edges* (1948) and *A Second-Hand Life* (1967).

27

Nial Kent, *The Divided Path*

Michael is a young boy, growing up in a small American town, confused as to his sexuality. He dreams of a divided path, "one fork seeming to lead downward into misty, shadowy depths which were somehow strangely, compellingly attractive by their mystery, and the other branch led uphill into the sunshine" (p. 252). Initially, Michael follows the uphill path. He has girlfriends—even loses his virginity to one—and refuses to follow through on a number of highly tempting gay proposals. His closest male friend is Paul, a young man with whom he swims nude, shares a bed, and, at one time, even kisses. However, Paul is apparently as confused as Michael, and the relationship leads nowhere—least of all to sexual fulfillment. The novel is quite remarkable for the number of occasions in which Michael finds himself naked and in bed with various naked, attractive young men, with each quickly falling asleep and never indulging in any physical contact beyond a chaste kiss.

Michael goes away to study music, comes to New York and becomes a medical orderly in a hospital when, at America's entry into World War II, he is rejected for the service because of a heart murmur. It is only in the big city that Michael finally comes to terms with his sexuality. He dines with and visits the apartment of his office manager, Mr. Page. Michael stays the night and in bed, "the mouth that suggested Paul's was pressed upon his own" (p. 276). He is careful to avoid revealing to Mr. Page that this is his first time and that he is pretending he is with Paul.

Michael's circle of gay friends grows, as do his sexual encounters, but still he yearns for Paul. The reader constantly wonders how many hundreds of pages must go by before the two are reunited. The outcome of the climactic final meeting—described by the author as "con abbandóno e belléza"—is foreshadowed well in advance. Michael writes his will prior to returning from New York to his hometown. As

Paul waits for him in his uncle's cabin, where the two young men had spent many happy hours, a thunderstorm arises. Paul finds Michael's car wrecked against a tree. He holds his friend's hand as it tightens its grip on his fingers.

The *San Francisco Chronicle* (November 27, 1949) compared Michael to Pollyanna, and there is something Pollyanna-ish about Michael's view of society. Even after sex with his girl in the backseat of the car, "at heart he was still a virgin" (p. 224). As if to cleanse himself from immoral thoughts, Michael takes endless baths. When he goes to an all-night café and hears the counterman and a customer joking about sex, he is disgusted. "Filth. Was there nothing in life but filth! Sex at its ugliest" (p. 120).

One of Michael's earliest loves is for a pen pal named Gerald. He believes he is saving himself for Gerald, as a girl waiting for Mr. Right to appear as a knight on a white charger.

Michael loves the human body with the love of an aesthete. He spends a lot of time at the YMCA pool with its naked male swimmers:

> The pool had a strong attraction for him, with its clear green waters and the strong smell of chlorine, the plunk and splash, and the echo of voices against the tile walls, the gleam of wet skin in the pool and under the showers—they all attracted him more than he liked to admit. He even liked and remembered some of the glances he got as he walked from the lockers to the pool. (p. 96)

An older and wealthy woman tries to force her attentions on Michael, an experience that the author uses as blame for the young man's distrust and fear of all women. His first abortive same-sex experience is equally negative, when he accepts an invitation for dinner with C. Roger Markham, a well-built man in his late forties who is head of the Boy's Seminary. Michael is shown photographs the likes of which he had not known existed. Markham gropes him to check on Michael's reaction to the images. He lowers his head toward Michael's lips. The young man breaks free and rushes for the door: "You . . . you swine!" he gasps as he slams it behind him (p. 118).

Only in Paul—in his image of Paul, in his memory of Paul—does Michael discover real love. "His sexual awareness had been early and premature. Always he had been older than his years in the knowledge of the subject. Nonetheless he had never been fully awakened, really stirred by sex, until now" (p. 146). Nonetheless, as with any popular romance, physical love is to be denied the pair. Death will most conveniently interfere, preventing any possible disappointment with the encounter for either young man.

The author is most comfortable once he has Michael firmly installed in New York gay society. The author is evidently as relaxed with it as Michael is to become. Two parties involving drag are described in considerable detail, with one character, Verne, a flight lieutenant in the Air Force, presenting a dazzling impersonation of Luise Rainer in the telephone scene from the film *The Great Ziegfeld*. There are jokes of a soldier in a private's uniform kissing another soldier on the couch, only to have a captain pull rank on him and take over the action.

At one point, Michael considers the "rare stories" that he might tell Paul if they meet again:

> John Page and his passion for blue sheets; Neil's friend who had sixty boys in one week at the steam bath; sitting alone in a corner watching Neil and Verne Talley rehearsing a number they were going to do at a party . . . Neil wearing black trousers and a white silk shirt open in a V to the waist, Verne far from being in full costume, wearing only a black brassiere, black net opera hose and spike-heeled shoes as they danced in front of the big mirror . . . the truly aphrodisiac quality of Verne's marble-like body as it went gracefully in the lifts, the way his hips gleamed above the black stockings like those of the Venus of Cyrene; the soldiers at Neil's parties who used to line up at the mirror before leaving to adjust their little overseas caps at exactly the right jaunty angle, like women putting on their hats, and the amusing things they used to tell, like the time in Paris at a bar patronized almost exclusively by gay officers when one had innocently taken a girl there, and an English lieutenant had screamed, "Oooh, a woman! Killit, killlit. Hit it with a stick!" (p. 439)

Michael is settled in a small New York apartment peopled extensively by gay men. Living next door are Rex and Jack, who met in the Army and are now a happily married couple. They urge Michael to marry and settle down, and look on as he has affairs with their friend

Lenny and, later, Nikki from Michael's hometown. But these lovers are not Paul.

There is some wonderful description here of New York gay life in the 1940s, but also there is much that is cheap and sentimental. It is often hard to wade through the first half of the book, with Michael rejecting relationship after relationship (both male and female) for little valid reason, but it is worth the struggle, although the trite ending disappoints.

Reviewers were scathing. In *The New York Times* (November 6, 1949), J. P. Quehl wrote,

> Mr. Kent's style is plain to the point of no style at all, and much of his story is unbroken narrative, which, perhaps, is a good thing, since his dialogue is artificial and weak. As a serious study of aberration, this novel misses by a mile.

In a similar vein, N. L. Rothman in the *Saturday Review of Literature* (December 3, 1949) complained, "Surely there is more to say of the world of the homosexual than this. It has been better said in at least half a dozen novels that come to mind."

Yes, but not said in such a sympathetic tone. *The Divided Path* (Greenberg, 1949) is very much a novel for gay readers of the day. There is no mention of the word "homosexual," but the author does utilize "gay" and he does provide some vivid descriptions of gay encounters, although the mores of the time do force him to draw down the curtain generally after the first kiss, be it on the mouth or the nipple.

Nial Kent is the pseudonym of William Leroy Thomas, about whom nothing is on record. He is presumably not the geographer and anthropologist of the same name who has authored a number of books.

28

Lew Levenson, *Butterfly Man*

"Butterfly Man" is the appellation bestowed on Ken Gracey by Chicago gangster Rocco, who bears no resemblance to any other gangster of fiction or nonfiction. Rocco takes Ken to his "den," where the young man dances for Rocco and his fifteen gang members. When Ken returns to consciousness the next morning, his clothes are torn and he has no recollection of what had happened to him the previous night. The implication is that he was the victim of a gang rape. The situation is both improbable and melodramatic, but typical of much that is contained in *Butterfly Man* (Macaulay Company, 1934). A great many things happen to Ken, which he does not remember the next morning, and which the moral standards of the day do not permit the novelist to record.

Nothing is known of the author Lew Levenson, which may well be a pseudonym. The Macaulay Company published both quality books and cheap fiction. *Butterfly Man* garnered no reviews on publication, but that might be, in part, because in 1934 the staff members of the Macaulay Company were on strike, the first such labor action directed at a publishing house. *Butterfly Man* is a novel that is strikingly explicit for 1934, and so entertaining to a gay reader not desirous of too much intellectual stimulation that it was reprinted in the mid-1950s by Castle Books (without a copyright notice) and again in 1967 by Tandem Books/Award Books.

Gay men might have found *Butterfly Man* appealing, but so might have homophobic right-wingers who believed that gay men were on the prowl to "convert" innocent young men to homosexuality. It is such a fictional character, Mr. Lowell, who arranges to take seventeen-year-old Ken Gracey away from his poverty-ridden Texas father and to introduce him to a new life of wealth and luxury in Los Angeles. It is not too long before Ken becomes aware of Mr. Lowell's sexual persuasion, but he manages to remain unsullied. "Keep out of strange beds," are Gracey's final words to his son (p. 9) and, at least around Mr. Lowell, Ken does just that. Later on, he does not display the same discriminating taste.

Ken Gracey is not a likeable hero. He is narcissistic and self-centered (albeit somewhat subconsciously). Despite rejecting Mr. Lowell, despite ignoring the suggestion of a poet friend of Lowell's that he accept himself as he is, when he leaves, Ken asks to take with him the clothes that Mr. Lowell has bought for him together with 100 dollars. He also leaves with an elderly woman, Anita Rogers, whom he has met at dancing classes, paid for by Mr. Lowell, and with whom he teams up as a vaudeville act.

Ken is praised for his dancing, but the act falls apart because of his partner's drinking, and the couple finishes up in Tijuana. In Anita's company, Ken does not necessarily become homosexual but he does become a misogynist: "he hated her because she was a woman" (p. 97). "The woman, Ken knew, was black as sin. She was unclean. She was conceived in slime. In slime she lived, into slime she would finally descend" (p. 107).

A chance encounter with a theatrical agent persuades Ken to leave for New York, and there he is hired as a specialty dancer for the Broadway show *Sweeter Than Sweet*. From this point onward, Ken begins the rapid descent into the hellhole of homosexuality.

The writer and producer of the show, Howard Vee, falls in love with Ken and very gradually a relationship begins, a partnership that is ended by an increasingly unstable and self-engrossed Ken, who is now twenty-three years old. Unsophisticated and gullible, Ken is quickly led astray by alcohol and, subsequently, drugs. When Howard Vee goes off to Europe to work on his latest production, Ken opts to stay behind, appearing in the touring production of *Sweeter Than Sweet*.

A wealthy forty-year-old Bostonian jeweler, Ernie Emerson, gives Ken a platinum wristwatch and blue diamond ring. When the touring company of *Sweeter Than Sweet* reaches Boston, Ken is invited to a drag ball, hosted by Emerson, at which, at the latter's request, he wears a cloth of gold gown, a Titian wig, and all the accessories. As Cara, Ken—identified as "Ernie's latest pansy" (p. 200)—wins first prize, a diamond bracelet, in the drag competition.

As is always the situation with Ken, it all ends tragically. He strips off his golden dress and dances naked for the crowd. Later in a room with Ernie Emerson, he does not recall what he has done, only "rang-ing torrents of passion, even blows" (p. 203). In the morning, as a Negro chauffeur drives him back to the city, Ken is ordered out of the car, forced to hand over the jewelry, and told to walk the rest of the way to Boston. Ernie Emerson's friendship does not extend beyond one night of passion.

Drunken evenings follow, as the melodrama of Ken's life continues. He rejects the opportunity to return to Howard Vee, and after insulting the English theatrical couple starring in Vee's latest production, it would seem that Ken's career is over. He returns to his father in Texas to rest and recuperate, and determines to return to New York and stay sober. On the train, he meets Tommy Cook, who seems a stable partner but infects him with syphilis. The downward spiral begins again, and Ken even considers posing for pornographic photographs. There are moments of sobriety but always a return to the gin bottle. Ken leaves his hotel room, dreaming of a return to Texas, and in true stereotypical gay style he drowns himself in the Hudson River.

Outrageous and often as offensive as is *Butterfly Man,* it is also a remarkably open and frank gay novel. Aside from Howard Vee, who is presented as the perfect nonstereotypical gay male, as well as the perfect gentleman, most of the gay men in the novel are effeminate chorus boys. There is an unusual moment when Ken decides he is homosexual and tells a fellow cast member, "I'm going gay" (p. 181), a phrase that cannot surely have been understandable to nongay readers of *Butterfly Man.*

A university professor (who, similar to so many older gay men in the novel, is forty) explains to Ken at one point the inevitable spread of homosexuality:

> It's the logical result of modern tendencies. . . . The feminization of men is due to the breakdown in the paternalistic world. A boy no longer can aspire to become an all-powerful head of his house. He envies his elegantly dressed toil-free mother, his gentle school teacher, his sheltered sisters, their colorful clothes and their lovely bodies. . . . What has the modern world to offer so completely uninhibited as the freemasonry of our kind? Women hate each other. We of the third sex enjoy perfect love, fruitless love. We are not fecund. We create no evil. For us, life is all. No false conception of immortality. No sons to jib at us. No soul to perish in eternal damnation. No jealous wives hovering over us, no laws barring our free association with each other. (p. 213)

29

Jean Lyttle, *Sheila Lacey*

The title character is born within the shadow of Ireland's Blarney Castle, and at an early age realizes she has psychic powers. She leaves for London to visit a sister who has shamefully married an Englishman who is also a Protestant, and is tempted by a career on the stage. Through a fellow performer, Sheila meets Australian-born Sunny Napier, who is as talented as either Noel Coward or Ivor Novello, and like those two gentlemen is "one of those" (p. 145).

Sheila Lacey learns about "those" from a character named Maude Tanner, presumably a theatrical dresser, who turns up out of nowhere, delivers a speech on the subject of sex, and equally conveniently disappears:

> Homosexuality is supposed to be a modern disease, but things have always been the same. . . . Sex is a poison, I tell you. I've seen young lads come into the theatre as manly as a man can be, an' in no time at all they'd changed completely an' be as feminine as you—more feminine than I am myself. Soon they'd have their boy-friends waitin' for them, after the show, jus' the same as the girls have their Johnnies. (pp. 146-147)

Maude is less tolerant of her own sex: "An' the girls that go homo—they're worse than the men. My God! How I hate the stuff!" (p. 147).

Sheila meets Sunny, and the two fall in love. Sheila tells him, "I've heard stories about your sex life" (p. 159), but he assures her that is all in the past. "He had eliminated the drop of pollution from the situation" (p. 160). The two marry, but Sunny must deal with his ex-lover Geoffrey Stapleton. Stapleton finds it hard to believe that all is over between them, but Sunny assures him, "I have a feeling of normal security for the first time in my life" (p. 176). Sunny arranges for

Stapleton to receive a cash settlement and also to be included in his will. How civilized can a born-again heterosexual be?

Tragedy strikes when Stapleton is invited to a party hosted by Sheila and Sunny. He and Sunny adjourn to the bedroom, where Stapleton declares, "I can't go on with you. And I won't" (p. 189). He takes a revolver, kills Sunny, and then turns the weapon on himself. Despite being a psychic, Sheila had no foreknowledge of what was about to happen.

She returns briefly to Ireland and is there when Britain declares war on Germany. She returns to England and becomes a nurse, and the author provides us with a potted history of World War II. Our heroine trains in psychiatry and is assigned to a ward for shell-shocked patrons. There she meets a Mexican-American aviator, Pepe, who was shot down over the North Sea. She understands that his "problem" is the inability to accept that he is a "hyphenate," a man born in Mexico but now proud to be an American. Once Pepe is persuaded that his fellow Americans regard him as one of them, Sheila looks at her own situation and realizes that she too is a kind of hyphenate—an Irish woman who is now an English lady. Sheila and Pepe marry. "She perceived that all created things, and all events, are signals that Life puts forth to make man realize itself" (p. 282).

Sheila Lacey (Creative Age Press, 1944) is pure romantic twaddle, and perhaps its only redeeming quality is that homosexuality per se is not totally condemned by any of its characters—it is just lesbians who are hated. Sheila Lacey comes to full self-awareness only through marriage to a gay man and his subsequent murder. According to a contemporary press release from the publisher, *Sheila Lacey* is a "fascinating picture of Women in the present time." Sadly, it is a far-from-helpful portrait of a gay man in the late 1930s.

The woman responsible for *Sheila Lacey,* which may very possibly be semiautobiographical, was Eileen Jeanette Garrett (1893-1970), who wrote under the name of Jean Lyttle and was an Irish-born trance medium. She was the founder and publisher from 1941 to 1951 of Creative Age Press, which, most conveniently, published *Sheila Lacey.*

30

Harlan Cozad McIntosh,
This Fine Shadow

This Fine Shadow (Lorac Books, 1941) boasts a wordy text, in which much happens—some of it incomprehensible or at least inexplicable—at sea and in New York. In the words of Marianne Hauser in *The New York Times* (February 23, 1941), it "is centered around homosexuality, which is about the most difficult and also most precarious theme for a writer." The hero, Martin Devaud, is a sailor who quits his ship in New York, is much too educated for such a lowly occupation, and is confused in both his sexuality and his liberalism. Martin's friend, a fellow sailor named Rio, provides a fairly accurate description of the first half of the novel:

> He [Martin] met a fag who had him fired, and he went off the deep end. He got drunk and the girl threw him over. I found him in the doghouse. I got hold of the fag and fixed him up a little and went to the girl's place.

The "fag," described as "temperamental," is named Roberts; the girl is Deane; and she, in turn, has two gay friends named Drew and Carol. Both Roberts and Carol are depicted as unattractive gay men. Drew holds "a drag," described in considerable detail, and it is attended by both Rio and Martin, dressed in female attire. The novel concludes with Carol a murder victim, Roberts suffering a stroke, Drew in Europe, and Deane still in love with Martin.

It is all very unsatisfactory, not the least because the author is so derogatory toward the obviously gay characters in the novel, and also because Martin and Rio are presented in such an ambiguous fashion. At one point, Rio asks Martin, "Are you a god-damned fairy with your god-damned eyes and the way you look at people? You looked queer in that draggy dress at the party, and you acted queer" (p. 263). To which Martin responds,

You asked me, didn't you, if I was queer, and although you're deathly afraid of it yourself, you hold such people in contempt. Did you think I was going to deny it as though it were intrinsically a shameful thing? . . . It exists. . . . It's part of life. It has its particular and its important position in the world. It has its stage and its stratas. . . . Created for balance . . . I didn't say they were balanced. I don't know that, because I don't know where the average begins or ends. I said they were created for balance. A necessary people forming a resilient salient between the rigidity of the sexes. (p. 264)

The description of homosexuality as a "resilient salient" is certainly an unusual viewpoint, but one more obviously directed toward the bisexual in society. It seems more than probable that both Martin and Rio are bisexuals, dealing with conflicting emotions, and hiding the turmoil within themselves through a negative response toward those who are openly, and obviously, homosexual.

"It is a curious book in many ways," commented Muriel Burns in *The New Republic* (April 28, 1941),

often muddled and obscure, containing some self-conscious, deliberately precious writing, yet illuminated occasionally by a beautiful passage or an exceptional flash of insight, and possessing a certain emotional power. Here is an explanation of the abnormal, the pathological in human life.

According to John Cowper Powys in his introduction to *This Finer Shadow,* Martin Devaud is "obviously a reflection of the author himself." The hero may be based on Harland Cozad McIntosh (1908-1940), but the book is dedicated to his wife Jane, suggestive of a bisexual torn between his hetero- and homosexual self. Jane denied that her husband was gay, and oversaw publication of the novel when he committed suicide on August 9, 1940, by jumping from the roof of his New York apartment building.

31

Compton Mackenzie, *Vestal Fire*

Set in the period 1905-1920, *Vestal Fire* (George H. Doran Company, 1927; first published in the United Kingdom in 1927 by Cassell) is an amusing, outrageous, and at times long-winded (by modern standards) study of the Anglo-American community on the Italian island of Sirene. A young Englishman named Nigel Dawson is identified as "one of those," and when he grows a beard and moves to the mainland, he is laughingly referred to as "the bearded lady." The central gay character and, indeed, the most influential figure in the novel is Count "Bob" Marzac Lagerstrom, who arrives on the island from his native France where, it is revealed, he had been convicted of pederasty. Not only is Count Bob addicted to opium, but also he is obsessed with his attractive Italian secretary, Carlo, whom he adopted when the boy was thirteen years old. As Compton Mackenzie explains of Carlo,

> To whatever there was abnormal in his relations with Marzac he had become easily habituated in that strange bisexual pause in the growth of normal adolescence. . . . The Latin individual is capable of what seems to the Anglo-Saxon a cynicism in sexual relations utterly beyond his comprehension. A decent Englishman would have despised Carlo; but a decent Italian would not have despised him, however much he might abominate his detestable situation. (pp. 212-213)

Count Bob is immediately taken up by two elderly American ladies, the Misses Pepworth-Norton, but, as his reputation becomes known, the majority of the residents snub him. Such behavior is rejected by the Misses Pepworth-Norton, who can find no fault with Count Bob. As a result, the island is split into two camps. The saga ends with the early death of Count Bob, and the passing of first one and then the other of the Misses Pepworth-Norton. However, World War I has also wrought a fundamental change to the island and its visitors. The deaths of the "old guard" mark the end of an era, with the "new guard" lacking both class and personality.

Sirene is, in reality, the island of Capri, upon which Compton Mackenzie and his first wife lived for a number of years, starting in 1913. Most of the characters in *Vestal Fire* are based on real-life residents of Capri. The Misses Pepworth-Norton are Kate and Saidee Wolcott-Perry and, more important, Count Bob is Count "Jack" d'Adelswaerd-Fersen, who like Count Bob was half-French and half-Swedish, an opium addict, and also a pederast imprisoned in France for offenses against minors.

Although his biographer, Andro Linklater,[1] denies that Compton Mackenzie had any physical interest in homosexuality, the novelist did keep company with quite a number of gay men, including Noel Coward and Ivor Novello; as a teenager Mackenzie met Lord Alfred Douglas and two of Oscar Wilde's most notorious gay friends, Robbie Ross and Reggie Turner. A bisexual actor named Dick Hewlett introduced the young Mackenzie to Adolf Birkenruth, whose studio was an infamous gay hangout. In his autobiography, Mackenzie wrote, "I am grateful to the opportunity I was given to observe homosexuality with a detached curiosity when I was sixteen, because now at eighty I recognize that it is quite possible to play with fire and yet avoid getting burnt."[2]

With his knowledge, Compton Mackenzie's first wife, Faith, indulged in a number of lesbian relationships. Some of her friends are caricatured in his novel, *Extraordinary Women* (1928), and it is not the first of his novels in which lesbians are found. The title heroine of *The Early Adventures of Sylvia Scarlett* (1918) and *Sylvia and Michael* (1919) is introduced in *Sinister Street* (1913) as a lesbian. When the screen adaptation of *Sylvia Scarlett,* directed by homosexual George Cukor, was released in 1935, the heroine, as played by Katharine Hepburn, displays no lesbian tendencies, although she does have a penchant for boy's attire. The film quite obviously contains a gay subtext, and has long been a camp favorite with gay audiences for reasons neither viewers nor critics have been able to explain.

It is remarkable how nearly always fatal prose is to the pretentiously styled Uranian temperament, which time after time shirks honest self-revelation in such a medium, but continually seeks by an endogenous understanding of women, an almost uterine intelligence, to atone for its inability to create men, (p. 246)

wrote Compton Mackenzie in *Vestal Fire.*

One day a novelist with that temperament will have the courage to write about himself as he is, not as he would be were he actually Jane or Gladys or Aunt Maria. And that will be a novel worth reading, not an obstretical feat. (p. 246)

He might not have had the right temperament, but Compton Mackenzie did, at the close of his writing career, produce another major novel with a central gay character. *Thin Ice* (Chatto & Windus, 1956) is the story of Henry Fortescuc, who suppresses his homosexuality in order to advance his political career. Henry Fortescue is based on a number of gay men of Mackenzie's acquaintance, including Harold Nicolson, Lord Lloyd of Dolobran, and Tom Driberg. *Thin Ice* has its origins in Mackenzie's anger that blackmailed homosexuals were frequent suicides, and his argument that no civilized society could consider homosexuality as more serious a crime than blackmail.

From *Vestal Fire* through *Thin Ice,* Compton Mackenzie demonstrates a remarkable empathy for gay men. Yet at the same time his characters are all too often stereotypes (effeminate, drug addicts, pederasts) and, because of their eminent positions in society, are generally immune from laws aimed at homosexual repression.

NOTES

1. Andro Linklater, *Compton Mackenzie: A Life.* New York: Basil Blackwell, 1987.

2. Compton Mackenzie, *My Life and Times, Octave Two.* London: Chatto & Windus, 1964, pp. 256-257.

32

William Maxwell, *The Folded Leaf*

Lymie Peters is thin, inept at sports, and a good student. Charles "Spud" Latham is intellectually an average student, but good at sports and a particularly proficient boxer. The two meet as high school students in Chicago in October 1923. Both go to college, and both fall in love with the same girl. Lymie apologizes to Spud for coming between him and the woman he loves and tries to commit suicide with a straight-edged razor.

Taking its title from a line of poetry by Alfred Lord Tennyson, *The Folded Leaf* (Harper & Brothers, 1945) is a delicate work dealing with human emotions. The triangular love affair, around which the final third of the book revolves, has its origins as much in Herman Sudermann's 1893 novel *Es War; Roman in Zwei Baenden* (filmed with Greta Garbo, John Gilbert, and Lars Hanson in 1926 as *Flesh and the Devil*) in so far as it has any antecedents in American literature. *The Folded Leaf* is not a gay novel per se—and was most certainly not perceived as such by contemporary critics—but the manner and the situations in which the author presents his two central characters is so appealing to gay readers that there can be little question as to the gay connotation. The schoolboy friendship between Lymie and Spud should, in the heterosexual world, have dissipated with their coming of age at college, but it does not. The author notes that had the two both been members of a fraternity, their closeness would have been recognized and efforts made to come between them. That Spud is an amateur boxer, with all the sexual energy that such a sport evokes, and that so much of his boxing takes place in front of Lymie suggests a further gay undertone.

Then there is the nudity, with which William Maxwell appears positively fascinated. Does there have to be quite so much of it? Does the author have to take delight in his description of these nubile and naked men? Lymie and Spud are first introduced in the nude, partici-

pating in a water polo match at school. Lymie nearly drowns and
Spud, a new boy at school, rescues him, his thighs around Lymie's
waist.

A little later, Lymie and Spud pledge a school fraternity. The initiation ceremony is described in great detail, and involves the pledges
being nude throughout. Blindfolded, the members of the group are
led around with their right hands on the shoulders of the boy in front.
Spud is behind Lymie—how appropriate a position for the dominant
member of the duo—and "With a kind of wonder Spud felt the fragile
collarbone moving, and the tendons, and made up his mind to follow
trustingly" (p. 49).

Later, the author acknowledges that Lymie had watched Spud
dress and undress hundreds of times:

> There is a kind of amazement that does not wear off. Very often,
> looking at Spud, he felt the desire which he sometimes had
> looking at statues—to put out his hand and touch some part of
> Spud, the intricate interlaced muscles of his side, or his shoulder
> blades, or his back, or his flat stomach, or the veins of his wrists,
> or his small pointed ears. (p. 115)

When Spud steps out of the shower after a workout, Lymie is always
there with a towel. The two young men often take showers together at
college, one bending over with his hands on his knees while the other
scrubs his back with a brush.

When Lymie and Spud first go to college, they board at a rooming
house owned by Alfred Dehner, an aging antiques dealer with a small
dog named Pooh-Bah. Even had he not been identified as effeminate,
there would be no question as to Dehner's homosexuality. At the
rooming house, Lymie and Spud share not only a room but also a bed.
Spud curls up against Lymie, with his fists in the hollow of the other's
back. The sharing of the bed is not only a money-saving proposition
but also a means of keeping warm during the bitter winter nights. At
no time is it suggested that there is anything sexual in the arrange-
ment.

In order to impress the girl, Sally, Spud joins a fraternity house. He
is not aware that Lymie has secretly loaned him the 100-dollar initiation fee. Spud does not enjoy the company at the fraternity house—
surprisingly the author does not document his initiation—and one
night, he returns to the rooming house and to Lymie's bed:

The bed has grown warm all around him. Spud's breathing deepened and become slower. His chest rose and fell more quietly, rose and fell in the breathing of sleep. Lymie, stretched out beside him, wished that it were possible to die, with this fullness in his heart for which there were no words and couldn't ever be. All that he had ever wanted, he had now. All that was lost had come back to him, just because he had been patient. (p. 206)

The threesome, Lymie, Spud, and Sally, spend much time together, with Sally joking that "Lymie's an old woman-hater. . . . He's the worst. But how could we ever get along without him?" (p. 163). When Lymie perceives that perhaps Sally cares more for him, he feels a sense of guilt. After visiting Spud at the fraternity house, Lymie returns to his room and tries to kill himself. With his act, all that exists—in a real or subliminal way—between the two men is exposed. Spud comes to Lymie's hospital room:

Neither he nor Lymie spoke. They looked at each other with complete knowledge at last, with full awareness of what they meant to each other and of all that had ever passed between them. After a moment Spud leaned forward slowly and kissed Lymie on the mouth. He had never done this before and he was never moved to do it again. (p. 284)

At this point, the relationship is returned to its relaxed and earlier status. Sally no longer comes between the two men; she is now the accepted third member of the trio. She also visits Lymie in the hospital, takes his and Spud's hands and announces, "Well, here we are!" (p. 289). Just where "we" came from and where "we" are going to remains somewhat elusive.

As noted, contemporary critics did not discuss the potential gay angle to the novel, but were generous in their praise. It was hailed by S. H. Hay in the *Saturday Review of Literature* (April 7,1945) as "a fine and moving book, full of true sympathy and understanding of human relationships." Richard Sullivan in *The New York Times* (April 8, 1945) wrote, "In a time of much loose and slap-dash writing it is a satisfaction to read prose always so admirably controlled, so governed with distinction, as that of William Maxwell." Only Diana Trilling in *The Nation* (April 21, 1945) complained that in the last third of the novel, Maxwell "becomes spare and even unconvincing."

The Folded Leaf was the third novel by William Maxwell (1908-2000), a writer best known as the poetry and fiction editor of *The New Yorker* from 1936 to 1976. If *The Folded Leaf* is in any way autobiographical, Maxwell is Lymie in that both have lost their mother at an early age. Similar to Lymie, Maxwell was slight of build, once described by John Cheever as "Fred Astaire-ish." Questioned as to why his fiction is influenced by his personal history, Maxwell explained,

> I came to believe that life itself, untampered with, always has a profound meaning and interest, and the less you rearrange the details the better, but unfortunately unanswered questions abound, and sometimes they are not questions that the writer has a right to avoid answering, artistically that is, and it has driven me to fall back on my imagination.[1]

Maxwell, who married the year *The Folded Leaf* was published and was to father two children, has never identified Spud as real or imaginary.

The Folded Leaf was first reprinted in somewhat different form by Vintage Books in 1959. A later Vintage edition, with slight revisions by Maxwell, was published in 1996.[2]

NOTES

1. Quoted in the *Los Angeles Times,* August 2, 2000, p. B8.
2. The page numbers quoted here are taken from that 1996 edition.

33

Richard Meeker, *Better Angel*

Largely autobiographical, *Better Angel* (Greenberg, 1933) recounts the story of Kurt Gray from the age of thirteen through twenty-two. Brought up in the small town of Barton, Michigan, Kurt has loving parents who care about him and are relatively undisturbed that he appears different from his playmates. He is more bookish, less interested in sports, and often accused of being a sissy. Part One of the novel deals with Kurt's adolescence with good humor and tolerance. One learns what it is like not so much to be different, but simply to be a boy growing up in small-town America in the mid 1920s. (As far as one can ascertain, the novel takes place in the mid- through late 1920s and the early 1930s.) There is something poignant and wholesome here, even in the pages dealing with Kurt's introduction to masturbation and the physical dangers he fears from it. This may not be Theodore Dreiser, as one gay critic has outrageously suggested, but it is a first-rate, firsthand account that can stand against any contemporary novel dealing with the maturation of any small-town American boy, gay or straight.

At college in Ann Arbor, Kurt meets Chloe Grayling and her brother Derry. Chloe is in love with Kurt, but Kurt is in love with Derry, and his love is not rejected. When Derry introduces Kurt to his friend David Perrier, Kurt is at first jealous but quickly a homosexual relationship develops among the three young men, with Kurt more properly paired with David.

En route to Paris, where Kurt is to study art, he meets a young actor with a Byronic appearance, Tony McGauran. When Kurt tries to talk with Tony of his sexual confusion, his love for both Derry and David, and now Chloe's declared love for him, the bisexual Tony tells Kurt of his many affairs—and then takes him to bed.

With hopes of an acting job, Tony travels to New York, and Kurt follows soon after, resuming his relationship with David and Derry.

From Tony, Kurt has learned that David's so-called guardian, Ozzy Brosken, is a notorious gay man, "an American Oscar Wilde" (p. 183). At his studio, "the boys" lie around in heaps, and David was Ozzy's special prize. David assures Kurt that his relationship with Ozzy is over, but he is troubled that Derry has now taken up with Ozzy and others of his type. As David described the boys at Ozzy's establishment, we have a curious indictment of a certain class of gay men and of a certain type of gay society that is as prevalent today as in the early 1930s:

> They're a sad lot, finding a feverish and hysterical kind of happiness in new associates—always new boys, new men. You're carried away with it when it's new, and sometimes even when you're older. There's a circle that's always getting wider. You get known, and sought after or avoided, but you get known. It's like some great and terribly secret society, with its own life, its own passwords and signs; and once you're in it, it's the very devil to break out. You get older, and you try to look younger. Your taste gets more and more jaded and you demand more and more perverse diversions . . . but the terrible part of it is, you're known and marked, wherever you go. (p. 226)

By now, Kurt has come to terms with his homosexuality. He has tried, unsuccessfully, to have sex with Chloe, and she, although at first trying to turn Kurt against David, has accepted the situation. Kurt obtains a position as a music teacher at an exclusive boys' school in Connecticut. An operetta that he had written with Tony is optioned for performance, and one of his serious pieces of music, an orchestral piece, is performed in concert.

Ongoing problems remain with both David and Derry. The latter is arrested for accosting a police officer for sex, but acquitted. When Kurt travels to New York to visit David, he discovers that David has gone to visit Ozzy. Yet as he sits reading in his school study, Kurt is aware that "the certainty of his love for David, of David's love for him, was as absolute and as right and as restful as this pale and now fading light of the March afternoon" (p. 283).

Because its author is not only gay but also intelligent and well informed, *Better Angel* is one of the most enlightened gay novels of the first half of the twentieth century. At the same time, it is not always as graceful in style as it might have been. The second part is crammed with too much action, too many situations, and the conclusion, although moving in its simplicity, is lacking in substance. Why has David gone to see Ozzy? Why does Kurt know that the two will spend their lives together? One may assume that David's visit to Ozzy is to force the older man to give up his hold on Derry, but no evidence suggests that such is the case.

Sex is, of course, limited to a chaste kiss or the holding of hands. There is no explicit physical contact among the four young gay men. What the author does get across is the "normal" promiscuity of life among young gay men. When Tony takes Kurt's hand and pulls him, "bemused and uncertain" (p. 181), for the first time into the bedroom, there is remarkable honesty here. For all his love for David, his affection for Derry, Kurt is a typical gay man and will have no problem enjoying a sexual relationship with Tony.

There is no criticism of gay life—except briefly and innocuously from a painter and his wife, from whom Kurt had rented rooms in Paris. Because of the time period, Kurt can share a bed with Derry at the home of the latter's parents and also his own—and neither group of parents would consider anything odd in the situation.

The word *homosexual* is used only once, when Tony confronts Kurt, and it is used as an adjective rather than a noun. Kurt responds, "I don't like that word . . . it makes me sound like a biological freak of some sort—to be classed with morons and cretins and paranoiacs" (p. 174). *Queer* is used a number of times, with thirteen-year-old Kurt describing his body as "a queer thing" (p. 26). Early in the novel, Kurt thinks of other boys "in gay pirate costumes (but none so gay as his)" (p. 16), a clear, early (and quite delightful) use of gay in the modern sense of the word.

Better Angel makes no attempt to deny the reality of gay life in the 1930s—stereotyping that continues to the present. When Kurt tells David of his discovery of a gay liaison between two of his pupils and the fear of the two boys, David responds,

> You've felt it, we've all felt it, the savage vindictiveness the normal man has toward our sort. We're all to him, like the street-corner "fairy" of Times Square—rouged, lisping, mincing. Those chaps too, once, had something in them too tender, and they went under. It's the army of us that doesn't quite go under that suffers, though. The street-walker doesn't, in his heyday, at least, any more than the prostitute. He can be open in his tastes

and obvious in his manner, and when the vaudeville comedian makes dirty cracks about him, he can laugh, somehow. It's we who can't laugh that matter. (p. 259)

Better Angel was published without critical comment, but it remained familiar to gay readers. In the 1950s, it was reprinted as a Universal paperback under the title *Torment*. (At that time, the *Mattachine Review* described its hero as "perhaps the healthiest homosexual in print.") In 1987, *Better Angel* was again reprinted—this time by Alyson Publications—and with an introduction by Hubert Kennedy, who makes the valid point that Kurt Gray "helped many others growing up gay to accept their kind of love as genuine and good." When Alyson again reprinted the novel in 1990, it contained an epilogue in which Forman Brown (1901-1996) revealed that he was the novel's author. He explained that using a pseudonym was the prudent and sensible thing to do at the time in view of his burgeoning career as a writer at CBS and in order to avoid hurting his parents.

Brown confirmed that the book was basically autobiographical. He identified the character of Tony as based on actor Alexander Kirkland. Primarily a stage performer, Kirkland was born on September 5, 1903, in Mexico City; he married Gypsy Rose Lee, later retired to Mexico, and his death has never been reported. Kurt is, of course, Forman Brown. Derry was Harry Burnett, his lifelong friend and partner who died in 1985, while David was Brown's lover, Richard "Roddy" Brandon, who died in 1993. The three men formed a working partnership that lasted their entire lives. It is very much prophesied in *Better Angel:*

> these three, David and Derry and Kurt, should be a priestly trinity. What they felt for each other was high and fine and worthy. No one outside the cathedral could understand this. They would sneer and perhaps even persecute, but the faith in the rightness of their strange creed must stand, shining and perfect. (p. 147)

The partnership that the three men shared was that of the Yale Puppeteers, with which they toured extensively, and for which they established the Turnabout Theatre in Los Angeles. The latter ran for fifteen years, from 1941 to 1956, consisting in part of a puppet show and then of a program of songs and sketches, usually written by Forman Brown and featuring Elsa Lanchester. Brown's songs for Lanchester are published in the latter's *A Gamut of Girls: A Memoir* (1988). The name "Turnabout" was given to the entertainment, because the audience was required to turnabout its seats in order to view either the puppet show or the live entertainment at each end of the theatre. The puppets are featured in the 1933 film *I Am Suzanne*.

The life and career of Forman Brown is the subject of a one-hour documentary, *Turnabout: The Story of the Yale Puppeteers* (1993), directed by Dan Bessie. It is not a great film, but it is a great record and reminder of one of the unsung heroes of the gay movement and a primary figure in gay entertainment history.

In the same year as *Better Angel* appeared, Greenberg also published Forman Brown's *The Pie-Eyed Piper and Other Impertinent Plays for Puppets*. Brown had earlier privately published in 1925 a book of poems, *Walls,* and also *Olvera Street and the Avila Adobe* (1930). He wrote three later volumes, *Punch's Progress* (1936), *Small Wonder: The Story of the Yale Puppeteers* (1980) and, most interesting, *The Generous Jefferson Bartleby Jones* (1991), a children's book on the subject of gay parents. When asked in old age of what he was most proud, Forman Brown responded,

> I think the most rewarding thing that has happened to me has been the rediscovery of *Better Angel,* and the realization that its message of hope, or the possibility of hope, is still pertinent and as warming as it proved sixty years ago.

Better Angel remained the only novel accepting of a relationship between a trio of gay men until William J. Mann published *The Men from the Boys* (Dutton, 1997), which features a very different triumvirate, but one that shares some of the same happy moments realized by its predecessors.

34

Ernest Milton, *To Kiss the Crocodile*

Ernest Milton (1890-1974) was once a prominent character actor of stage and screen. Born in San Francisco, he made his U.S. stage debut in 1912, and his British stage debut in 1914, at which time he took up permanent residency in the United Kingdom. Milton appeared in a handful of films between 1919 and 1957, and from 1918 to 1952, he was a longtime member of London's Old Vic Company. His wife, Naomi Royde-Smith, was both an actress and a novelist. Ernest Milton wrote a 1924 play, *Christopher Marlowe,* and one novel, *To Kiss the Crocodile* (Harper & Brothers, 1928), first published in London by Duckworth in 1928.

A strange, meandering affair, *To Kiss the Crocodile* is the story of Roy Ffolliott, Irish born, but brought up and educated in Canterbury after the death of his father. In the early chapters of the novel, the reader is introduced not so much to Roy as to his overprotective mother. As the story progresses, most of the other women that Roy encounters are similarly possessive.

After Roy leaves Canterbury for London, he becomes involved with the theatrical community, which admires his good looks and quiet personality. He meets the middle-aged Vernon Moore, who tries to persuade Roy to visit his home, but Moore is rebuffed by one of Roy's friends: "I won't have you annexing Roy to your court of jaded and over-sophisticated young men" (p. 108).

However, on a hot summer's day, when most of Roy's friends are out of town, Moore insists that the young man accompany him for a weekend in the country at the home of a friend, Drovesnap. The latter and the majority of the weekend visitors at his home are representative of a certain type of gay men. They are middle aged or older, generally overweight, and inclined to refer to each other in feminine terms. One of the gentlemen present is called Auntie Clara. The conversation is of the dance, of the latest "pajama suitings," of the latest fancies, and of fabrics, such as "charmeuse, pongee, linen, China silk, paisley" (p. 152).

The house party also includes a number of younger gentlemen, aged between eighteen and twenty-eight, dressed by London's most exclusive tailors and haberdashers. Drovesnap is persuaded to recite, and after he has "minced his way" (p. 156) through several pieces by Verlaine and Austin Dobson, "slowly a feeling of great uneasiness and discomfort" has crept over Roy, "though he couldn't tell why" (p. 155).

A young man named Edgar Loring approaches Roy and apologizes to him for what is taking place:

> The face that confronted him was of a high intelligence and idealism. The mouth was sensitive, with lines of suffering. The eyes were full of pain. There was a sort of good looks, too, which some tragic need, some repudiation of circumstances, some hungry desperation, had written into this trustful mask. (p. 156)

Loring asks that Roy stay, arguing that the two have much in common. Looking at the assembled company, he explains, "it's this sort of people who make life impossible for the rest of us." Loring talks of "beautiful friendships, . . . full of the truest feelings and trust and virility, too" (p. 157), of the Greeks, of some of the greatest soldiers, statesmen, and artists, and concludes by asking if Roy has read Walt Whitman's *Leaves of Grass*.

Roy, who has not read *Leaves of Grass,* assures Loring that he will always be his friend and that he will stay at the house. That night, after dinner, the butler enters with the news that Loring has thrown himself from his bedroom window and broken his neck. Roy rushes to Loring's side and can barely be separated from the body. He is obsessed with the young man whom he has known only a few hours: "This pleasant, quiet, gifted young man, who knew all about the Greeks and painted beautiful pictures, and badly, very badly, wanted a friend" (p. 166).

Roy returns to London in a daze. In bed that night, he thinks of Loring and of the others at the house party. He realizes that what Loring wanted was no different than was evidently wanted by all those present. Roy is obsessed with the belief that if he had not accompanied Moore to that party, Loring would still be alive: "Had it been a sin to succumb so easily? . . . His easy descent with Moore down the paths which Moore trod? Perhaps he, Roy, after all, because of this sin, had killed Edgar Loring?" (p. 182).

Unable to stay in his rooms, Roy visits an old schoolmate from Canterbury, but is asked to leave when the newspapers publish the story of Loring's death and Roy's presence at the house is mentioned in the article. Roy's theatrical friends rally around him, despite his notoriety, but the young man remains confused and unhappy. He wanders down to the docks, and, after hearing a young boy weep after having signed on to work on board a schooner, asks to take his place.

At this point, the tenor of the novel changes dramatically. What we have here is now a seagoing adventure, as we follow Roy onboard ship to Rio de Janeiro, Hawaii, Hong Kong, and, eventually, to Marseilles. In a village just outside of Arles, Roy (rather suddenly) dies of pneumonia. At the end, he realizes he has been kissing the crocodile, "and with every kiss it had torn him limb from limb, and he had refashioned himself from the bleeding tatters and shreds of his flesh around some persistent core of life" (p. 333). His last thoughts are of the women in his life and also of Edgar Loring:

> The strange disciple of some complex and clipped-winged Eros . . . the world Edgar lived in offered no place, afforded no temple, for his strange creed, no resting-place for his curious love, no time to consider his desperate demands . . . the world had rejected him as something abhorred. . . . Poor Edgar, who had looked for real love and real life as he saw these things—as he was evidently born to see them, in a world that would not admit that *his* life or *his* love could be real at all. (pp. 338-339)

To Kiss the Crocodile does not know where it is going and changes course, with neither rhyme nor reason, when Roy suddenly decides to escape the sophisticated world he has been inhabiting to become a sailor. The long-winded story of Roy's mother and life in Ireland is tedious and serves little purpose in the narrative. The opening and closing parts of the novel frame a story line that could well stand on its own, and might well interest readers more if they did not have to wade through such a large amount of irrelevant verbiage. Roy is never completely of interest because we have no physical image of him. He must have been attractive to both men and women. Of the actor Raymond Clitheroe, who introduces Roy to theatrical society, the author tells us he has hairy legs, a good amount of hair on his chest, and wears a "cellular kind of shorts" (p. 69), but we have no such description of Roy. In search of gay characters in *To Kiss the Crocodile,* one might be inclined to latch upon Clitheroe, whose attachment to Roy, after one meeting, is hard to justify. Yet Clitheroe is later identified as heterosexual.

The author's approach to his obvious homosexual characters at the house party is at first somewhat offensive to the gay reader, with its emphasis on certain gay stereotypes. Edgar Loring's reaction to these stereotypes is also unfortunate and his suicide hardly justified and totally unexpected. Why should Loring kill himself immediately after identifying Roy as his friend? It is that same old plot device: introducing a sympathetic gay character and then conveniently having him commit suicide? Although here, of course, it is not a cliché because it is used perhaps for the first time in a gay novel.

And what of Roy's sexuality? Is he perhaps a latent homosexual? If his attachment to Clitheroe and later Loring is any clue, the answer might well be yes. The author pointedly notes that Roy dies a virgin. When he is in Rio, a fellow sailor tries to persuade him to lose his virginity with a prostitute, but Roy, much to the sailor's initial disgust, cannot go through with the act. From the night of Loring's death, Roy thinks constantly of him; his fleeing England and, ultimately, his own death can be linked to his meeting with Loring. At the same time, at the end, Roy recalls a young woman he had met and realizes that she was the only one he had loved, despite her being a relatively minor character in the story and probably being forgotten by most of the readership.

One must agree with Eugene Lohrke in the *New York Herald Tribune Books* (May 20, 1928), who praised Milton in that

> he has treated sincerely and tragically a situation that has hitherto been largely reserved for discussion in psychiatric textbooks. There is no reason why it should not be treated in fiction provided it is approached with understanding. This Mr. Milton has done; and in this much *To Kiss the Crocodile* is a singular and noteworthy achievement.

Generally, criticism of the novel on both sides of the Atlantic was negative. The reviewer in *The New York Times* (May 13, 1928) wrote,

There is a sense of neither restraint nor design in this overflow-
ing book; adjectives pour out unendingly, sentences pile up one
upon another, sensory details mingle with quaint information.
In the end the whole thing grows tiresome and overdone; one
cries out for a simple style and for swift story-telling. A very
good book in germ has become, in the doing, a very indifferent
one.

The Times Literary Supplement (August 9, 1928) commented,
"Mr. Ernest Milton does not at present possess the gifts that make a
good novelist. *To Kiss the Crocodile* is an untidy, hysterical book."

It is unfortunate that perhaps the reviews discouraged Ernest Milton from attempting a second novel with a primary gay character.
With his theatrical background, Milton was obviously very familiar
with the homosexual scene and with gay men. He has nothing for
which to be ashamed in *To Kiss the Crocodile,* particularly in view of
the decade in which it was published, and his suggestion of a gay
house party suggests that he might later have written an amusing dis-
course on this type of event and the gay men to which it appealed.

35

Willard Motley, *Knock on Any Door*

A highly descriptive and powerfully moving novel, *Knock on Any Door* (D. Appleton-Century Company, 1947) is the story of Nick Romano, an altar boy in Denver, whose family faces ruin, who is sent to reform school, and ends up a petty criminal in Chicago, where he is executed for the murder of a policeman. In Chicago, Nick haunts West Madison Street and, to make money, allows himself to be picked up by gay men, described as "phonies." One such "phoney"— the word "homosexual" is never used—is a quiet man named Owen, who becomes Nick's friend and even finds the courage to visit the young man as he awaits the electric chair in his prison cell. "Owen was somebody who understood," writes Willard Motley, "Maybe because Owen, in his way, lived outside the law too" (p. 189). Motley finds no fault with Nick, despite his life of crime, and the only criticism that one might direct at his presentation of Owen is a somewhat stereotypical description of him "with pitifully sad eyes, long blond hair . . . fleshy body" (p. 371).

Critical reaction to *Knock on Any Door* was generally favorable. Only *The New Yorker* (May 24, 1947) complained that Motley was "neither a subtle nor an imaginative writer." H. R. Clayton in *The New Republic* (May 12, 1947) described the novel as a "monumental work. . . . The wealth of material and the writer's great compassion for the human spirit are unequalled in anything that has been produced on the Chicago scene." In *The New York Times* (May 4, 1947), Charles Lee hailed Motley as "an extraordinary and powerful new naturalistic talent. . . . *Knock on Any Door* achieves a powerful, although rude, vitality. It will absorb the individual reader as it will challenge society to mend its body and soul."

Willard Motley (1909-1965) was indeed an extraordinary talent. *Knock on Any Door* and his three later novels give no indication that the author is African American and brought up in a middle-class Chicago neighborhood by his grandfather, a Pullman porter, and his grand-mother, a deeply religious woman. The book is, as its author described it, "a raceless novel," but one that owes much in its detail to Theodore Dreiser and certainly to Richard Wright, the author of *Native Son*. Motley may have been classified early in his career as a black author, when, as a teenager, he wrote a weekly column in the African-American newspaper, the Chicago *Defender,* but such categorization is too narrow for a man who was to declare, "My race is the human race," and, very obviously, unlike his contemporaries, also considered gays and lesbians to be a tangible part of the human race.

By 1950, *Knock on Any Door* had sold 350,000 copies. It was filmed in 1949 as an independent production by Humphrey Bogart, with John Derek as Nick Romano, and Nicholas Ray directing. The character of Owen, of course, disappeared in Hollywood. A sequel novel, *Let No Man Write My Epitaph,* which contains a handful of characters from *Knock on Any Door,* published in 1958, was also filmed—in 1960.

In 1952, Willard Motley moved to Mexico City, where he lived for the remainder of his life. His last novel, published after his death, is *Let Noon Be Fair* (1966), in which the small Mexican seaside community of Las Casas is exploited and destroyed by both American tourists and the Mexican hierarchy. *Let Noon Be Fair* contains its share of gay characters, some of whom are Americans exploiting young Mexican boys but others of whom are native born. There are two anti-Catholic comic stories, both with gay themes, and a long de-scription of a gay bar in Las Casas, in which can be found the gentle *alegre,* "the gay people."

Motley has a strong fascination for gay characters, but demonstrates a critical weakness in his handling of females in his novels; writing of *Knock on Any Door,* P. L. Adams in *Atlantic Monthly* (July 1947) com-plained, "The women characters are all stereotypes." Further, Motley never married, but did adopt a Mexican boy as his son. It would be satis-fying to "out" Willard Motley as a gay author, but the evidence is all cir-cumstantial. He would appear to have written himself into *Let Noon Be Fair* as exiled American writer Tom Van Pelt—but Van Pelt's behavior is ambiguous: he visits the gay bar, has an attractive Mexican houseboy, but also enjoys sex with visiting American women. The trail is cold, and perhaps that is how Willard Motley would prefer it. His novels are raceless, and neither can he conveniently be placed in any sexual com-partment.

36

Blair Niles, *Strange Brother*

Mary Blair Rice (188?-1959) adopted the last name of her second husband, Robert Niles Jr., for her work as a historical and romantic novelist. She was also a travel writer, and her approach to homosexuality in *Strange Brother* (Horace Liveright, 1931) is almost that of an anthropologist. She spends much time documenting gays in history and discussing, in semiacademic terms, writers with something to say on homosexuality, love, or both, from Plato to Walt Whitman.

The pivotal gay character is compiling an anthology of *Manly Love* (based on Edward Carpenter's *Iolaus: Anthology of Friendship*), and he quotes verses by Harlem Renaissance poet Countee Cullen, who was subsequently revealed to be gay. There are references to August Forel's *The Sexual Question* and Havelock Ellis's *The Psychology of Sex*. Nor is Blair Niles' anthropocentric gaze limited to homosexuals. An equal amount of space is devoted to the Harlem Negro, observed in his or her native habitat. What perhaps Blair Niles did not realize is that as the scion of one of the first families of Virginia, she was comfortable in the company of the rich, and her observations on the wealthy young things of New York society are just as fascinating to a modern readership.

It is one of the latter, June Westbrook, who is the central player in the novel. In love with Seth Vaughan, who does not return her affection, she becomes close to Mark Thornton, a young gay man from the Midwest who has come to New York in the hope that he will feel less of an outsider here. June and Mark first meet at a nightclub in Harlem. They both witness the arrest of Nelly, one of five young Negro men, all of whom

> had carefully marcelled hair, all had their eyebrows plucked to a finely penciled line, all had carmined lips, all were powdered and rouged, all had meticulously manicured nails, stained dark

red, all had high voices and little trilling laughs, and all expressed themselves in feminine affections and gestures. (p. 49)

Mark is both repulsed and fascinated by these effeminate gay men. He discovers where Nelly is to be arraigned and hears him sentenced to six months imprisonment on Welfare Island. Mark visits the New York Public Library to uncover the law under which Nelly was arrested and found guilty. Looking in the *Penal Code* and *The Code of Criminal Procedure,* he discovers on page 223 of Section 690, "Crimes Against Nature," punishable with an imprisonment not exceeding twenty years.

> His mind rebelled. "By what right is anything pronounced a crime against nature?
>
> "Words," he reflected, "words can do anything. They can make it fine and noble and glorious to kill men in battle but a crime to kill a private enemy. They can make love romantic or loathsome. They can make virtue appear as sin and sin as virtue." (p. 124)

It is because of what he has just read that Mark reveals his secret to June. She is the only one to whom he feels he can turn, despite their having met only the previous evening. He tells her of his life in Narova City, of an older man named Tom Burden, who has since gone abroad and who pointed out to Mark that the two were both gay. Mark recalls his aunt discussing Tom with his mother:

> "He hadn't ought to be at large . . . his sort hadn't. There's no saying the harm they do. How'd you like it if Mark? . . ."
>
> "My Mark? Why if my Mark . . . I just couldn't bear it. I'd rather see him dead. Mark must be like his father; a man every inch." (p. 138)

Through June, Mark meets a number of young, affluent New Yorkers who enjoy his company and one of whom admits she has fallen in love with him. He also meets Professor Irwin Hesse, who speaks of his experiments with animals and his conclusion that "sex differences are chemical" (p. 177). After hearing Hesse speak, Mark feels invigorated: "We can't then . . . be crimes against Nature, after all! . . . We are experiments, and it's a wonderful thing to be one of Nature's great experiments" (p. 178).

Mark is not a stereotypical gay man of early-twentieth-century literature. He is not effeminate; he wears neither makeup nor women's clothing. He is presented almost as an outsider within the recognizable gay community. He meets a chorus boy named Lilly-Marie, who includes him in the phrase "our sort" (p. 274). But Mark is not attracted to effeminate men; he is secretly in love with June's heterosexual friend, Phil. When Lilly-Marie takes Mark to a party, the young man is "disgusted" by the effeminate company. It does not fit his concept of "manly love" (p. 314).

Earlier, Mark had turned down June's invitation to go with her to a drag ball in Harlem: "June, Mark said, would realize how painful it would be to him to see his kind thus on exhibition, like animals in the Zoo, like freaks in the side-show of a circus" (pp. 210-211). The ten pages that Mrs. Niles devotes to the drag ball provide one of the most detailed, contemporary, nongay accounts of such gatherings. The drag ball also reveals to June that the husband from whom she is divorced is gay; he is there dancing with a half-nude boy.

Mark's world is shattered when a young greengrocer accuses him of homosexuality and threatens to expose him to the head of the Settlement House, where Mark teaches. He thinks of Walt Whitman's letter to John Addington Symonds, in which the poet denies his homosexuality: "Whitman had disavowed it all as damnable" (p. 318). And what of Mark and Lilly-Marie? What of his "Loathing of his own species . . . when he should have been compassionate and understanding" (p. 318). Mark takes his grandfather's gun and kills himself. As he dies, he is discovered by the kindly janitor at the Settlement House, who holds his hand through the final moments.

As powerful and fascinating as *Strange Brother* is, the ending is as stereotypical as the effeminate gay men whom Mark encounters. Mark deserves a little happiness and, for that matter, a few moments of sexual release, of which the novel is singularly lacking. Ultimately, Mark and June both end up alone—but June, being heterosexual, is allowed to live on, with Mark's spirit providing her courage to continue.

Quite rightly, gay critic Henry Gerber wrote in 1934, "The author causes him [Mark] to go through as many mental sufferings as she can, then puts a pistol in his hand and lets him shoot himself and end the book. Again an ideal anti-homosexual propaganda."[1]

It has been suggested that *Strange Brother* is set in 1927 in that the Harlem nightclub entertainer, Glory, sings the 1927 Duke Ellington classic, "Creole Love Song." However, Blair Niles provides us with a more reliable clue as to the year in which the story takes place. A movie house is screening *Born Reckless,* which was released by Fox in 1930. It has also been suggested that the character of Glory is based on Adelaide Hall, who introduced "Creole Love Song," but, again, this is perhaps unlikely because Hall herself is mentioned in passing. She and Beatrice Lillie, whom the crowd believes to be at the drag ball, are the only two contemporary entertainers mentioned in the text. Both were known to be sympathetic to gay men and women.

Reviewers were mixed in their reaction to *Strange Brother,* but none were offended by the theme. The anonymous critic in the *Saturday Review of Literature* (October 31, 1931) wrote, "A panorama of abnormality is unrolled with the utmost tolerance and sympathy, though never with approval. *Strange Brother* is interesting and informative, though not particularly meritorious as a novel." In the *New York Herald Tribune Books* (August 23, 1931), D. C. Tilden wrote,

> Perhaps because of Mrs. Niles's very eagerness to state the case of the men of whom she writes, neither the book as a whole nor any of its people ever come really alive . . . as a detailed account of the persecutions and self-imposed tortures that a homosexual suffers in a modern civilization—it is an admirable and interesting job.

Strange Brother proved popular enough to receive a British publication (by T. Werner Laurie in 1931). In 1979, the British journal *Gay News* began offering the book for sale, having obtained a quantity of the original American edition with "dust jackets slightly worn." In *Gay News* (January 25, 1979), Ben Duncan wrote, "The book remains and is welcome now, as a monument of good reporting." In 1991, *Strange Brother* was reprinted in the United Kingdom by the Gay Men's Press, with an introduction by Peter Burton.

NOTE

1. Blair Niles, *Strange Brother.* London: Gay Men's Press, 1991, p. v.

37

Eugene O'Brien,
He Swung and He Missed

The writing style of *He Swung and He Missed* (Reynal & Hitchcock, 1937) is certainly unpretentious. As L. J. H. Jr. wrote in the *Saturday Review of Literature* (August 28, 1937), "The story is told in the oversimplified style of an elementary-school primer. No characterization is attempted beyond the rudimentary, and the only intellectual attitude expressed is that of a man with a grievance." The central character has not got much beyond the elementary school primer and looks at life with about the same amount of innocence and inexperience.

The man with the grievance is young Toby Brent, who leaves the family farm in Illinois to join the Navy, where he expects to get an education at the Naval Academy. The only education he receives is in the severity of naval life. With a fellow sailor, he takes a blood test. The results are switched, and poor Toby is diagnosed with syphilis. The treatment Toby receives for his nonillness is horrific and described in graphic detail. The more the doctors work on him, the sicker he becomes. He denounces the Navy, serves time in the brig, goes AWOL, and spends more time in the brig. When at last it appears that Toby Brent can leave the Navy and go home, he discovers that the family farm has not been doing well and the money he has been sending home for a future education has been spent.

What makes *He Swung and He Missed* of interest is that while on shore leave in Hampton Roads, Toby and his buddy, Rebel, share a double bed at a hotel. Toby wakes up in the middle of the night, feeling a hand creeping over his body. He pushes the hand away, but it comes right back. Toby tells Rebel he will go and sleep over at the YMCA. Rebel knocks him out and the strong implication is that he rapes Toby. When Toby wakes up, the underwear he had worn to bed is lying on a chair and Rebel is gone.

Toby blames all that happens to him later on that one night with Rebel: "Then he tried to look at it sensibly. He told himself that almost every boy had an experience of that sort. Sometime. They must. How could they avoid it? It made him shiver when he thought of it" (p. 155).

Prior to Rebel, Toby had enjoyed one sexual experience with a woman. After Rebel and the syphilis scare, no further sex is documented. *He Swung and He Missed* requires effort on the reader's part not to lose interest after the first few pages. After Rebel and syphilis, it is difficult not to give up on the book altogether.

Despite the claims by Dorothy Brewster in *The Nation* (October 23, 1937) that here is "A first novel that swings and doesn't miss," the book is weak in writing style and construction. As with Toby and his life, *He Swung and He Missed* is, in the words of F. T. March in *The New York Times* (September 5, 1937), "Immature and rather pointless."

The publisher had high hopes for the novel, but sales were disappointing. It is rather odd that just as Toby accepts his rape by Rebel, so did the publisher claim that here was "a note of emotional experience common to all men." Life was perhaps a little more unpredictable in and out of the Navy in the 1930s than one had realized. A female librarian at the Los Angeles Public Library opined in an in-house evaluation that "Men will certainly want it." But few men did, gay or straight. Eugene O'Brien tried his luck with one further novel, *One Way Ticket,* published by Doubleday Doran which, similar to *He Swung and He Missed,* also had a naval setting.

With America's entry into World War II, other novels about service life appeared, and these would sometimes contain secondary gay references. For example, Frederic Wakeman's *Shore Leave* (Farrar & Rinehart, 1944) is the story of a group of war-weary veterans on shore leave in San Francisco. There might appear to be ample opportunity for gay life and characters here, but there is only one incident when a couple of heterosexual heroes visit a nightclub frequented by "fairies." One of the men comments, "I like to pal around with fairies when I'm feeling low. I feel so superior to a fairy that it helps my morale." The narrator confesses, "They bother me a little, I don't feel at ease around them" (p. 238). Orville Prescott in *Yale Review* (Summer 1944) was right, "*Shore Leave* is vulgar and cheap by any standard."

38

Elliot Paul, *Concert Pitch*

Ernest Hallowell is the narrator of *Concert Pitch* (Random House, 1938), set in 1920's Paris. While sipping his wine one evening, he is joined by Lucien Piot, who is, like Hallowell, a music critic, but far more successful, and also an entrepreneurial teacher of young musicians. Hallowell, who has recently written that piano music is dead and has advocated a return to the harpsichord, is flattered that Piot wants him to attend a party at his apartment. Piot is gay, identified as such by his painted eyebrows, and by the comments of a post-Dadaist poet named Evrard, who announces that Piot's place "reeks of fairies" (p. 35).

At the party, Piot becomes fixated with a young pianist named Robert Maura, so much so that he ignores another young man whom he had been grooming for fame and also, presumably, his bedroom. He launches Maura's professional career in Paris and later takes him to the United States. In the meantime, Hallowell is more interested in Robert's mother, Elizabeth, an American-born widow. While Robert is abroad, the two marry. The poet Evrard asks whether Piot is "still chasing that American boy" (p. 151). When Hallowell protests, he points out that it has given him free reign with the mother.

The novel is vague as to the circumstances, but Piot apparently tries to molest Robert in Detroit, and the young man strikes his mentor and flees back to Paris. Here he contacts Hallowell and begins an affair with Hallowell's housekeeper, Berthe, primarily in order to prove there is nothing wrong with him sexually. The advances made by Piot have had some psychological impact on the boy; when Hallowell tries to steady him with his arm, Robert cries out, "Don't touch me! I can't bear it!" (p. 237). Piot also returns and is gravely ill for awhile. Hallowell concerns himself with Piot's recovery, and also helps Robert find work with funding provided by an American patroness. As Piot recovers, Hallowell asks him why he did not display more restraint in dealing with Robert. "Do you think I didn't try? I had to control myself every moment of the day and night. The wonderful boy! He didn't understand at all. . . . Can't you understand how I love him?" responds Piot (p. 270).

Elizabeth becomes obsessed with her son's well-being and eventually leaves Hallowell. The latter appears somewhat less upset by this than by his housekeeper's leaving to take up residence with Robert. He knows that Berthe is making a mistake because, as he explains to Piot, Robert is too self-centered to fall in love. At the novel's somewhat curious finale, Hallowell realizes what certainly all gay readers of the novel had been aware of for some time—that Robert is a selfish bitch-of-a-boy. He had used Hallowell, his mother, and the housekeeper, just as he had used Piot. "You knew all the time about Piot," says Hallowell. "I knew and I didn't care," responds Robert (p. 413).

Initially, the author, through Hallowell, is condescending of Piot and his homosexuality but, gradually, Hallowell (and the author) acknowledge and do not condemn the man. It is secondary characters, such as Evrard and a modern composer named Gurevitsch, who are negative in their responses to Piot: "That pansy" is how Gurevitsch refers to Piot, while asking, "is the kid queer, too?" (p. 190). Reintroduced to Robert, Gurevitsch reminds him, "The last time I saw you was in that fairy joint [Piot's apartment]. . . . You didn't act like a nance" (p. 274). Fittingly, Evrard commits suicide, and Gurevitsch's latest composition is attacked in Paris, forcing him to take it to Moscow, where the response is more positive.

There is the possibility that Robert's mother, Elizabeth, has left Hallowell because of a lesbian relationship with an aging Spanish pianist named Vallejo. This is very unclear. She had been Robert's tutor at one time, and there is a closeness between the two women that cannot be denied.

Elliot Paul (1891-1958)[1] was an expatriate American living in Paris in the 1920s and 1930s. There he co-edited the journal *transition,* which published Gertrude Stein, James Joyce, and others; he wrote many mystery novels and the autobiographical *The Last Time I Saw Paris* (1942). He described *Concert Pitch* as his favorite novel because it features Paris and music, the two elements with the most appeal to him. *Concert Pitch* is filled with musical commentary—after all, its two principal characters are both critics—and the Paris music scene of the 1920s is admirably captured. The full complexity of composing and performing serious music in Paris of the period is discussed— from the American patrons of the arts, through the modern composers with their new instruments, to the concert halls and their audiences. The Paris gay scene is less favorably reproduced. There is only one gay character here, and the enthusiasm for him wanes and waxes, according both to the narrator's feelings at the time and to the response of the reader. Berthe reminds Hallowell that there are plenty of *tapettes* available to Piot—that "There couldn't have been less than a thousand in the Salle Gaveau that evening" (p. 255).

Contemporary reviewers stressed the author's knowledge of the musical world. In *The New York Times* (March 20, 1938), Louis Kronenberger wrote,

> Mr. Paul's stage is brilliantly compact—a small world of characters who impinge half pathologically upon one another, with the Paris of the boulevards with the studios kept unostentatiously in the background. . . . While *Concert Pitch* is pessimistic in tone and wholesale in its scrapping of a world run down, it does emerge with a positive and affirmative theme.

Less enthusiastic was Theodore Purdy Jr. in the *Saturday Review of Literature* (March 26, 1938):

> Mr. Paul lavishes his excellent style and sound knowledge of music, musicians, and Paris on this odd and improbable story. . . . The whole thing is ingeniously written and worked out with exceptional care, but in spite of some striking scenes and at least two remarkable portraits (the French critic and a Spanish woman pianist), it is not a first rate musical novel. The central figures remain unreal and the drama static.

The reviewer in *The Nation* (April 30, 1938) was also less than impressed:

> With its variety of virtuosi, critics, impresarios, patrons, and composers, its concerts, its music theorizing—this, it should be said, is fresh and vigorous—and its musicians' shop talk, *Concert Pitch* is a fairly complete picture of the milieu it deals with.

As a novel, however, it is no more than a competent account of a tenuous love affair between two curiously unimpressive characters.

NOTE

1. The career of Elliot Paul is well covered by Philip H. Eppard in the *Dictionary of Literary Biography: American Writers in Paris, 1920-1939*. Detroit: Gale Research, 1980, pp. 304-310.

39

Thomas Hal Phillips,
The Bitterweed Path

The setting is Mississippi. The date is somewhat obscure, probably around the turn of the twentieth century, when the Civil War is still a strong memory, and those who fought it are still alive. Two boys, Darrell Barclay and Roger Pitt, meet for the first time—naked—while changing into tracksuits to compete in the Vicksburg Spring Race. Pitt's father is wealthy and determined to get richer, while Darrell is poor, a sharecropper's son, soon to move with his father and grandmother onto Pitt land.

As Darrell becomes alienated from his abusive father—who at one point kills his puppy—he becomes closer to Roger, and Roger's father, Malcolm, taking a liking to the boy, becomes his mentor. As the years pass, Darrell's father eventually dies, Malcolm Pitt helps Darrell prosper, and Roger goes off to school and later college. Malcolm Pitt is accidentally killed. Roger marries and becomes a doctor. It seems as if Darrell may marry Roger's sister; instead, he marries another woman who gives him two sons, but dies in childbirth when a daughter is stillborn.

Roger has become heavily in debt, but is helped by Darrell in a reversal of roles. In Vicksburg, the two men walk along the street together. "Are you drunk?" asks Darrell. No, replies Roger. "Are you my brother?" he asks. Yes, replies Roger. "Have always been?" "Have always been" (p. 307). The two men check into their hotel room. They undress, naked as they had been the first time together. They climb into bed together. They kiss. They hold each other. The following morning . . .

> In the bright light of day their eyes burned with a tenderness against each other, as if to say: now it is done; we have reached

the just-beyond; there is no going back to something less; there is no ending. (p. 312)

After saying goodbye to his mother and sister, Roger leaves. Darrell is now alone with his two sons, and with the light from the Pitt house showing him the way to the future.

The Bitterweed Path (Rinehart & Company, 1950) is a novel whose strength lies in its description of life in the deep South for two white families at very different levels of society. Darrell cannot and does not really want to break free from his father and his grandmother. The former's death is convenient, but his grandmother remains with him to warn of the threat she sees from the Pitt family. "You're too beautiful, Darrell Barclay," she tells him, "and any time the Lord give a body too much of anything he has to pay and pay and pay" (p. 67).

Malcolm Pitt loves Darrell like a son—and more so. He does not in any sense reject his own son, but the fire within Darrell is like his own fire (p.150). Roger is the intellectual, the professional man. Darrell and Malcolm stay at home; they belong to the land and build a cotton empire together. The relationship between Malcolm and Darrell can be viewed on many levels. It is of a father and son, a mentor and his student, and, perhaps, an older man and his younger lover. On a number of occasions, Darrell and Malcolm share a bed. They first sleep together on board a boat from Memphis to Vicksburg. Malcolm asks if Darrell is cold and then invites the teenager to join him.

> Malcolm pulled him close so that Darrell could feel the great maleness of him, soft and warm and weighty. . . . His heart began to pain him with its wild beating, for now he touched the great clean strength of Malcolm Pitt. . . . Their hands touched for a long time, as if it were part of some old ritual binding them together. . . . He could feel Malcolm's lips against his cheek, partly touching his ear, saying, "You go to sleep . . . honey-boy." (pp. 83-84)

The Bitterweed Path succeeds in its subtlety, in its refusal to define relationships. They might be gay or they might (but probably not) be nothing more than examples of pure male bonding. Here is familial and paternal love on a high plane, extending beyond the family to an "adopted son."

The reviewer in *Library Journal* (June 15, 1950) had no doubt as to the subject matter of *The Bitterweed Path*: "Unfortunately there is no better word than homosexuality to describe the basic theme of this unusual novel. The connotations of such a term will undoubtedly either repel or attract a reader." The trade publication *Kirkus* (April 1, 1950) praised the author for "A skillful skirting of the distasteful, a recognition of the psychological shadings."

The critics with the major publications were mixed in their response. The most positive came from Thomas Sugrue in *The New York Times* (September 10, 1950), who wrote,

> Mr. Phillips has made the action of his story flow as effortlessly as time itself; he has brought Louisiana [sic] life during the early years of the century into the sort of believable reality which other Southern writers carefully avoid. He knows the country he describes, its colors and moods and seasons, its odors and winds and dirts, its flowers and trees and grasses.

To N. L. Rothman in the *Saturday Review of Literature* (August 5, 1950), "With all the sincerity and aspiration that he possesses, Mr. Phillips has yet been unable to fashion a novel out of one emotion." George Miles in *Commonweal* (July 21, 1950) opined that, "There isn't much development either of character or situation." *The New Yorker* (June 10, 1950) complained that

> Some of the early scenes of Darrell's home life are very real, but after a short time too much emotionalism, too faithfully recorded, puts an end to the story; from then on we just have a kind of mournful, pointless reminiscing. One finishes the book with the strong impression that Mr. Phillips has been unable to get a grip on the problem that besets him, and that all this is a prelude to another book, yet to be written.

Thomas Hal Phillips (born 1922) wrote *The Bitterweed Path* as a master's thesis while in the creative writing program at the University of Alabama. Through grants from the Julius Rosenwald Fund and the Eugene F. Saxton Trust, he was able to revise the manuscript for publication. It was the first of five novels and successful enough to be published in a paperback edition. Phillips worked in Hollywood as a screenwriter and script doctor, responsible for the mediocre *Tarzan's Fight for Life* (1958).

In 1958, Phillips entered politics, serving on the Mississippi Public Service Commission, heading the Mississippi Film Commission, and managing his brother Rubel's Republican gubernatorial campaign. He can be heard as the voice of the populist presidential candidate in Robert Altman's *Nashville* (1975). A bachelor, Phillips always refused to answer questions about his personal life.

In 1996, the University of North Carolina published a new edition of *The Bitterweed Path,* with an informative introduction by John Howard (from which much of the biographical material on Phillips is taken). "I just wonder how I had the nerve to complete it," Phillips said of his novel to Howard.

40

Mary Renault, *Promise of Love*

Promise of Love (William Morrow, 1939) is a romantic novel with a twist. The heroine, Vivian Lingard, is a nurse. Through her gay brother, Jan, she meets Mic, with whom Jan is temporarily living, and who has supplanted an earlier lover, Alan, in his life. After Jan has departed, a relationship develops between Vivian and Mic. When the latter first kisses her, it is because she reminds him of Jan—"I forgot you're not accustomed to women," says Vivian cruelly (p. 77)—but soon the couple is in love and sleeping together. They split up when Vivian commences an affair with Mic's boss in the hospital pathology lab where he works. Jan returns to town, and his death following an automobile accident brings Vivian and Mic back together.

A subplot involves a nurse named Colonna Kimball, who is in love with Vivian. The two do sleep together, but Colonna simply caresses Vivian as she falls asleep. "I wonder why I thought I wanted to make love to you," she asks. "I don't, at least not physically. There's something queer and rare about you. I don't know what I want" (p. 27).

Lesbian attachments within the nursing fraternity are treated as commonplace here. Despite the very explicit nature of the affair between Vivian and Mic, much of what takes place is described in the most abstract of terms. We learn that Vivian is pregnant only when she tells Colonna, "It's the third week now" (p. 168). When she aborts, Vivian drinks "thick black stuff out of a vial" (p. 171).

The author is equally vague in describing the homosexuality of the men. There is no explicit reference at all. When he has a blood transfusion, Jan asks who the donor is. Told it is a Miss Pomfret, he laughs when told "about a pint" of him is Miss Pomfret (p. 320). Mic's continuing love for Jan is hinted at only by the poetic description when he sees his friend on the examination table: "Jan stripped well. A skin tanned like thick brown silk, over sleek hard curves of muscle; open shoulders, narrow waist; the down of his chest and belly golden with sun" (p. 309).

Promise of Love, published in the United Kingdom as *Purposes of Love* (Longmans, 1939), is the first novel of Mary Renault. Although the developing love affair between Vivian and Mic is at times hard to accept, the relationship is described in surprisingly modern terms.

Mary Renault (1905-1983), the pseudonym used by Mary Challans for all her books, is, of course, something of a gay icon. Many of her fifteen novels are historical ones, set in Greece, and with prominent gay characters and recurring gay themes. *The Charioteer* (1953), *The Last of the Wine* (1956), and particularly *The Persian Boy* (1972) quickly became best-sellers within the gay community, although Renault was not always happy with the gay reverence her novels evoked.

Promise of Love is based in part on Renault's experiences as a nurse, and it was in that profession in 1934 that she met her lifelong companion, Julie Mullard. The author writes of lesbian love in *The Middle Mist* (William Morrow, 1945), first published in the United Kingdom with the more interesting title of *Friendly Young Ladies* (Longmans, 1944).

When *Promise of Love* was first published in the United Kingdom, it created a storm of controversy. Its depiction of the harsh conditions under which nurses worked was criticized by matrons at hospitals around the country. A writer in the *Sunday Times* argued that studies of the sexually abnormal such as this should be confined to the consulting room, but a critic in *The Times Literary Supplement* (February 25, 1939) hailed Renault for her "peculiarly feminine sensitiveness."

Promise of Love was well received in the United States. E. H. Walton in *The New York Times* (March 12, 1939) described it as "An unusually excellent first novel." The *New Republic* described *Promise of Love* as "A well written novel of young and very serious love done with full modern accomplishments and lots of analysis." Renault's biographer, David Sweetman, argues that *Promise of Love* is the first best-seller to reach "a large and appreciative audience" of gay men and women.[1]

Mary Renault was somewhat ambivalent in her attitude toward gays. For one thing, she disliked the word *gay* in a homosexual sense. For another, she was most uncomfortable with the gay liberation movement, denouncing the notion of "sexual tribalism."[2] She was, however, very affirming in regard to homosexuality, suggesting it was positively beneficial. Renault argued that all men should love someone of their own sex until just over twenty, at which age they should marry and raise a family. In middle age, the men should return to their own sex.[3]

NOTES

1. David Sweetman, *Mary Renault: A Biography.* New York: Harcourt Brace, 1993, p. 76.
2. Ibid., p. 273.
3. Ibid., p. 227.

41

Janet Schane,
The Dazzling Crystal

There is perhaps something autobiographical in the central character here. Janet Schane was interested in fashion and design, and her heroine, Judith Forrester, is interested in work as a commercial artist. After the death of her professor father, Judith comes to New York and meets novelist Nicky Hoffmann. The two marry and Judith becomes part of his affluent New York set, moving into Nicky's apartment, which comes complete with a Chinese live-in house servant.

Judith meets Nicky's first publisher, Mark Sauter, and, gradually, as she tries to comprehend her husband's dislike for him, she realizes the two men had once been lovers. Nicky had been Sauter's protégé, just as now Sauter is promoting a naive, twenty-three-year-old poet name Rollo Cantrell. The relationship between Nicky and Sauter is revealed in the most general of terms. There is no reference to sex. When the two lived together, they had separate bedrooms. Sauter is, in fact, married, living a life separate from his wife, but still sharing accommodation. Sauter had taken Nicky to Europe and gradually introduced him to the better (and more expensive) things in life.

The relationship between Sauter and Rollo is equally devoid of any vulgar, crude, or sexual inference. As Sauter looks at Rollo, enjoying himself like a small child in the snow, he thinks,

> To be frank, Rollo's only conceivable interest lay in his extreme and admittedly appealing youth, and his unbelievable attractiveness. . . . No one had to make excuses for admiring beauty, as such. Certainly there was beauty in youth, tinged as it was with sadness. And a true love of symmetry admitted no distinctions. One could admire a handsome species of woman, of porcelain, as one could be touched equally by a perfectly wrought man. (p. 65)

Judith's first inkling that something is odd in her husband's relationship to Saunter is at a party, when a poetry editor comments that Mark had forgiven Nicky "with his usual nobility" (p. 133). When Judith presses him for details, he tells her that Sauter had punched him in the jaw for a negative review of one of her husband's books. Unaware that Judith is Nicky's wife, he explains that Nicky, in marriage, is "accepting the challenge of convention, a temporary illusion of heaven in the flight from himself" (p. 133).

Judith learns that the manservant had been hired by Sauter, and that immediately after providing Nicky with his first advance the two men had sailed for Europe. Sauter jokes of Nicky's love for his first typewriter, adding, "I'm sure he would have slept with it under his pillow if I'd have allowed it" (p. 173). The suggestion that Sauter should have dictated Nicky's actions, that he should have control of what Nicky could do in the bedroom, destroys Judith.

The reader, but not Judith, is told of the flowering of Nicky's relationship with Sauter in Europe:

> That night in Paris he had vowed that anything he could do to make Mark proud of him he would do, that if Mark wanted his life he could have it. . . . He did not care to journey through life unless Mark was to be there beside him to see with, unless Mark was there to turn to with thoughts to share. (p.195)

Both Rollo and Nicky had tried to escape from their mentor, and both had, but with hideous consequences. Rollo kills himself. Nicky is separated from Judith, but, at the novel's close, it appears that the two will be reunited. Nicky had finished with Sauter prior to meeting Judith, but only with her did he have courage enough to make the break permanent.

The gay life as enjoyed by Mark Sauter is not in any way promoted in *The Dazzling Crystal* (Reynal & Hitchcock, 1946). When Nicky confronts Sauter after Judith has left him he tells the other man that he is alive, which is more than Sauter will ever be. Sauter tries to tell him that he is Nicky, and Nicky is him, but the suggestion is angrily rejected. Nicky points out that by letting his wife know of the former relationship between the two, he has found himself: "Mark and Mark's world would die—they would die because they had not deserved to survive" (p. 236).

Does the novel reject homosexuality, or does it reject simply the notion that an older gay can proselytize younger men who may or may not be gay? What the novel does not make clear is why the younger men should accept the advances of the older one. It is, of course, to advance themselves and their careers, but, in so doing, they are presenting themselves as no better than the "enemy." In reality, *The Dazzling Crystal* could easily have been rewritten with Sauter straight and Nicky and Rollo as young women. It is more adventuresome for its day to present the story line as it is here, but the basic premise is far from original and the writing style forgettable.

The "theme, which, though never named, is perversion," noted *Library Journal* (August 1946), but, as the reviewer, B. V. W., wrote in *The New York Times* (September 8, 1946), *The Dazzling Crystal* is "perverse without being perverted." There is not one single action of the part of Sauter that one can wholly condemn even if one is the most extreme right wing of religious bigots. An oddity about contemporary reviews is that, although unimpressed, all suggested that the novel was for a female readership. "For feminine tastes, which are also fastidious, this offers delicacy and discernment," commented *Kirkus* (June 24, 1946). Presumably that recommendation also extended to gay men with a discerning love of romance.

42

Rex Stout, *Forest Fire*

Gay (and quite a few heterosexual) readers of classic mystery novels have pondered the relationship between Rex Stout's private detective hero, Nero Wolfe, and his young, good-looking assistant, Archie Goodwin. Wolfe is so much a misogynist that he will not even shake a woman's hand. He and Archie share that famous brownstone home on New York's West 35th Street. They do not share a bedroom, although they have certainly slept together in the same room on the few occasions that Wolfe has agreed to set foot outside his home. And what about those phallic-shaped orchids with which Nero Wolfe is obsessed? It is fun to speculate, outrageous as the speculation might be, and despite critics denouncing such gay subtext conjecture as requisite of immediate dismissal. Everyone appears to agree that Wolfe and Archie have a father-son relationship, but what that implies on a heterosexual level may not be the same as the implication as seen from a gay or Freudian viewpoint. To confuse the issue further, there is the question of which character is modeled after Rex Stout. In physical appearance, Stout is Nero Wolfe, but in terms of personality he is Archie Goodwin. Rex Stout is both Nero Wolfe and Archie Goodwin—and what does that make of any psychological interpretation of the Wolfe-Goodwin relationship?

Few fans of Rex Stout and Nero Wolfe are aware that back in 1933 the author published a novel—his fourth—in which one of the two principal characters is gay, or at least bisexual. The idea for *Forest Fire* (Farrar & Rinehart, 1933) dates back to November 1931 when Stout wrote to the U.S. Department of Agriculture requesting information on the Forestry Service. He did not advise them of his planned story line.

Similar to the Nero Wolfe novels, *Forest Fire* concerns the relationship between an older and a younger, good-looking man. Stan Durham is a senior fire ranger in Montana, noted for protecting his territory from forest fires and his ability to fight them should they arise. He is married with a son who has left home and in whom Durham has no interest. He is boorish and lacking in original thought or action. As in most activities, he is mechanical in his lovemaking with his wife. Durham's most notable attribute is his snub-nose, which has gained him the nickname of "Nosey," a moniker given him also because of his habit of unexpectedly checking up on the duties of his men.

Stan Durham is doing precisely that on blond, blue-eyed Henry Fallon, a nineteen-year-old summer recruit to the service, when the novel opens. Finding Fallon derelict, Durham fires him, but later relents after suggesting he should instead punch his subordinate out. Fallon stands ready to receive a blow to his jaw, refusing to put up his hand, but Durham cannot let his fist connect wth the young man's face.

At this point, both Durham and the reader realize there is something special about Fallon, something boyish and appealing. Durham is no longer sure of himself: "All he could tell was that things were happening which it was impossible to understand; something was breaking loose inside of him" (p. 115). Later, Durham will hit the boy—an act of love based on the discredited theory that there is little difference between love and pain, shades of *Carousel* and its source, Ferenc Molnar's *Liliom,* and that to both assailant and recipient a blow can feel like a kiss.

> He had heard many of the forest and prairie epithets and phrases and jokes regarding intimate relations between men, or between men and boys, but knew nothing whatever of the actual facts on which they were based. He was aware that to most men there was something both shameful and funny about it, but to him it was neither the one nor the other. . . . He knew that a cross-eyed bull was a man who was supposed to be unable to distinguish— for certain practical purposes—between a woman and a boy; or able to distinguish, preferred the boy. (p. 119)

Durham is fixated with Fallon. He recalls that when the young man first came to him he had rested his hand on Durham's leg just above the knee, and that while Fallon's hand was there Durham had the impression that he had nothing covering the joint. He looked in the young man's eyes, and could not bring himself to shift his leg.

Durham is not the only individual attracted to Fallon. His wife, Elsie, is not unaware of Fallon's looks, but it is the arrival of Dot Fuller on vacation and her fascination with the young man that serves as a catalyst for the tragedy that ensues. She camps near Fallon's cabin and tries unsuccessfully to persuade him to sleep with her. Durham becomes hysterical with jealousy when he discovers the two together, innocent as the situation actually is. A lighted cigarette discarded by Dot leads to a major forest fire, which indirectly kills Fallon. When Durham, who has lost his skill in fighting the fire as a result of his confused sexual identity, attempts to detain Dot for her part in the conflagration, she tries to shoot him with Fallon's gun. But it is Elsie Durham, arriving on the scene, who fires the fatal shot, killing her husband. Ultimately it is revealed that it was Elsie who set the fire.

Elsie's shooting of her husband has nothing to do with his "love" for Fallon. She is unaware of it, unlike one of Durham's fellow rangers, Al Disney. When Elsie rides out to the cabin, believing her husband is about to harm Fallon, he tells her, "Stan ain't going to hurt Henry Fallon, and what he may be going to do to him is none of my business" (p. 140).

What Durham is going to do is present Fallon with a love gift in the surprising form of a potted geranium. It is laughable, but at the same time symbolic of the naive, and trusting, love that Durham has for the boy. It is as if Durham was going courting for the first time—he has even taken a clean bandana with him—and there is something both tragic and endearing about Durham's actions. One does not have to be gay or even tolerant of homosexuality to sympathize with the ranger, confronted for the first time in his life with a pure and overwhelming love. Durham has little sexual experience—he has had only three women in his life—and has no feelings about his body except that he likes to keep it clean. The idea he has for expressing his love for Fallon is a simple letter: "You are the only man I have ever wanted for a friend. Yours sincerely, Stanley R. Durham" (p. 147). When Durham and Fallon spend a night together, sleeping in their nonglamorous underwear in separate bunks, the most Durham can do is sneak a peek at Fallon, wondering if he sleeps with his head toward the wall.

Henry Fallon has no knowledge of Durham's love. He is a personable and probably virginal young man, who confesses that he does not know how to make love to Dot. He is pure of heart and soul, trapped by the desires of others that he does not understand and, eventually, too good to live.

The lack of physical contact between the protagonists leaves the reader somewhat unsatisfied. One would like to know more of Durham's physical characteristics. The author even avoids any scenes in which Fallon strips down to his shorts. If he takes off his shirt, it is to reveal a long-sleeved vest. When Fallon takes a swim, he dons a self-made bathing suit that covers most of his body, although we are slightly titillated with the revelation that the material clings to his rear in a revealing fashion.

Forest Fire is to a large extent pure melodrama, with the theme of conflagration brought on by sexual desire obvious and overwrought. Gay love is not to blame here, but the raw, unrequited desire of three individuals—one man and two women—for the unattainable. At the same time, the writing is good enough to hold one's attention, despite too much detail given to the rather dreary fighting of the forest fire.

Critical response was mixed. The *Saturday Review of Literature* (April 29, 1933) commented,

> If in the end it is doubtful, in spite of much excellent material and straightforward writing, whether *Forest Fire* is a good novel, it is largely because of the lack of imagination. The whole is convincing and workmanlike, but not memorable, and Mr. Stout's people, always a little flat and abstract, follow too often a preconceived line of conduct, and too little the devices of their own hearts.

To the reviewer in *The New York Times* (April 16, 1933), "the book drags sadly much of the time, and on other occasions skirts melodrama. Mr. Stout is an interesting novelist, but his emphasis on abnormality in this instance seems misplaced and strained." The reference to "abnormality" is as close as any critic got to the topic of homosexuality as presented here.

The publisher of *Forest Fire,* Farrar & Rinehart, promoted the book with publicity as incendiary as the story line:

> This novel rips aside the film of normality covering the deranged mentalities of sexually-starved people living in a circumscribed, primitive environment. . . . In the forest reserves of

Montana, the emotions and deep inhibitions of four people were tinder as dry as the trees themselves one waterless summer . . . thrown together, they struck forth a spark which brought tragedy to two of them, which made the forest a red-mouthed inferno.

Forest Fire is the only gay novel from Rex Stout (1886-1975), who would doubtless have disapproved of my description. It is important in his career, because it is followed by *Fer-de-Lance,* the first of the Nero Wolfe detective mysteries. Although *Forest Fire* sank into obscurity, the later books guaranteed Rex Stout immortality.

43

L. A. G. Strong (Leonard Alfred George), *The Last Enemy: A Study of Youth*

Divided into three segments, *The Last Enemy* (Alfred A. Knopf, 1936) is a study of a young Englishman, Denis Boyle, from the age of twenty through approximately twenty-five. The first part deals with his leaving Oxford because of World War I in order to take up a teaching position at a preparatory school, and his return to Oxford to appear before a medical board to confirm he is unfit for military service. That one day in Oxford influences his thinking as he realizes how a class-ridden society discriminates against the uneducated and the weak. The third part of the novel has Boyle falling in love with the wife of one of the other masters at the school and his death in a motoring accident as he travels for a meeting with her that will consummate their relationship. The transfer of Boyle's spirit from one life to the next is movingly described, and one can well understand why critic Dayton Kohler once described Irish-born poet and novelist L. A. G. Strong as possessing "the poetic romanticism of the Gael." The novel's final chapters reveal the reasoning behind the title, taken from 1 Corinthians 15:26, "The last enemy that shall be destroyed is death."

It is the middle portion of the book that has a strong gay interest, although there are suggestions that some of the students with whom Boyle becomes reacquainted in Part One are gay. After the end of World War I, Boyle returns to Oxford, gains his degree, and is welcomed back to the school where he first taught. One of the new and much-admired masters is Gordon Fane, who had served with distinction during the war, and is now head of one of the houses into which the school is divided. He invites Boyle to be his second in command, obviously enjoys the company of a younger man, and is even jealous of his friendship with other masters. Fane also enjoys the company of some of the older schoolboys.

Boyle realizes something is wrong when, one night, he is seated in the bedroom with a small group of boys, reading them a story. Quite innocently, one of the boys takes Boyle's hand and places it between his thighs. A shocked Boyle gently removes his hand, and expresses his concern to Fane, who reassures him. Shortly thereafter, the father of another boy comes to the school, protesting that his son has been molested by Fane. Fane takes a revolver and kills himself.

This might appear all very straightforward and all very obvious in terms of Fane's behavior and its outcome, but the author does not consider it from the established modern outlook on what is termed "child molestation." The two boys involved, Jimmy and George, are fifteen or sixteen years old. Fane leaves a suicide note for the latter, and Boyle has no hesitation in removing it prior to the arrival of the police, and delivering it to George. The contents of the letter are not revealed, but for George, "It is a wonderful letter. . . . I shall keep it all my life" (p. 295). George also reassures Boyle, "He didn't do me any harm" (p. 294).

George's reaction to Fane is mirrored by that of the school-teacher's wife, with whom Boyle will later have an affair:

> It remains to be seen how much harm has really been done . . . Gordon loved that boy: probably both of them. This didn't happen from the worst sort of reasons. It wasn't mere—whatever the word may be. It was because he loved them. . . . If George had been a girl, it would have been all right, wouldn't it? . . . When a thing happens because people love one another, then, however wrong it may be, it's not a quarter as bad as when it happens for the mere sake of the thing itself. There's all the difference between a man going with a prostitute and with a woman he loves and who loves him, whatever there may be against it otherwise. (p. 265)

For 1936, it is quite an extraordinary philosophy to espouse, one that would be grossly politically incorrect a half-century later. Even at the time, Peter Quennell in the *New Statesman and Nation* (July 4, 1936) complained that everything here combined "to produce a slightly uncomfortable atmosphere." The tolerant response of Boyle, George, and the master's wife is further emphasized by another master at the school, who talks of Fane's killing himself "for a trifle like that" (p. 282). The master goes on to reveal that he had done something far worse—what he's done is not explained—and that he had even served a prison term: "One can survive anything. It doesn't even take will power. Time does it for one, I've proved that" (p. 282).

Even the cold and unfriendly headmaster adopts a conciliatory tone. In an act of charity and courage, he orders that Fane's funeral be held at the school, and the headmaster asks his pupils to "try to remember only all the good about him, and how kind he was" (p. 293).

Critical response to *The Last Enemy,* which was first published in 1936 by leftist British publisher Victor Gollancz, obviously influenced by the thinking in the first part of the novel, was mixed. *The Times Literary Supplement* (July 4, 1936) found the novel "curiously fragmentary and incomplete," and yet, of course, it is the very incompleteness of the book that is its strength. We don't need to know what took place between Fane, George, and Jimmy, and it is better we do not read what Fane writes in that last note to his boy lover. More accurate in his response is Maurice Joy in the *New York Herald Tribune Books* (October 11, 1936), who praised the novel as "a fine achievement. Mr. Strong has written with noble courage, with brutal force at times, and at times with subtle beauty, of the hopes, fears and ordeals of youth in a period of tragic and wasteful stress."

In a foreword to this his seventh novel, L. A. G. Strong is quick to point out,

> The story, the episodes, the characters, and above all the school, belong to fiction. I repeat and affirm this, not only because of the school in question, but for the benefit of a type of reader who regards all fiction as autobiography. For the benefit of a related type, who attributes directly to the author everything said by the characters, I would like to emphasize the story's sub-title—A Study of Youth—reminding him that the opinions and discoveries of Denis Boyle are conditioned by his age, his temperament, and the years in which he lived.

44

André Tellier, *Twilight Men*

Twilight Men (Greenberg, 1931) is the tragic and overmelodramatic story of Armand, the illegitimate son of the Comte Edmond de Rasbon, a slim, blond, somewhat effete, and languid young man. He is very much a poseur, tossing curls back from his forehead. It is not difficult to understand why heterosexual men might find him irritating and outrageous. He is far from appealing to a modern gay readership. Armand—his last name is never confirmed—is positively precious in the manner in which he loves the beautiful things of life, the flowers, the trees—and the gardener Henri (Shades of Lady Chatterley!).

In the novel's first chapter, Armand is brought by his uncle and guardian, Josef Bironge, to meet the Comte, his relationship to whom he is unaware of. Armand explains to the Comte that he does not like women and that he gets his inspiration from the fields and trees. Not surprisingly, the Comte tells Josef to keep his relationship to Armand a secret: "If we were seen together it would set all Paris talking" (p. 12). The Comte makes available funds for Armand's upkeep but announces that "Henceforth Comte de Rasbon's son will be known as your nephew" (p. 36).

Armand lounges around in his uncle's library, enjoying the pleasures of a large estate, hurt that he is mocked by all excepting Henri, the gardener, with whom he shares the occasional (presumably chaste) kiss. Armand and Henri stroll the grounds at night, anxious to see what the elder-blossoms are doing. Armand leans against Henri's shoulder while the gardener smokes his pipe. Eventually, Henri is sent away, and Bironge thinks, "Sometimes I wish I had told him [Armand] more about the perversions that beset people like him" (p. 62).

The Comte's nephew, Lucien, comes to visit Armand and his uncle, and Armand is immediately attracted to him: "Armand glanced covertly at Lucien's lips. He would love to touch them, to feel the thrill that welled up with the touching, as it did when Henri pressed him to his shoulder with sudden tenderness" (p. 32). Lucien does not share Armand's feelings and instead suggests to Bironge that they all head for London, where Armand will get these strange longings out of his system, and where Lucien will fix him up with a woman.

In the meantime, the Comte has approached thirty-five-year-old Marianne Dodon, a well-known Parisien seductress, and suggested that she might try and make a man of his son. Armand does visit Marianne and he has his first sexual experience with her. The problem is that the encounter has more of an impact on Marianne, who falls in love with her victim.

In London, Bironge and his extended family rent a house on Hampstead Heath, where Armand and Lucien enjoy long walks. The author does not consider it necessary to explain, as every gay man in London knows, that Hampstead Heath is a notorious gay cruising ground. Lucien sets up Armand with a prostitute, but Armand runs away from her. "We could lie together. . . . I'll lie in your arms tonight just to show you," Armand urges Lucien (p. 58), but Lucien laughs in his face. An ambiguity exists in the Armand-Lucien relationship. The two take pleasure in each other's company, but the reader is never certain whether they eventually bed down together. (A problem throughout the novel is trying to develop a clear sense of when Armand is actually enjoying a sexual relationship or when it is purely platonic. About the most sexual of acts to be found here is a kiss!)

Bironge is far from well, but he does decide to hire a tutor for Armand, a Jean Mareau, who makes Armand happy in that the young man is now loved by both Lucien and Jean.

> Armand found resistless attraction in Jean's supple, well-knit body, in his broad, muscular shoulders, in his manly height, and to Jean the frailness of Armand was appealing—his slimness, his incessant, nervous restlessness. . . . The super-abundance of passionate life in all his actions and gestures was insistently provocative. (p. 72)

Suddenly, with little warning or explanation, Lucien dies, followed shortly thereafter to the grave by Uncle Josef. Jean takes Bironge's body back to France, and Marianne Dodon seizes the opportunity to move in with Armand. Marianne is not surprised when Armand tells her that he is never going to marry. Aware that Armand is in love with Jean, she warns him, "Men like Mareau don't love; they destroy. . . . It's filth he offers, can't you see! It's lust of the most perverted kind" (p. 79). In anger, Marianne reveals to Armand that the Comte de Rasbon is his father. "I can't believe you are a homosexual. I am sure if you were away from Jean you would find that your reaction against such perversion is as strong as mine" (p. 81).

Jean returns to London and Marianne moves out, but there is no happiness in the household. Jean believes he must leave in order that Armand will be "happy and unmolested" (p. 95) back in France. The manner of Jean's leaving is more than a little melodramatic. With a storm raging outside, Jean flings open the bedroom window and jumps to his death. Armand's response is to take a boat to New York.

En route, Armand is taken up by a wealthy New Yorker, Lady Beverton, who persuades him to move into her apartment overlooking Central Park, despite the disapproval of her husband. After six months with the Bevertons—which must have been trying for all concerned—Armand leaves. He moves down to Greenwich Village and moves in with writer Stephen Kent, whom Armand had met while communing with nature in Central Park.

Armand is introduced to the gay denizens of Greenwich Village, and also the delights of alcohol, drugs, and cheap sex. Stephen Kent encourages Armand to write and publish his poetry, but Armand fails to recognize the love that Stephen has for him and his disapproval of Armand's hedonistic lifestyle. At a party, a group of friends persuades Armand to dress in drag and parade around the block. As a result, Armand is arrested by the police. Stephen contacts a gay judge, Adrian Ware, who arranges for Armand to receive nothing more than a reprimand. The primary result of the court appearance is that Armand falls in love with the judge, unaware that his savior is keeping another gay man, pianist Pedro Mecardi.

In the midst of all this gay frivolity, Marianne Dodon arrives on the scene, still in hot pursuit of Armand. She is again rejected. Next to arrive in New York is the Comte de Rasbon, who asks that Armand visit him at his hotel. The two argue, and the Comte points out that Armand's lifestyle is financed by him. "You've turned into something more filthy than I ever knew existed," says the Comte (p. 233). He tells Armand that he is a drug addict and that he intends to have him confined in an institution: "if you weren't such a vile, perverted little animal, it wouldn't be necessary to lock you up" (p. 234).

In anger and under the influence of drugs, Armand takes a heavy candlestick from the mantelpiece and bashes in his uncle's skull. He rents a cheap room on the West Side and overdoses on morphine. Stephen Kent learns of the Comte's murder from Marianne Dodon and of Armand's death from the judge, who, as usual, takes care of everything. Armand at one point fancies himself as a romantic who dies for love. In truth, he is a weak-willed murderer, who dies rather than face the consequences of his actions.

Twilight Men is a rather silly novel. When something happens, it happens very quickly, but generally there is nothing more than page after page of triviality (perhaps as befitting the trivial personality of the central player). As one of the few novels available with a principal gay character, it must have had tremendous appeal to gay men back in 1931, and was successfully republished by Greenberg in 1948 (running through two printings). There was even a further reprint, from Pyramid, in 1957. The novel did not attract the attention of contemporary reviewers. However, a librarian at the Los Angeles Public Library read the novel for its potential purchase and found it "more informative than *Well of Loneliness*. . . . A very acute story of this type, very melodramatic but very possible situations, but distasteful because of the absence of any kind of normal sexual emotion."

In reality, there is an absence of any normal gay emotion. Armand is a type influenced by Oscar Wilde's lover, Lord Alfred Douglas, more than by gay men of the 1920s. He is twenty-three years old at the novel's close, and it is probably best that he should die, because he most certainly would not have looked forward to life as an aging homosexual male.

One of the most offensive paragraphs in *Twilight Men* deals with aging gay men. Armand is at one of the many Greenwich Village parties at which he wastes his creative and emotional life:

> Armand gazed intently at the dancers as he drank. They were of all ages. Once he caught a glimpse of a young, fresh-faced boy dancing in the close embrace of an elderly, loose-lipped man. For a moment he was displeased and wished they had not come there. He rather expected all affection, all love, to cease at a certain age. To him, as to almost all young persons, the thought of sexual passion in a man past forty was abhorrent. Armand did

not realize that he was seeing the most tragic figure that haunts the shadowy, hysterical world of the temperamentally misfitted, the homosexual who had lived past the age of physical attraction and must depend upon wealth and willingness to forego affection and respect in his attempts to dispel loneliness. (p. 147)

Who was André Tellier? He was presumably gay and, similar to Armand, he lived in both France and the United States. *Twilight Men* is not translated from the French, but written in English by the author. The writing style is generally as overly graceful as the posturing of Armand. Neither have stood the test of time well. There are sentences in which Tellier utilizes a French word rather than an English-language equivalent, and he gets completely muddled when trying to quote the American folk song, "Oh, Susanna." Born in 1902, Tellier authored two other novels prior to publication of *Twilight Men: The Magnificent Sin* (1930) and *Witchfire* (1931). He published no further novels in the United States.

45

Ward Thomas, *Stranger in the Land*

Homosexual blackmail is the subject matter of *Stranger in the Land* (Houghton Mifflin, 1949). The victim is Raymond Manton, a twenty-eight-year-old English teacher in a small New England town. The blackmailer is a twenty-year-old youth named Terry, with whom Raymond has what is more a friendship than a sexual relationship. When a wealthy, elderly townsman, Orville Finch, is arrested for the sexual molestation of fifteen-year-old schoolboys, Terry reminds Raymond that he, also, is underage. When a bank clerk and then a commercial artist are also arrested, it is obvious that a witch-hunt is under way in the town. Others are arrested, all unmarried and all disqualified for military service. The bank clerk commits suicide in jail. Raymond pays Terry ten and then fifty dollars. He contemplates suicide, but realizes an easier solution is to kill Terry. He lures the young man out for a nighttime swim in a local reservoir and drowns him: "I, Raymond Manton, am a murderer—a homosexual and a murderer, a double menace to the peace of the godly, doubly damned and estranged from the world that never accepted me" (p. 371).

Raymond Manton makes a fascinating and sympathetic character study. He lives with his aged mother, and has been rejected for the draft after being labeled a "psychoneurotic." His father, now deceased, despised him. At school, he had fallen in love with a fellow pupil, who rejected him when his mother discovered a letter that Raymond had written the boy. At graduation, the other boy greets him with cruel words, "Oh, hello, Manton, you big fairy, where's your wings?" (p. 307). On a scholarship to Yale, Raymond falls in love with his roommate, but, again, there is tragic and semipublic rejection.

Through it all, Raymond remains bright and generally cheerful. His intellectual prowess over those around him is evidenced repeatedly in his conversations with his mother, Terry, and others. He is something of a misogynist when it comes to his female pupils, but equally deplores the lack of interest from his male students in poetry. They offer no apparent sexual attraction to Raymond, and at one point when he loses control of his class—fixated with the problem of Terry's blackmail—the students attack him because he is not in military uniform.

He does not give in to Terry's blackmailing and has the courage to fight back:

> You're vulnerable, too, Terry, in your own way. . . . You're making liquor your substitute for love. We're both going to destroy ourselves, but your way won't be any prettier than mine. You've poisoned my life so thoroughly that it's no good to me any more. I only hope you get some of that poison back before you die. (p. 272)

Raymond's relationship with Terry is a strained one, and, prior to the latter's attempts at blackmail, seems about to end. Terry is younger and better looking, but he is very much Raymond's intellectual inferior. Raymond, outraged at the town witch-hunt against gays, asks would they have called Shakespeare normal, Michelangelo, Christopher Marlowe, Walt Whitman? "Or practically any other great name in art or literature you can think of—they may not all have been queer in my way, but they all looked terribly queer to their neighbors and their contemporaries." "I don't know nothing about those guys," replies Terry, "Maybe they were all queer, too" (p. 179).

Ultimately, Raymond knows that

> "Guys like you" could so easily become more brutal synonyms when spoken in private to others. . . . No, there was no dignity in being an invert. There was only the filthiest abasement, such as few men but lepers and pariahs knew as their daily lot. It did no good to remind oneself of Plato and Michelangelo; that was too specious a consolation, appeasing only to the conceit. (p. 195)

Unlike many gay men in other works of fiction from this period, Raymond Manton has many positive characteristics. He is a closeted gay man, typical in that sense of his time, but also one that is not stereotypical, certainly not effeminate, and very much his own person. When Terry makes reference to "your type," Raymond responds,

"Call me an invert, if you can think of it, or a plain fairy, if you can't. Even that sounds better than 'your type.' You see, I'm not a type at all, I'm an individual" (p. 81).

Contemporary criticism was largely positive. In the *New York Herald Tribune Weekly Book Review* (June 19, 1949), Richard Match wrote, "the force of its honesty is enough to override many of its inadequacies as a novel. Mr. Thomas is careful to not exploit his 'sensational' theme for any purpose other than to illuminate the life of a tragic individual."

In *The New York Times* (June 19, 1949), Hilda Osterhout wrote,

> Ward Thomas is one of the first writers to deal with homosexuality, so recurrent a subject in modern letters, on a socially conscious plane as the problem of a minority ostracized by the group. But *Stranger in the Land* is less a homosexual novel than the story of the demonic friendship between the hunter and the hunted, a Dostoevskian situation in suspense and intensity.

The New Yorker (June 18, 1949) complained on the novel's length—thirty pages shy of 400—but considered the author's "analyses of a small town, and of his hero's dilemma . . . most perceptive."

In a patronizing review in the *Saturday Review of Literature* (July 9, 1949), Harrison Smith described *Stranger in the Land* as

> a powerful and dramatic revelation of the nature of a man who knows he is doomed. . . . The author does not ask for mawkish pity or even sympathy for the Raymond Mantons of the world. But he is deeply sincere in asking the rest of us to treat them like human beings for whom we must show the consideration we should give to any stranger who crosses our path.

Despite its theme, most contemporary gay men must have read *Stranger in the Land* with deep satisfaction. It is not published by Greenberg, specializing in novels for the homosexual market, but rather the major publishing house of Houghton Mifflin, noted for its great literary works. The reader admires Raymond Manton, and wishes he might have his way with words. Terry is not a character deserving of total dislike, but it is satisfying to read of Raymond's slowly drowning him. At the same time, the reader worries that our hero has left too many clues as to who the guilty party is. Why did he drink with Terry at a bar that night? Why did he take a bus to the lake with Terry? The police in that small town seem more obsessed with victimless crime than with real violence, and so, hopefully, Raymond may escape the law, if not his conscience.

46

Loren Wahl, *The Invisible Glass*

The title *The Invisible Glass* (Greenberg, 1950) is taken from W. E. B. Du Bois's *Dusk of Dawn,* and is a reference to the divide between blacks and whites who see but do not know each other. It is a phrase that might, of course, also be applied to gays and straights. In full, the quotation reads, "Some thick sheet of invisible but horribly tangible plate glass is between them and the world"—and "them" might easily refer to the gay community. But just as the phrase, which after all comes from the writings of a black scholar and educator, more strictly applies to prejudice against African Americans, so does the novel, despite its major gay content, document white-black prejudice more than straight-gay prejudice. To be gay and in the U.S. military during World War II was to be relatively at ease with oneself compared to the hatred and bigotry that African Americans experienced.

The novel takes place in American-occupied Italy toward the close of World War II, primarily in the small town of Bassano. *The Invisible Glass* begins with the dedication "to Eddie, who is Chick, and George, who was Steve." Chick is an educated African American from Los Angeles, who has spent two years at UCLA. He is drafted into an all-black regiment, constituted entirely of poorly educated Southerners who are used to obeying orders from their white masters. That white master here is Captain Randall, who despises Chick because of his education, and treats his soldiers just as he would if they were working for him in Greenville, South Carolina. Steve is Lieutenant Steve La Cava, who had known Randall at officer training camp and who, following a leg injury, has persuaded the captain to request his joining the regiment. The author suggests that because Steve is also from California—in his case San Francisco—he has a totally different attitude toward African Americans.

Steve is gay and has been involved with a sergeant named Phil, who was killed at Rapido. As he awaits Chick's arrival to pick him up at Group Headquarters in Verona, his thoughts are of Phil. He has no notion at this point that he is joining a Negro unit, but he is immediately aware of an attraction for Chick:

> A good-looking colored lad. His nose and lips weren't as broad and large as with most Negroes he had seen. Slender, not particularly tall, and solidly built. He could tell that from the way the soldier's sweat-soaked woolen shirt clung to his arms and chest. (p. 25)

Except for their color, Chick's strong hands and slender fingers are exactly like those of Phil.

Steve tries to talk with Chick, but is initially rebuffed as the soldier looks on his new lieutenant as just another bigoted white officer. Chick's attitude changes during the jeep ride back to Bassano, as Steve shares a whiskey bottle with him, drinking immediately after Chick and not wiping the mouth of the bottle. To Chick, this is symbolic of tolerance, but it might also be considered as evidence of Steve's growing desire for the young soldier, the pleasure of tasting Chick's lips on the whiskey bottle. The jeep is nicknamed "Lena Horne," and Chick is impressed that Steve has not only met the singer but also danced with her.

Steve goes into town and meets Chick's Italian girlfriend, Anna, just as her brother, Angelo, a partisan, returns from the mountains with the news that the Germans in Italy have surrendered. Angelo, who is obviously outraged that his sister is sleeping with a Negro, looks curiously at Steve. He reveals that he was at Monte Cassino along with Steve. One day, he was watching the hills through his binoculars, and had seen a lieutenant and a sergeant hiding in a foxhole. After drinking, the two had moved closer together and put their arms around each other. Steve leaves, but, as he walks back to camp, he is accosted by Angelo, who resumes the story, adding, "and I wished it were I that was with you. . . . It is still the same, now that I have seen you again" (p. 100). Angelo puts his arm around Steve's waist and leads him into an olive grove.

Steve receives permission to visit Italian relatives who live near Milan and he is able to take Chick along as his driver. At the home of the relatives, Steve and Chick eat and drink well, and retire to a room with one bed. Steve watches as Chick undresses, noting his lack of underwear, his beautifully proportioned body, the ridges of muscle without hardly any hair. Steve joins Chick in bed, and as the two men lie together, Chick examines the expensive Swiss watch that Steve is wearing, a watch given to him by Phil. In a moment of love-obsessed generosity, Steve gives the watch to Chick. In the dark, Steve stretches out his toes to reach Chick and his hand brushes the soldier's side. Chick turns toward Steve, who draws him closer. He kisses his neck, his shoulders, his breasts, and comes to rest on his thighs. "Chick, Chick . . . I love you," he murmurs (p. 200). As far as can be surmised, he performs oral sex on the soldier.

In the morning, Steve discovers that once he fell asleep, Chick had left the bed and spent the night on the floor. Chick is sullen and distant as the two men drive into Milan. Steve arranges that Chick will pick him up the next day, and begins to explore the city. He sees effeminate Italian men, identified as *finocchi,* who smile at him and cause him to blush. He wanders into a bar only to discover it is a gay establishment, and rejects the advances of an air force sergeant.

Disillusioned, but for the first time fully accepting of his homosexuality, Steve meets up with Chick, and decides to drive back to Bassano. Chick tells Steve to forget what has happened, but an angry Steve points out that Chick had not rejected his advances the previous evening. In anger, Steve tells Chick that he will never be able to marry Anna, that the captain has refused Chick's request—although the captain is, in fact, unaware of the relationship between Chick and Anna—and, responding with anger, Chick imitates a Southern drawl and suggests that he might become a pimp for the lieutenant: "If you so crazy bout black meat, I'll introduce you to some of the sweet boys in the Company" (p. 224). As Steve begins to cry, Chick looks at him in disgust. He promises he will keep Steve's secret, but takes out a gun given to Steve by his relative, and makes the suggestion that Steve shoot him—after all, "A white man in a nigger outfit can get away with anything" (p. 224). Chick stops the jeep at the camp, and, as he walks away, Steve takes the Beretta and kills himself.

Immediately, Chick is confronted by Captain Randall, accused of killing the lieutenant and stealing his watch. Chick runs off into town and pounds on the door of Anna's home. It is opened by Angelo, who spits in his face and slams the door. Chick collapses in the piazza and is found there by Captain Randall.

The Invisible Glass is a gay novel, but, more important, it is a harsh indictment of the manner in which African-American soldiers were treated during World War II (and, of course, earlier and later). John Cournos in the *Saturday Review of Literature* (March 11, 1950) described the book as "another story of man's inhumanity to man." The inhumanity is not directed at gay soldiers, but at Negro soldiers. The language that Captain Randall uses to describe his men and the manner in which he adopts Negro patois is incredibly offensive to the modern reader. The soldiers are called "menz" not "men." The corporal and sergeant who take care of Captain Randall are stereotypical Uncle Toms. "Nigger" and "jigaboo" are the accepted names for the men of Randall's company. Chick cannot gain promotion because he is educated, because he displays the decency and intelligence that Captain Randall lacks.

Captain Randall is unaware of Steve's homosexuality, and accepts the story that the lieutenant is having an affair with Chick's girlfriend, Anna. Randall sees nothing odd in his remembrance of Phil walking around the barracks in a grotesque impersonation of a woman and crawling into bed with Steve. He is aware of gay activity among his men and does not condemn it. After Steve has conducted a bed check, he reports to Randall that Sergeant Washington is in bed with Corporal Carney:

> The Captain chuckled. "Oh, that! Those two have been having a wild affair for months. Let them have their fun. But I'd like to know who does what to whom!" He rolled onto his back and snickered. "Yep, Steve, we've even got them in this nigger outfit." (p. 168)

Up to a point, the Italians are willing to fraternize with the African-American soldiers, just as they are relatively tolerant of homosexuality. It is ironic that at the novel's close, it is the gay Angelo who rejects Chick, unaware—or perhaps because he knows—that Chick is loved by Steve, the man whom Angelo loves.

In Milan, Steve spends time at the Yankee Bar, which, at first, he does not realize is gay. As he drinks his cognac, he becomes aware of the many effeminate characters there—a chubby infantry sergeant who admires Steve's "basket," a corporal with a look of Veronica Lake and who uses the same first name—all of whom disgust him. Only the technical sergeant who buys him a drink is different:

"Husky, handsome, with a deep and pleasant voice. A crew haircut accentuated his masculine appearance. There was nothing, outwardly, to suggest the feminine. And yet he too was as gay as the others" (p. 210).

The implication is that Steve is not gay in the sense that the effeminate men in the bar are gay. Only when he encounters another "masculine" soldier does he get a sense of belonging to the gay community. He leaves the bar, but would have returned and picked up the sergeant had he not encountered Chick.

Loren Wahl devotes ten pages to the Yankee Bar, and his description obviously begs comparison with that of the gay bar in John Horne Burns' *The Gallery*. The latter has more description and boasts a better writing style, but the two places are surprisingly similar in atmosphere and clientele. At least in American-occupied Italy at the end of World War II, gay bars were predominantly effeminate, camp headquarters, so to speak.

The Invisible Glass is not a great work of literature in the manner of *The Gallery*. It is at moments—such as Angelo's description of Steve and Phil together, and Steve's seduction of Chick—little more than a trashy gay novel. Only when the author discusses the treatment of the African-American soldier, or in the early conversations between Chick and Steve, does the novel rise in stature. As Herbert Mitgang wrote in *The New York Times* (March 12, 1950),

> One of the less explored sides of the war is the role of the Negro soldier, his bravery despite those who branded him yellow because he is black, his relationship to white officers and foreign civilians. With boisterous goodwill Loren Wahl attempts to tell that story. If his novel is sadly inadequate, the plot rather than the intention is to blame. . . . [When] the theme switches to homosexuality the story becomes unmotivated and unreal.

A similar comment was offered by the reviewer in the *San Francisco Chronicle* (April 2, 1950):

> Though Mr. Wahl lacks a sense of structure and proportion in form, he displays real power in characterization. . . . At times one is reminded of a bad movie by this book; what with the innumerable interludes of searching for a cigarette, lighting it and inhaling it—or of opening a bottle of liquor, pouring it out and

drinking it. This sort of trick is used in Hollywood to hide lack of action in the story itself. It should not have been necessary here; there is enough powerful material to furnish real story-movement.

Loren Wahl was the pseudonym of Lawrence Madalena (1919-1983), who, under the name Lorenzo Madalena, wrote a second novel, *Confetti for Gino* (1959). It was set among the Italian Americans of the tuna-fishing community of San Diego, within which Madalena grew up. Lawrence Madalena did serve as a captain in the U.S. Army Reserve in Italy at the end of World War II, and in 1957 he returned to Italy as an English exchange student under a Fulbright fellowship. *The Invisible Glass* was reprinted by Washington, DC-based Guild Press in 1965.

47

Sylvia Townsend Warner,
Mr. Fortune's Maggot

Although told in nonsexual terms, and without any suggestion of sexual impropriety, *Mr. Fortune's Maggot* (The Viking Press, 1927) is the story of the infatuation of a middle-aged missionary for a young Polynesian male. It might well be compared to Somerset Maugham's 1921 short story "Miss Thompson" (which became the play and film *Rain*) in which another missionary in much the same part of the world falls in love with a prostitute, Sadie Thompson. The difference, of course, aside from the change in sex, is that the object of Mr. Fortune's love is pure and unspoiled. Sadie Thompson seduces the Reverend Alfred Davidson, whereas Mr. Fortune is neither the seduced nor the seducer, but simply the besotted. His affection is returned, but without the returnee being full comprehensive of just what is being asked of him. In a pure, unspoiled society, male-male love is not subject to Christian bigotry. Those who have never been taught wrong cannot commit a wrong.

A "maggot" is defined here (according to the *New English Dictionary*) as "a nonsensical or perverse fancy," and that is what the Reverend Timothy Fortune finds on the remote island of Fanua. A former bank clerk, Fortune became an ordained deacon and spent ten years in St. Fabien, a port "on an island of the Raritongan Archipelago in the Pacific" (p. 2)—presumably one of the Cook Islands. He persuades his archdeacon to permit him to go to Fanua in an attempt to convert the natives, who are described as both childlike and immoral, and who have no word for either chastity or gratitude. Mr. Fortune takes over an abandoned hut as his home, and on the first morning there he is surprised and delighted to find a young man, Lueli, kneeling in prayer beside him.

The boy is welcomed with a kiss and renamed Theodore, meaning "the gift to God." With the approval of Lueli's mother, the boy moves in with Mr. Fortune and introduces him to island life and customs. Mr. Fortune has the vague hope that Lueli has adopted a Christian lifestyle, but the boy explains that here no god is supreme, and every islander has his or her own unique god; and Lueli clings to his idol, at first without his mentor's knowledge.

"Despite more than sixty degrees of latitude and over thirty years between them" (p. 62), Mr. Fortune and Lueli become the most intimate of friends. In Lueli's company, Mr. Fortune becomes "glorified and gay" (p. 158), and when he believes (wrongly) that Lueli has committed suicide, he is grief stricken:

> I loved him. . . . From the moment I set eyes on him I loved him. Not with what is accounted a criminal love, for though I set my desire on him, it was a spiritual desire. I did not even love him as a father loves a son, for that is a familiar love, and at the times when Lueli most entranced me it was as a being remote, intact, and incalculable. (pp. 186-187)

After three years on Fanua, Mr. Fortune realizes that he has made no converts to Christianity, not even Lueli, and so he returns to St. Fabien. He leaves Lueli, urging him to take a wife. Thanks to Lueli and Fanua, Mr. Fortune goes back a far more human and a considerably more heathenized individual.

The intimacy between Mr. Fortune and Lueli involves their living, eating, and sleeping together. The only suggestion of any bodily contact or appreciation occurs when Lueli introduces Mr. Fortune to the pleasures of massage with scented oil, which the missionary initially rejects as effeminate. Everyone of the island is apparently nude and in time Mr. Fortune has lost sufficient inhibition to bathe naked in front of the local inhabitants. Perhaps it is both Mr. Fortune's Christianity and his basic Englishness that prevent him from more fully enjoying other delights that Lueli is very willing to offer. The truth, sadly, is that Mr. Fortune is not so much an old queen as an old fart.

Mr. Fortune's Maggot is the second of three novels by Sylvia Townsend Warner (1893-1978) that helped establish her as an outstanding prose stylist; those early works have been described by scholar J. I. M. Stewart in *The Times Literary Supplement* as "one of the most notable achievements of English fiction in the 1920s." *Mr. Fortune's Maggot* did not transcend the sales of Warner's first novel, *Lolly Willowes,* but it did confirm her as a major commercially and

critically successful novelist of the 1920s. *Mr. Fortune's Maggot* is
satire at its best. There are passages here—particularly those delightfully malicious ones, of which there are many—that still cause the
reader to laugh out loud. There is so much truth here in regard to
Christianity, innocent love, and English reticence that it is easy to dis-
miss *Mr. Fortune's Maggot* as a novel without a clear content. Truth
can be very simple and very engaging, and those are precisely the
charms of *Mr. Fortune's Maggot*.

One can well understand T. E. Welby in the *Saturday Review*
(April 30, 1927) asking why "so much careful craftsmanship should
have been lavished on a story that worked up to no point." Or why
Edwin Muir in the British publication, *The Nation and Atheneum*
(June 4, 1927) should complain that the novel "reads like an imitation
of an imitation, laboriously done." Far more perceptive of Sylvia
Townsend Warner's accomplishment was Clifton Fadiman in *The
Nation* (May 25, 1927):

> Her satire, so humorous, so warm, so finely feminine, has the
> depth and reach that brutally naturalistic rendition of a life-sur-
> face can never attain; and the fairly-like locale of her story, her
> impossible islanders, and her slightly made quixotic hero ad-
> mits the entrance of beauty and wit—two qualities which Amer-
> ican satire . . . does not largely possess.

Aside from her work as a novelist, Sylvia Townsend Warner was a
major contributor of short fiction to *The New Yorker*. Following the
breakup in the 1920s of her relationship with her music teacher, Sir
Percy Buck, Warner enjoyed a long and sometimes turbulent relationship with Valentine Ackland, which lasted from 1930 until
Ackland's death in 1969. The two women published a collection of
poetry together, *Whether a Dove or a Seagull* (1933).[1]

NOTE

1. Their relationship is documented in *The Letters of Sylvia Townsend Warner,*
edited by William Maxwell (Viking, 1983), *The Diaries of Sylvia Townsend Warner,*
edited by Claire Harman (Chatto & Windus, 1994), and in Wendy Mulford's *This
Narrow Place: Sylvia Townsend Warner and Valentine Ackland* (Pandora Press,
1988).

48

Denton Welch, *Maiden Voyage*

Maiden Voyage (L. B. Fischer, 1945) is a semiautobiographical novel, based in part on the life of its author, but primarily taking its story line from the author's fantasy world. This is not what happened to Denton Welch, but rather what he wishes might have happened to Denton Welch. The narrator is a schoolboy, fifteen years old, who briefly runs away from his English public school, Repton (where Welch was a pupil), agrees to return if he is allowed to leave permanently at the end of the term, and travels to China with his older brother on a visit to their father. The time period of the novel is unclear, but Welch went to Repton in 1929 at the age of fourteen, and so, presumably, the novel is set in 1930-1931, certainly long before the Japanese invasion of Manchuria and any thoughts of World War II.

This is not a gay novel per se. There is not one overt reference to homosexuality within its pages, but it is very much the story of a young man with more than a passing interest in other young men—a young man who, although he may not fully realize it yet, is gay. The narrator thrills in his descriptions of the men that he encounters. Soldiers hold a particular fascination for him. He is a "pretty boy," so described more than once in the novel. At school, he is attracted to an older pupil, who has scratched his shoulder while running. The narrator cleans the wound with his handkerchief in semierotic fashion, entranced by the red scratch on white flesh and the beads of blood. The older boy presses against him hard, "rubbing his cheek against mine. I could feel how warm and moist his body was, and the touch of his eyelashes was like feathers. He spoke harshly and yearningly and shut his eyes" (pp. 63-64). The older boy hitches up his shorts and runs off:

> In the steaming changing room afterwards I felt happy about life. The room was full of the nice smell of bodies, and gay

shouts rang out. I sank down into the hot bath which twenty other people had already used. The thick, muddy water stroked my flesh. (p. 64)

Later, in China, the narrator is staying with a married couple. He and the husband use the bathroom at the same time, with the latter suggesting that the boy use the tub while he shaves. The narrator stares at the husband, lays back as he watches the silky muscles running over his back. The husband takes a loofah and scrubs the narrator's back, rubbing his skin roughly, and then ducks him under the water, holding his head in place.

The erotic prose here is filled with youthful male desire. Seldom does one read, outside of a pornographic magazine, of a locker room so vibrant with sexuality, the smells of masculinity, the dirty water loving to the touch.

"Certainly the publishers of this astonishing book will not be found guilty of describing it as the autobiography of an English public school boy who deserts his Horace and goes off on a holiday to China," reads the opening descriptive paragraph on the dust jacket. The copy goes on to compare the author to Evelyn Waugh and Aubrey Beardsley—a heady combination—but plays it safe by emphasizing the heterosexual aspects of the work, including a visit to a Chinese brothel and the consoling of a homesick lady missionary.

Aside from an enthusiastic dust jacket, *Maiden Voyage* boasts a foreword by Edith Sitwell, in which she announces that "This is a very moving and remarkable first book, and the author appears to be that very rare being, a born writer." One can well imagine this doyenne of the Bloomsbury set being entranced by the young, personable, and gay Denton Welch.

In part thanks to the dust jacket copy, reviewers were unsure as to whether *Maiden Voyage* was a novel or an autobiography. (Librarians were similarly confused, and the Los Angeles Public Library system to this day insists it is an autobiography.) In *The New Republic* (January 19, 1945), James Stern wrote that

A less good, less honest writer would be bound to have fallen into the temptation of dramatizing himself, falsifying facts, in such a situation. Mr. Welch never does. You believe every word, every sensation: the fear, the futility and the inevitability of the dismal return to the dismal school clothes.

However, of course, Denton Welch does falsify the record, and it is because he is such a good storyteller that the reader, critic or not, believes in him and his adventures.

Not surprisingly, the narrator of the novel is named Denton Welch, an author whose fame has dissipated with the passing years, despite a remarkable record as both a writer and a gay man. Denton Welch (1915-1948) was a pixielike character, almost emaciated in appearance, with a pair of spectacles dominating his face. His very thinness suggests ill health and Welch was indeed unwell often. He has been described by *Contemporary Authors* as the "pioneer of sexually frank autobiographical fiction with a confessional bias," and, after reading *Maiden Voyage*, one has to agree that "No gay writer more demands literary resurrection."[1]

This is an author whom William Burroughs acknowledged as a major influence in his work—and the 1985 edition of Welch's second novel, *In Youth Is Pleasure* (first published in 1945) contains a foreword by Burroughs. *Maiden Voyage* was reprinted by Penguin in 1983, and Welch is the subject of a major biography, *Denton Welch: The Making of a Writer* (Viking, 1984) by Michael De-la-Noy, who also edited *The Journals of Denton Welch* (E. P. Dutton, 1984). Unfortunately, both the biography and the journals are singularly dull, with the homosexuality of the subject underemphasized, and this despite the promise that the journals are published for the first time in unexpurgated form.

Maiden Voyage emphasizes two types of sexual activity with which Denton Welch was intrigued, if not an active participant. He was fascinated by sadomasochism, hence his treatment of soldiers, the "rough trade" of the novel, and his lingerings on the canings routinely delivered to the bottoms of the young boys at Repton. After each caning, the youth would return to his dormitory, where he would be urged by the older boy in charge of the room to drop his trousers and underwear and show off his markings.

Denton Welch may also have been a closet transvestite: in *Maiden Voyage,* he takes advantage of a stay in the bedroom of the daughter of one household. He puts on a thin woolen dress; a wide scarlet, leather belt; snub-nosed, high-heeled shoes; a tight felt hat; and appropriate makeup:

> I sat down at the dressing-table and began to work on my face. It was as absorbing as redecorating a room. I was not at all re-

strained. I used everything I could find. I sunk my eyes in wells
of blue eye-shadow and arched thin black eyebrows over them. I
covered my cheeks with brick-red rouge and my lips with scarlet lipstick. (p. 243)

So attired, Welch wanders the streets of Shanghai, alternately terri-
fied by and fascinated with his appearance. Such female impersonation suggests that here is a novel with a subtextual title. *Maiden Voyage* implies femininity, and also has the reader pondering if our hero
is more than a little maidenish.

Contemporary reviewers ignored or remained oblivious to any gay
subtext to *Maiden Voyage*. In the *New York Herald Tribune Weekly
Book Review* (April 1, 1945), Iris Barry wrote that

> It is written with limpidity and directness, setting down a record
> of sensations, embarrassments, little failures and fears, with a
> detachment and candor rarely encountered. Though it is evi-
> dently to be taken as autobiographical, it presents its hero in the
> cruelly objective light of a laboratory: we see the human mecha-
> nism in its alarming and utter nakedness responding to a succes-
> sion of mostly disagreeable stimuli. Its very defenselessness
> makes it curiously pitiable and disconcertingly instructive.

W. H. Auden in *The New York Times* (March 18, 1945) responded in
similar fashion:

> A combination of scientific objectivity with subjective terror, I
> think makes *Maiden Voyage* a revealing comment on our histor-
> ical situation. Are we not all emotionally what Mr. Welch is in
> fact—orphans, each traveling alone on a journey which, if it
> headed in the right direction of unknown dangers, at least is
> leading one away from the fears one knows?

NOTE

1. "Welch, (Maurice) Denton 1915-1948," volume 148, *Contemporary Authors*.
Detroit: Gale Research, 1996, p. 474.

49

Calder Willingham, *End As a Man*

End As a Man (The Vanguard Press, 1947) is the study of life at a Southern military school, identified as The Academy, and seen primarily through the eyes of cadet recruit Robert Marquales. Marquales becomes involved in a gambling scandal thanks to Sergeant Jocko de Paris, and the book concludes with his facing possible expulsion.

One neither likes nor dislikes Marquales, who seems easily manipulated, but one is very much manipulated, in turn, by the author into disliking the two gay men at The Academy, senior Carroll Colton and sophomore Perrin McKee. Some contemporary critics suggested that Marquales is weak; in reality, he is just an ordinary guy, not terribly strong, who has found himself in a tough situation. Colton is under the spell of McKee, who is presented as thoroughly despicable. He has evidence of de Paris's infecting a woman with syphilis and threatens him with exposure unless the handsome young sergeant agrees to an assignation: "Do not be afraid, I am gentle with virgins," McKee writes (p. 143).

The author's purpose in injecting the letter into the story line is difficult to understand. Jocko de Paris is not going to be seduced or threatened by the text in any way. As has been pointed out by others, he is not vulnerable because he is a sociopath with an incarnate streak of evil.

When Marquales visits McKee at the family home, to which the latter has been taken as a result of a heart attack and a fall, he is verbally attacked:

> You certainly must have realized early in the evening, if indeed you didn't know it all the time, that I am that dismal, depraved, unhealthy, and the all-the-rest-of-it thing—a practicing homo-

sexual. And not a repressed one like yourself, I may add. (p. 236)

Marquales is indignant, just as he had angrily responded no, when asked by other cadets if he is gay. (Presumably he is not.)

The sadomasochistic activities at The Academy may appeal to quite a few gay readers, but there is nothing appealing in the author's attitude toward gays. As he has de Paris explain it, "It's all in the brain. They have the brain of a woman but the body of a man" (p. 166). Another cadet, Albert Wilson, calls Perrin "the petunia" (p. 242), adding for effect, "A pansy is on the level of an ape" (p. 243).

At the novel's close, after de Paris and others have been expelled, the head of The Academy, General Draughton, explains, "No youth can pass through four years at The Academy and not end as a man" (p. 350). If not spoken aloud, the implication is very clear: the men The Academy graduates are not gamblers, not fornicators and, most certainly, not gay.

End As a Man is remarkable for the honesty of its language—there are four-letter words here—and the realism in its depiction of cadet life. "This first novel is the work of an artist, written with power, honesty and courage," wrote J. T. Farrell in *The New York Times* (February 16, 1947). To J. M. Lalley in *The New Yorker* (March 8, 1947), "with all its technical crudities and philosophic immaturity, this is a novel capable of evoking, even in a seasoned reader, something like cathartic terror." Referring to the confrontational scene in which homosexuality is revealed and reviled, John Woodburn wrote in the *Saturday Review of Literature* (April 5, 1947), "Any young man who can conceive, execute, and sustain such a scene as Marquales's visit to the home of Perrin McKee, to say nothing of the rest of this vivid, brilliant, exasperated book, is someone to watch steadily."

As Calder Willingham's widow, Jane B. Smith, expresses it,

> The question of the book . . . is what makes a man? Is it aggressiveness and cruelty? Is it honor and discipline? Can sometimes these negative and positive influences be mixed up in an environment? The book was an indictment of the military, at least some aspects of it, but Calder didn't intend the commander's speech at the end in an entirely satirical sense. The commander was something of a pompous fool, but some of what he said rang true.

Calder Willingham (1922-1995) attended The Citadel from 1940 to 1941, and that establishment obviously serves as the model for The Academy as, in more recent years, it has served as the basis for Pat Conroy's *The Lords of Discipline* (1980), which can certainly trace its lineage back to *End As a Man,* although it is quite different in purpose and tone. *End As a Man* also reminds one of Lucien K. Truscott IV's *Dress Grey* (1979), although the homosexuality there is crucial to the story line and here could easily be deleted. Willingham presents it as an almost natural part of cadet life, but one that does not overshadow all the dishonorable activities—particularly gambling—taking place among the would-be soldiers.

End As a Man was Willingham's first novel, which he also developed as a play. He has been compared by critics to Norman Mailer and James Jones, but also denounced as a purveyor of smut and trash. As far as his widow is concerned, "I think there are many readers who do not understand Calder's work. They are put off by his sexuality and style." Willingham is perhaps better known as a screenwriter, responsible for such major motion pictures as *Paths of Glory* (1957), *The Vikings* (1958), *One-Eyed Jacks* (1961), *The Graduate* (1967), and *Little Big Man* (1972). *End As a Man* was filmed in 1957 by Horizon Productions for Columbia release as *The Strange One,* directed by Jack Garfein and starring Ben Gazzara, Pat Hingle, Mark Richman, and a very young George Peppard in his screen debut as Robert Marquales. The director and a number of cast members came from the original Broadway production. The film version retains the two homosexual characters and contains considerable homoerotic overtones. Some sequences were considered too provocative, and three minutes were deleted from the original release prints on orders from the Production Code Administration (better known as the Hays Office). It has been suggested that *Sorority Girl* (1957), remade as *Confessions of a Sorority Girl* (1994), is a female version of *The Strange One.*

50

J. (John) Keith Winter,
Other Man's Saucer

First published in the United Kingdom in 1930 by William Heinemann, *Other Man's Saucer* (Doubleday Doran, 1930) takes its title from the habit of cigarette smokers who deposit their ashes in another man's saucer. One reviewer suggested that the title was a sign of the author's "desperate originality," but it seems more deliberate obfuscation in that the point is far from obvious. It would appear to emphasize nothing more than the selfishness of the leading character, Shaw Latimer, who accepts but never returns a friendship.

The Latimer family is precocious and upper middle class, consisting of a mother, who is barely visible in the novel and in her family's life; two daughters; three sons; and a dead and forgotten father. They fascinate the reader in that they serve almost as a parody of a certain class of English society, referring to "the lower classes, in the form of the maids and chauffeur" (p. 8), and existing in an idyllic world—between the wars—in which reality seldom intrudes.

At public school, Shaw Latimer becomes friendly with Gerald Marcus, a prefect two years his senior who has "the most disturbingly wonderful face that he had ever seen" (p. 70). Although Marcus appears to like the younger man, the relationship between the two verges on the sadomasochistic as Latimer is frequently punished and often caned by Marcus for minor school infractions. The association between the two teenagers reaches its climax and its conclusion when Marcus orders Latimer to his study. He ties Latimer's wrists and ankles, pulls off his clothes, and thrashes him. The sense of the loss of friendship "seemed to hurt far more than the thrashing he had given me" (p. 95), Latimer tells his sister, Jetta. The implication is that Latimer was also raped by Marcus. "Have you told me everything, Shaw?" asks Jetta. "At least everything that can be told," responds the young man (p. 96).

190

The relationship with Marcus changes Latimer. He now has "a deep-rooted conviction of the essential beastliness of his fellow beings" (p. 110), as he goes up to Oxford. There, Latimer develops what would seem to be platonic relationships with a number of handsome young men. In the chapter titled "Kink," the reader learns more of Latimer's other friends, friends who will buy meals and luxuries for him and others, including Mickey with "his Byronic beauty" (p. 159), Findlatter who hosts parties at which the Oxford graduates turn out the lights and begin kissing each other (p. 160), and George, "with a smooth white face and exquisite clothes," who is described as "like a great white slug—disgusting" (p. 155)

Eventually, Latimer develops a close and troubled friendship with Orm Lind. When Lind visits the Latimer family, it is Shaw Latimer's brother David who seems to recognize the potential homosexual relationship between the two men:

> David affected what he imagined to be a feminine voice.
> "Of course his face is alluring—if you like that type. Personally—personally," he repeated, sweeping his hand extravagantly over his hair, "I thought him a little too near to nature, if you see what I mean.
> "I mean if I was to wake up one morning and find that on my pillow," he shrugged his shoulders—"Well, imagine my embarrassment." (pp. 317-318)

Latimer and Lind go swimming, and Latimer considers drowning the latter, because for him there is no peace with such a friend. Instead, it is Lind who drags Latimer from the ocean. Lying on the beach afterward, Latimer realizes the world is upside down. An equal partnership has developed between the two men, a partnership that may continue purely as a friendship or extend to something else.

Other Man's Saucer is engrossing and never fails to entertain, but it is very much a first novel, with all its faults and all the failings of youth, which is what most of the contemporary critics noted. In London, *The New Statesman* (June 14, 1930) dismissed it as "hardly worth writing." To the reviewer in *The Times Literary Supplement* (September 11, 1930), "There is a restless brilliance and an ease of dialogue in this first novel of Oxford life, but they have been expended upon a theme of very doubtful interest. Moreover Mr. Winter handicaps himself by the uncertainty of his intentions."

"I detect only the yearnings of the immature aesthete," complained Guy Holt in *The Bookman* (December 30, 1930). "A fairly routine piece of youthful highjinks and sophomoric audacity, always exciting and sometimes even brilliant, but hardly ever shocking," opined Edwin Seaver in the *New York Evening Post* (November 22, 1930).

Hugh Walpole, the British novelist and critic who once shocked his contemporaries by admitting that he had wet dreams about child actor Freddie Bartholomew, noted both the good and bad points of *Other Man's Saucer* in the *New York Herald Tribune Books* (August 17, 1930):

> Mr. Keith Winter's novel is as young a book as any one is ever likely to publish. It has all the very young determination to tell the whole truth, it has young poetry and young style and young characters. The fable, such as there is of it, is unconvincing and the hero most unsatisfactory. Nevertheless, in spite of these things, it is a most encouraging work, encouraging because it shows the real gifts of the novelist, the power to create character, to be dramatic, to make the reader want to turn the page, to call up atmosphere out of the vasty deep.

John Keith Winter (1906-1983) was a Welsh-born novelist and dramatist, who spent two and a half years as an assistant master at a preparatory school before going to Oxford in 1927. He wrote *Other Man's Saucer* while in his last year of reading history there. There is, presumably, something of Winter in Shaw Latimer, who like his creator writes a first novel while at Oxford. Winter certainly understood life at an all-boys public school, when he wrote,

> Because Gerald was a prefect and Shaw was not, a tradition stronger than any written law kept them apart. The Public School feels very strongly about these matters. On the assumption that friendship between boys of different ages is unnatural, not to say wicked, the Public School recognizing regretfully the inevitability of such friendships decrees that they shall at least be conducted in decent secrecy. The authority that has driven boys underground like so many rabbits is then surprised to find them behaving like rabbits. (p. 73)

The novelist realized that once *Other Man's Saucer* was published, he would never again be allowed to resume his career as a schoolteacher. Instead, Winter turned to the stage and eventually, in the early 1940s, to Hollywood, where he had a brief career as a screenwriter. His best known film, however, is the British production of *The Red Shoes* (1948), the script for which Winter cowrote with Emeric Pressburger.

Dropping the initial "J" Keith Winter is also responsible for a second novel of some gay interest, *Impassioned Pygmies* (Doubleday Doran, 1936). The impassioned pygmies of the title are those who feed on the great, represented here by E. L. Marius, who has just taken up residence on the Mediterranean island of Miramar (and the author provides sufficient clues to identify it as Majorca). Most contemporary critics agree that E. L. Marius is based on D. H. Lawrence, just as it is very obvious that another visitor to the island, Andrew Jordan, is based on Noel Coward. Winter brilliantly recreates Coward-like dialogue. His frequent use of "gay" in describing Andrew Jordan—at one point it is said of him, "About as gay as a vulture emulating the morning activities of a lark" (p. 145)—cannot be coincidental. In London, *The Times* (April 6, 1936) commented, "As a satirical portrait of Noel Coward, *Impassioned Pygmies* is first-rate. As a caricature of Lawrence's biographers it is catty but accurate. As a novel about real human beings it is less than fair." As an exposé of the bogus and dishonest, *Impassioned Pygmies* is quite brilliant, and quite desperately cries out for reappraisal.

Appendix

Titles in Chronological Order

Greenmantle (1916), by John Buchan
Bertram Cope's Year (1919), by Henry Blake Fuller
The Dark Mother (1920), by Waldo Frank
The Western Shore (1925), by Clarkson Crane
Vestal Fire (1927), by Compton Mackenzie
Mr. Fortune's Maggot (1927), by Sylvia Townsend Warner
To Kiss the Crocodile (1928), by Ernest Milton
Revelation (1930), by André Birabeau
A Strange Love: A Novel of Abnormal Passion (1930), by George Eekhoud
Other Man's Saucer (1930), by J. (John) Keith Winter
The Opening of a Door (1931), by George Davis
Strange Brother (1931), by Blair Niles
Twilight Men (1931), by André Tellier
This Man Is My Brother (1932), by Myron Brinig
Gentlemen, I Address You Privately (1933), by Kay Boyle
Better Angel (1933), by Richard Meeker
Forest Fire (1933), by Rex Stout
Butterfly Man (1934), by Lew Levenson
Dwell in the Wilderness (1935), by Alvah Bessie
Shadows Flying (1936), by John Evans
The Murder of My Aunt (1936), by Richard Hull
The Last Enemy: A Study of Youth (1936), by L. A. G. Strong
Serenade (1937), by James M. Cain
He Swung and He Missed (1937), by Eugene O'Brien
Concert Pitch (1938), by Elliot Paul
Promise of Love (1939), by Mary Renault
This Fine Shadow (1941), by Harlan Cozad McIntosh
Sheila Lacey (1944), by Jean Lyttle
The Brick Foxhole (1945), by Richard Brooks
The Folded Leaf (1945), by William Maxwell
Maiden Voyage (1945), by Denton Welch

The Fall of Valor (1946), by Charles Jackson
The Dazzling Crystal (1946), by Janet Schane
The Great Light (1947), by Larry Barretto
The End of My Life (1947), by Vance Bourjaily
The Gallery (1947), by John Horne Burns
The Sling and the Arrow (1947), by Stuart Engstrand
Knock on Any Door (1947), by Willard Motley
End As a Man (1947), by Calder Willingham
The Welcome (1948), by Hubert Creekmore
All Things Human (1949), by Stuart Benton
The Christmas Tree (1949), by Isabel Bolton
The Gay Year (1949), by Michael de forrest
The Dark Peninsula (1949), by Ernest Frost
The *Divided Path* (1949), by Nial Kent
Stranger in the Land (1949), by Ward Thomas
Quatrefoil (1950), by James Barr
The Night Air (1950), by Harrison Dowd
The Bitterweed Path (1950), by Thomas Hal Phillips
The Invisible Glass (1950), by Loren Wahl

Bibliography

Austen, Roger. *Playing the Game: The Homosexual Novel in America*. Indianapolis: Bobbs-Merrill, 1977.

The Book Review Digest. New York: H. W. Wilson Company, 1916-1951.

Contemporary Authors: A Bio-Bibliographical Guide to Current Writers in Fiction, General Nonfiction, Poetry, Journalism, Drama, Motion Pictures, Television, and Other Fields. Detroit: Gale Group, 1964 to 2001.

Cory, Donald Webster. *The Homosexual in America: A Subjective Approach*. New York: Greenberg, 1951.

Cowley, Malcolm. *The Literary Situation*. New York: Viking Press, 1954.

Garde, Noel I. *The Homosexual in Literature: A Chronological Bibliography, Circa 700 B.C.-1958*. New York: Village Press, 1959.

Harris, Daniel. *The Rise and Fall of Gay Culture*. New York: Hyperion, 1997.

Kurnitz, Harry J. and Howard Haycraft. *Twentieth Century Authors: A Bibliographical Dictionary of Modern Literature*. New York: H. W. Wilson Company, 1956.

Malinowski, Sharon and Christa Brelin. *The Gay & Lesbian Literary Companion*. Detroit: Visible Ink, 1995.

Norton, Ricter. *The Homosexual Literary Tradition: An Interpretation*. New York: Revisionist Press, 1974.

Sedgwick, Eve Kosofsky. *Between Men: English Literature and the Male Homosexual Desire*. New York: Columbia University Press, 1985.

Seymour-Smith, Martin and Andrew C. Kimmens. *World Authors, 1900-1950*. New York: H. W. Wilson Company, 1996.

Slide, Anthony. *Gay and Lesbian Characters and Themes in Mystery Novels: A Critical Guide to Over 500 Works in English*. Jefferson, NC: McFarland, 1993.

Slide, Anthony. "Gay and Lesbian Mystery Fiction," in Robin W. Winks (Ed.), *Mystery and Suspense Writers: The Literature of Crime, Detection and Espionage*. New York: Charles Scribner's Sons, 1998, pp. 1069-1088.

Tebbet, John. *A History of Book Publishing in the United States*. New York: R. R. Bowker, 1978.

Young, Ian. *The Male Homosexual in Literature: A Bibliography*. Metuchen, NJ: Scarecrow Press, 1982.

Index